Happy Birthday
you ol' devil !.
love n' etc.
Victoria

*S*aturn
*a new look
at an old
devil*

LIZ GREENE

SATURN
a new look at an old devil

Liz Greene

SAMUEL WEISER, INC.
York Beach, Maine

Samuel Weiser, Inc.
P.O. Box 612
York Beach, Maine 03910

ISBN 0-87728-306-0

Book design by
Peretz Kaminsky

Printed in the U.S.A. by
Noble Offset Printers, Inc.
New York 10003

"When the disciple
knows Saturn as the God
who offers opportunity
and does not only
feel him to be Deity
who brings disaster,
then he is on the path
of discipleship in truth
and in deed
and not just
theoretically."
Alice A. Bailey,
Esoteric Astrology

TZ Sat 18° Aqu 23'

8th House

TH Sat Aqu
JS Sat 10° Aqu 52'

Contents

Introduction

In the tale of Beauty and the Beast, it seems somehow right, familiar, and fitting that the Beast, for all his ugliness, his sternness, and his capacity to inspire fear, should at the end turn into the Handsome Prince and marry the heroine. This feeling of rightness is characteristic of the response that fairytales evoke because the stuff from which myth and fairytale are composed is a symbolic portrayal of the values of the collective unconscious psyche of man. They are apparently innocent, yet have a curiously compelling and familiar quality. Beneath the many cultural differences which provide the superficial detail of these stories, there lies a bare simplicity of plot and character, for these are portrayals of man's inner psychic experiences, the bare bones of his subjective life. There is always the same hero, the same beautiful princess, the same stupid giant, the same treasure buried underground. The Beast is always the dark face of the Handsome Prince.

This kind of paradox seems to be an obvious facet of life, and it is acceptable when found in myth or fairytale and also acceptable in other kinds of symbolism, such as many religious themes; however, this quality of duality does not seem to have permeated our modern astrological viewpoint to any degree. There are still bad planets which are wholly bad and good planets which are wholly good; and even if we allow a little ambiguity to enter in, a little greyness among the stark black and white, it is still only a little. There remains a certain flat, two-dimensional quality to many of our traditional interpretations of the birth horoscope. There is also the tendency to interpret the birth chart according to our society's moral tenets so that there are honest and dishonest charts, moral and immoral aspects, and positive and negative behaviour. In astrology things tend still to have an "either-or" quality. Carl Jung once wrote that before Christianity, evil was not quite so evil, and it might be said that in Christianising astrology, we have lost many of the subtle paradoxes which this rich symbolic system contains. Most maligned of all astrological symbols is Saturn, whose face as the Beast is well-recognized but whose alternate face as the Handsome Prince is not often considered; however, without both of these, the symbol cannot communicate its meaning, and the interpretation has only a flat and two-dimensional value for the individual.

Saturn symbolizes a psychic process as well as a quality or kind of experience. He is not merely a representative of pain, restriction, and discipline; he is also a symbol of the psychic process, natural to all human beings, by which an individual may utilise the experiences of pain, restriction, and discipline as a means for greater consciousness and fulfilment. Psychology has demonstrated that there is within the individual psyche a motive or impulsion toward wholeness or completeness. The state of wholeness is symbolised by what is called the archetype of the Self. This symbol does not suggest perfection, where only the "good" aspects of human nature are incorporated, but instead implies completeness, where every human quality has its place and is contained in a harmonious way within the whole. This archetype stands behind much of the symbolism of the various world religions and may also be found in folklore and in fairytale in every civilisation and in every era of history. It is always intrinsically the same, although its outer ornamentation changes as man develops. The psychic process which Saturn symbolises seems to have something to do with the realisation of this inner experience of psychic completeness within the individual. Saturn is connected with the educational value of pain and with the difference between external values—those which we acquire from others—and internal values—those which we have worked to discover within ourselves. Saturn's role as the Beast is a necessary aspect of his meaning, for as the fairytale tells us, it is only when the Beast is loved for his own sake that he can be freed from the spell and can become the Prince.

In traditional astrology Saturn is known as a malefic planet. Even his virtues are rather dreary—self-control, tact, thrift, caution—and his vices are particularly unpleasant because they operate through the emotion we call fear. He has none of the glamour associated with the outer planets and none of the humanness of the personal planets. In popular conception he is devoid of any sense of humour. He is usually considered to be the bringer of limitation, frustration, hard work, and self-denial, and even his bright side is usually associated with wisdom and self-discipline of the man who keeps his nose to the grindstone and does not commit the atrocity of laughing at life. By his sign and house position Saturn denotes those areas of life in which the individual is likely to feel thwarted in his self-expression, where he is most likely to be frustrated or meet with difficulties. In many instances Saturn seems to correspond with painful circumstances which appear not to be connected with any weakness or flaw on the part of the person himself but which merely "happen", thereby earning the planet the title, "Lord of Karma". This rather depressive evaluation remains attached to Saturn despite a most ancient and persistent of teachings which tells us that he is the Dweller at the Threshold, the keeper of the keys to the gate, and that it is through him alone that we may achieve eventual freedom through self-understanding.

The frustrating experiences which are connected with Saturn are obviously necessary as they are educational in a practical as well as a psychological sense. Whether we use psychological or esoteric terminology, the basic fact remains the same: human beings do not earn free will except through self-discovery, and they do not attempt self-discovery until things become so painful that they have no other choice. Although few astrologers would consider Saturn a very cheerful bedfellow, the necessity of Saturnian experience is grudgingly recognised. That there can be joy in this kind of experience is usually not so easily recognised. Anyone who enjoys his pain is considered to be a masochist; however, it is not enjoyment of pain which Saturn fosters, but rather the exhilaration of psychological freedom. This is not often recognised because not many people have experienced it.

Everyone has at some time experienced the repeated delays, disappointments, and fears which usually coincide with a strong Saturnian influence; however, there is not much response to the question of what these experiences mean and how they can be used as opportunities, other than the usual advice of patience and self-control. The ordinary answer to this question, when it is not the wholly useless reply of chance, is the equally useless idea that because these experiences represent the individual's karma, the present completion of an action or cycle begun in some past incarnation, he had best endure his disappointments, grit his teeth, do nothing, have faith, and in this way pay off his debts and find the path into the light. Even those astrological consultants who allow for some freedom on the part of the developing human being find it difficult to offer any advice for Saturn other than patience, calmness, and a positive attitude. Perhaps what is really asked of us by Saturn, and by our psyches, is that, like Parsifal when he finds himself in the enchanted castle and sees the Grail, we try asking why. It is possible that each delay, disappointment, or fear may be utilised as a means for greater insight into the mysterious mechanisms of the psyche, and that through these experiences we may gradually learn to perceive the meaning of our own lives.

There is much that goes on within a human being of which he remains unaware, and this does not apply only to repressed emotions. The world of the unconscious only begins with that peripheral level which Freud explored. Man creates his world all the time, according to the thought patterns he generates, and he brings about a reality which is the outward expression of these patterns. The experiences which an individual encounters are in some mysterious way attracted into his life by the creative power of his own psyche, and although we do not fully understand the synchronous fashion in which the inner and the outer reflect each other, we know that it happens in every person's life. One has only to observe an individual undergoing a process of self-development to see that the outer circumstances of his life always follow in an immediate fashion the inner psychic changes which he undergoes. He does not consciously create these circumstances; it is the larger self, the total psyche, which is the dynamic energy behind the individual's unfoldment. If the individual makes no effort to expand his consciousness so that he can understand the nature of this total unfoldment and can begin to cooperate with it, then it will seem that he is the pawn of fate and has no control over his life. He can only earn his freedom by learning about himself so that he can understand what value a particular experience has for the development of his whole self. And nothing stimulates a man into this kind of exploration faster than frustration, which is the gift of Saturn.

The majority of us are not yet at that stage where the dense molecules of matter move instantaneously at the bidding of our thoughts. Those of our race who have arrived at this point in evolution usually have their experiences or existence vehemently denied. Or, they are given the dubious honour of being considered not as teachers who express what is potential in all of us, but as freaks of nature whom the religions of the world have placed in the precarious position of explaining our sins to God. Most people see their creations return to them as physical reality through indirect channels which appear to be someone else's fault; or through happy circumstances which we attribute to the cleverness of the conscious intellect; or through sickness or accident which can be blamed on chance, bad luck, bacteria, or a poor diet. All of these channels are the means through which Saturnian experience comes, along with his favourite channel, loneliness. Usually these experiences are far more difficult than they need to be, and often very little is learned of the meaning or inner value of the experience. Only caution or practical wisdom is learned. There is nothing we hate so much as accepting responsibility for our actions and our fate, although man wants so desperately to believe that he is free. And when responsiblity is taken, it is usually coloured black and called sin, which is an equally useless attitude.

Merely wanting a problem to change, and understanding the superficial reasons for its existence, will not make the problem go away, particularly if it is not really a problem at all but an attempt on the part of the inner psyche to establish balance or a more inclusive viewpoint. The unconscious side of a human being always strives for wholeness and integration and will work through whatever channels the conscious man makes available. It is only when his conscious ideas of what is right or suitable come into direct conflict with the underlying path that he is unconsciously following that real pain begins, and this is usually the gnawing inner pain of a sense of futility and purposelessness. There are many men pitted against themselves, where regardless of what they believe they want in life, they continue at the last moment to do something to destroy the dream before it blossoms. Often this destructiveness is connected with guilt and fear, and this is one side of Saturn's expression. Equally often, behind the guilt and fear, there lies another purpose which is perhaps wiser and more meaningful a path than the one which the conscious man has chosen. Usually all that is seen is the destructiveness. It has often been termed evil and given personification as an external energy or person known as Satan—who is of course very close to Saturn, complete with the hoofs and horns of Capricorn the Goat. The nature of this conflict between conscious and unconscious, dark and light, is neither good nor evil; it is necessary for growth because out of it comes eventual integration and greater consciousness. The duality which a man finds in himself below the threshold of consciousness is usually very disturbing for we are likely to forget that anything standing in the light casts a dark shadow. God and Satan, whether they have objective existence or not, most definitely exist as impulses within the human psyche, but they are not what they at first appear to be.

There is no fast and easy method of making a friend of Saturn. In many ways the ancient art of alchemy was dedicated to this end; for the base material of alchemy, in which lay the possibility of gold, was called Saturn, and this base material, as well as having a concrete existence, was also considered to be the alchemist himself. Modern psychology, which is paralleling more and more the path of the alchemists, also seeks to make a friend of Saturn although here he is called by other names. But if one is persistent, it is possible to extract the gold, and in the end one may find, if the effort is made, that Saturn has a sense of humour after all—when we have become subtle enough to understand his irony.

1 *in the watery signs and houses*

A traditional reading of Saturn in the signs and houses may be found in a number of textbooks. Some are more psychological in their orientation, but the majority are concerned with his limiting and delaying influence upon the material plane or the world of events. This is certainly a valid method of interpretation as he unquestionably coincides with hindrances and the frustration of the even flow of material and emotional comfort in life. An analysis of Saturn's effects by aspect is also available from many sources, and this area also has been well documented through observation, experience, and tradition. The form side of Saturn's expression has in fact been most adequately covered and will continue to be so as further research is done in the areas of midpoints, harmonics, and medical astrology; however, it is the inner meaning which here concerns us.

No interpretation of Saturn by sign, house, or aspect can be complete, of course, since it is necessary to synthesise these elements and align them with the combination of Sun, Moon, and Ascendant first of all, corresponding with the individual's conscious expression, his unconscious or instinctual reactions, and his behavioural patterns. These isolated factors in combination with Saturn become the spinal column of the natal chart from the point of view of character. They will in a very concise manner shed light on what the individual wants (the Sun), what he needs (the Moon), the style in which he goes about getting these things (the Ascendant), and the thing within the man which causes him either to fail or to be dissatisfied once he has achieved his desire (Saturn). This is, of course, grossly simplified, and entire volumes could be filled on all the known meanings of the Moon alone; however, from this relationship of four factors—and every trinity must in the end be integrated by a fourth factor, a psychological as well as an esoteric law—we may gain insight into the meat of the individual struggle toward greater consciousness indicated on every birth chart. There is no chart which does not contain Saturn, however dignified and admirably aspected he may be, and there is no life without struggle.

We are taught in esoteric doctrine that the physical plane is the plane of effects, the last and densest of a progressively more subtle series of states of consciousness. Many people conceive of these planes as having a location spatially, but they have never been described in this way: the planes refer to states of being, or of awareness, rather than of place, and all coexist simultaneously at the same time and all the time, in all planes, and at the same point. This is a difficult concept for the rational and one-pointed intellect to grasp as it contains a paradox and must be perceived through the intuition which is capable of reconciling the opposing ideas inherent in a paradox and seeing them as one unit. This concept of the planes does not contradict the findings of psychology although the terminology used by both ways of thought is different. The man who is following the devotional path will find the language of the esoteric teachings comfortable with its references to soul, to spirit, to illumination. The man who is following the path of mental development may find it more acceptable to think in terms of conscious and unconscious, of repressions and peak experiences, and of the total integrated self rather than the Monad. It does not matter particularly which set of terms is used to understand the development of man. The worlds of the body, the feeling nature, the mind, and the intuition are essentially the same as the physical, astral, mental, and spiritual planes.

No event or mundane circumstance can occur without having first been set in motion by an idea, charged with emotion, and then manifested as an action. Beyond these three stages of an experience lies the meaning of the experience in relation to the whole, which it is the function of the intuition to perceive. The world of feeling lies directly behind the world of events, and it is this world with which the watery signs and houses are concerned. The astral plane symbolises the "wish life" or feeling nature of humanity, and the astral body—or feeling nature—of an individual man is often the world of causes for everything which happens to him in external life. He is, however, largely unaware of the potency of this feeling nature, particularly at the present juncture where emphasis is placed on external behaviour rather than on the quality of desire. As long as something is not "done", the individual will convince himself that he has no desire to do it; consequently, the power of the feelings increases because they are forced underground, into the realm of the unconscious. From this subterranean position the feelings will force a man to action or attract certain kinds of illnesses or behavioural patterns which he does not understand, and which may hurt him, and which appear to be coming from somewhere else. Psychic energy, like physical energy, cannot be destroyed; in fact they are the same, both kinds of energy, and will merely follow a different channel of expression if the usual one is blocked. Blockage on the level of the feeling nature is symbolised by Saturn in a watery sign or house, and true to form the psychic energy which would ordinarily seek release through expression of feeling must take another channel of expression—frequently through the physical body or through certain kinds of events.

The concept of different planes or states of consciousness which are all part of one life, but which may not be clear or known to the conscious mind, is most helpful in understanding the kind of responsibility which Saturn requires. As the majority of people are polarised in their feeling nature and are motivated by desire, it is particularly important to understand this principle if any sense is to be made of a watery Saturn. It is useless, of course, to tell the average man, come for an astrological consultation, that his pain is, finally and ultimately, part of the growth and evolution of a larger life of which he is a part; it does not help him to overcome his personal problem in terms that he can understand. Nor is it likely that he will be interested in the fact that the soul of the earth itself is preparing for initiation into a higher sphere of consciousness and that his personal struggle is intimately connected with this larger struggle. He will simply want to know why his wife left him, or why he has arthritis, or why his business has collapsed. If he can understand, however, that there is more to him than the small and feeble spark of his conscious awareness and that in coming to terms with that in him which seeks expression but which he has blocked through fear, he may be able to accept his experiences as a positive and necessary phase of growth and prevent their future repetition, he can acquire a sense of meaning and purpose in his life. He may even find that his wife comes back.

There is an aspect to Saturn which is given insufficient attention yet which holds much of the key to his meaning. This is his penchant for disguise, beautifully symbolised by the Egyptian myth of Osiris who, in flight from the wrath of Set, first changed himself into a sea-serpent and then into a crocodile—the original bestial symbol of the sign—to avoid detection. We may see the remnants of this disguise in the mountain goat who has a sea creature's hind quarters. A goat he may be, and his natural habitat may be the barren slopes and crags of the highest mountains, but when necessary, he can swim in the water of the emotional world and can effectively disguise himself in the face of necessity as some other sort of creature. There are many other references to this deliberate duality which is unlike the natural instinctive duality or flexibility of the mutable signs. One is the Roman god Janus, god of gateways, for whom the predominantly Capricornian month of January is named and who was possessed of the remarkable attribute of two heads—so that he could look backwards and forwards, ostensibly, guarding where one has been as well as where one is going, but also because he was, figuratively as well as literally, two-faced.

There is also no sign other than Capricorn which is represented by two distinct glyphs, drawn in totally different ways. This may seem like a small point, but those acquainted with either the esoteric realm or the realm of psychology in its deeper aspects will recognise the fact that there are no coincidences.

We are familiar enough with that innate trait of the strongly Capricornian individual to justify the means by the end and to accept willingly the outward trappings of submission for a period of time if these will eventually help him to earn the fruits of his ambitious. Yet Capricorn is not ordinarily considered a deceptive sign, in the sense that the Piscean in his vague elusiveness is deceptive, or the Geminian in his tendency to work his way into an intellectual corner and trick his way out again, or even the Scorpian who cloaks his essential emotional vulnerability and sensitivity with a barrage of false clues. It would pay to look twice at our hard-working, self-disciplined mountain goat for no one overcompensates as readily as he. We have many signs and planets which change colour like chameleons: all of the mutables, also Cancer, the Moon, Neptune, Mercury. But all these are instinctually changeable and fluctuate because it is their nature to do so whether the circumstances require it or not. Only Saturn calculates his defense, in the same manner as a competent solicitor, both to protect himself from the attack of the environment and to protect himself from the conscious discovery of the individual himself. Yet it is the individual who initiates the protection in both cases.

It is the free will of the individual, contingent upon the degree of his self-knowledge, that decides whether Saturn will be lead or gold or any of the intermediate states. His position at birth may be read in either of two ways, or both simultaneously, and his contact with other planets may bring out two apparently contradictory modes of expression at the same time. Freud termed this state ambivalent emotion; he was the first to postulate the idea that we may both love and hate someone at the same time and one does not negate the other. Things are never as they appear with Saturn; and whenever there is light, there is shadow. The understanding of his innate duality, and the necessity and value of this duality, alleviates much of the pain of the struggle.

Cancer, Scorpio, and Pisces and their corresponding houses—the fourth, eighth, and twelfth—are directly concerned with emotion and with motivations which lie below the surface of consciousness. Saturn in any of these signs or houses is extremely elusive because the average individual is rarely aware of the unconscious emotional frustration which lies behind his actions; he only knows that he is isolated and emotionally vulnerable, if he knows even that much. Saturn in these signs and houses is most typical of the kind of pain on the feeling level which finds its way to the therapist's couch, for often an objective viewpoint is needed to help guide the man through the mazes of his own feeling nature.

Saturn in Cancer
and the fourth house

The fourth house, corresponding to Cancer and the Moon, is the domain of childhood, origin, family, and roots. As the base of the astrological chart it represents the base of the individual himself both literally—in terms of the home he has come out of—and symbolically in terms of his inner sense of security and safety. This house describes the emotions and atmosphere which surround him before he is old enough to make a conscious and rational choice about whether he accepts them or not. This house may be associated with the Jungian idea of the personal unconscious and with areas of conditioned instinctual reactions imposed by the early environment.

Because of this association with influences that occur prior to the development of the discriminating mind, any planet placed here is highly suspect because it points to something in the psyche which must be first discovered and brought up to the surface before it can be dealt with constructively. The influence of this house lies like a great moving subterranean river beneath the surface of the later personality which is developed in accord with the Sun and Ascendant; and this river may be powerful enough to dominate the behaviour without being seen. It is a wholly personal house and does not seem to have much to do with the larger area of collective unconscious streams which affect the group emotional life. Because it is so personal, it is that much more difficult to approach with a clear and unbiased eye.

The fourth house is generally considered to be the indicator of the father and his relationship with the individual. This is of course subject to much argument, and the only clear statement which has so far come out of the confusion is that the fourth-tenth house axis refers to both parents. In some ways it is immaterial which house goes with which parent as problems with one automatically create compensatory problems with the other; however, I am inclined by experience to assign this house to the father as it is he who establishes the backbone of the family, gives it his name, and determines by his presence or absence the security or instability of the child's early life. It is rare that a child loses his mother except by death; but when a marriage fails, or there is no marriage in the first place, it is generally the father who leaves and whose support is withdrawn. The background of a difficult or broken home in childhood is usually coincident with afflicted planets in the fourth house or the fourth sign.

It will be obvious that having Saturn working as an unconscious factor from the plane of the feelings is rather difficult as he is very slippery. He is usually considered, in Cancer or in the fourth house, to suggest conditions of coldness, limitation, authority without love, separation or isolation, and a generally unsympathetic early home life. This is often in a very literal fashion, where the father dies or the parents are divorced or where the father is forced by circumstances to be away much of the time. The isolation may also occur in a symbolic fashion where the father is very much physically present but can offer no love, sympathy, or emotional support—or where he may be loving and kind but is a burden or a great disappointment through alcoholism, sickness, weakness of character, or an emotional pattern which destroys the peace of the home. Or there may be undue emphasis on material development and little on emotional expression.

There are many possible avenues on the mundane level in which a fourth house Saturn may find reflection. The forms are as varied as are individuals. Regardless of which means of outward expression occurs, however, the inner reaction is generally the same; the sense of security, the feeling of protection needed by a developing child as a base on which to build the evolving ego, is denied or frustrated, and the natural expression of feeling which seeks to find unity with family and a sense of heritage is blocked.

It needs little further reasoning to see that this kind of situation, working on unconscious levels, can effectively cripple a part of the individual's emotional nature for the remainder of his life if it is not understood. The mistrust of any emotional intimacy, particularly the kind which revolves around a domestic situation, is usually pronounced; at the same time a craving for something secure and permanent and tangible in the emotional life is also pronounced. It is a rare individual who is aware of this polarity existing within him; he will see one end or the other. He may either be inordinately tied to his family and the place of his birth, or he may hate them or display coolness and detachment. He is never truly indifferent, however, for something which was necessary for his emotional development was missing, and the entire structure of his psyche has had to develop lopsided to compensate for the loss.

There is often great emotional instability with Saturn in the fourth house, and a definite feeling of having been unloved, unwanted, is common. This may not be wholly conscious, however. Nevertheless it will show, in a very obvious fashion, to the perceptive observer. There is also often resentment toward men in general as the father is the first man or symbol of masculinity encountered by the child. This can, of course, wreak havoc with a man's understanding of his own masculinity and a woman's understanding both of men and of her own unconscious male half. This is particularly true if the father is actually absent from the home; for then, however justified she may be, the mother must play both roles, and consequently, whether she is temperamentally suited to the role or not, she must become a dominant or authoritative figure. This is as much true of the weak or inept father as it is of the vanishing one. The areas of the emotional life which can be affected in adulthood are much greater than the sphere of the home, for the fourth house is one of the angles and is therefore more significant in terms of the expression of the man on the physical plane.

Saturn in the fourth house is also often concurrent with a compulsion to accumulate land. In this way the need for some sense of security on the emotional level is reduced to a physical fact—a common translation which Saturn very often attempts to make. The translation usually fails, however, for material things cannot satisfy an emotional need. But to the person carrying this emotional burden, land is solid and unchangeable, a home which is owned cannot be taken away in the same fashion that emotional support can suddenly be torn away by death or absence. The unchecked crystallisation of a feeling value will eventually, as the individual hardens and grows older, lead to that which has been referred to as a "lonely end to life".

It will be obvious from this that a fourth house Saturn—and to a lesser extent Saturn in Cancer for his influence seems to be more obvious in the houses than in the signs—can rule the life with an iron although invisible hand by undermining the sense of self-worth and making it difficult for the individual to permit any close emotional contacts. It is the meaning of the position that is necessary if it is to be utilised in a constructive way.

By denying a component which ordinarily comes from the environment, Saturn's influence forces an individual to create that missing component himself if he is to have any peace. He must gradually withdraw identification of the value with the external world and find its reality within himself as a part of his own psyche. Thus the opportunity is offered, when Saturn is in the fourth house, for the person to build an inner sense of security and self-acceptance based on an understanding of his real origin. This solid inner psychic structure cannot be destroyed or shaken by circumstance; unlike the support and confidence given by a loving parent which fosters emotional dependency on others later in life—the worst aspect of Cancer—this inner strength becomes the inviolable possession of the soul. What begins as an emotional value must remain an emotional value, but the field of its expression is expanded.

This kind of security on the feeling level is extremely rare. The great majority of individuals bear many scars because of the loss of security in childhood, or they are dependent on loved ones for a constant supply of it. Only the individual with Saturn in the fourth house is likely to have developed it on his own, and this because he has had to. There is some amount of trust required in the guidance or wisdom of the inner self who has chosen this particular experience. Without this trust, there is no possibility of understanding the meaning of the experience. Saturn always drives a man to understand the nature of his pain. With a fourth house Saturn he must understand the vulnerability of his own feeling nature and the needfulness which underlies his apparent coldness toward all family and domestic matters. It is then necessary to accept the experience as a positive means to an end which will be worth the pain and the effort since the pain is relative to the dependency on others in the first place. The very personal and intimate world of the feelings must be acknowledged and encouraged. This is particularly difficult for men to do, and for this reason a fourth house Saturn is more dangerous on a man's chart; but in compensation, a man with Saturn placed here who has taken the time to descend into his own emotional depths, as do the heroes of mythology into the underworld, will display that rare integration and serenity which comes from a balancing of the masculine and feminine sides of the nature.

Saturn in Scorpio and
the eighth house

The symbolic progression of man's evolution from Aries to Pisces has been described in many sources. There is a similar progression within the three signs belonging to one element, and here the progression represents the stages of development in that particular sphere of consciousness. The first sign or house belonging to that element is generally the clearest and most direct in meaning and relates to the development of the individual personality and its integration. The second sign of that element denotes a point of crisis for here the individual must take his own experience and integrate it into the group of which he is a part. This is rarely done without struggle, for this too is an expansion of consciousness from the personal to the universal. The third and last sign or house refers to the larger unit of the group and infers the final purpose of the particular level of consciousness symbolised by that element.

The watery signs and houses do not contradict this. In the fourth house a man is first subjected as an isolated unit to emotional forces and pressures from the environment which shape his future growth as a personality. He has the opportunity of building a base within himself so that the projection into circumstance is withdrawn and inner security on the feeling level becomes a permanent possession of his character. In the eighth house, the man must take his feeling nature as a channel of expression and contact and begin to function in personal relationships with others. The flow of feeling is now between him and another. Finally, in the twelfth house he has the opportunity of taking the wisdom he has acquired from his experiences and offering it to the group in service for the group development. He is no longer an isolated unit but part of a larger evolving life. This is a helpful way of viewing things which is useful to remember in considering Saturn in the eighth house for this house is probably the most misunderstood and maligned of all the houses in the horoscope.

This house is primarily described as either the house of physical death—which suggests that it has no value or activity outside that brief moment when we take leave of the physical sheath—or as "money received from others", a description which is an insult to the complexity and power of the sign and planet associated with the house. Both interpretations are valid as far as they go, but they do not help in an understanding of Saturn placed in the eighth beyond the reading of a death in old age and the denial of inheritance; and both of these readings are frequently mistaken. The interchange of finances between two people in partnership may be one of the by-products of the house, but it is only when the meaning of money as a symbol of emotional values is understood that the more complex meaning of "money received from others" becomes clear. Death itself does indeed come under this house, but there are many kinds of death, and most of them are not physical; and every death is followed inevitably by a rebirth because it is only the form, and not the life which inherits the form, that dies.

As a watery house, the eighth deals primarily with emotional exchange. As opposite from the second house, that which has physical value and meaning and which constitutes stability and self-sustenance becomes that which has emotional value and which constitutes stability of feeling. It is in the eighth sign, Scorpio, that we may find a clue to the significance of this house in matters of sex, emotional crises, and the death and rebirth of the instincts as purified desire.

This is primarily a house of crisis and refers to those points in life where the emotional ties to others force a man to the realisation of some vital area of his own feeling nature which must be recognised, examined, and purified. Here money becomes a symbol of emotional dependence or freedom, for in our society it buys freedom or bond-age in marriage, and our sexual values are largely coloured by our finances. So often in the eighth house there exists the enactment of a struggle which appears purely material and which is really emotional in origin. It is no wonder that Freud attributed such significance to money in dreams and why psychology continues to recognise the relationship between monetary and emotional generosity or tight-ness.

It is common to find the individual with afflicted planets here tied to a difficult financial situation following upon a broken marriage or to chronic problems with partners who take advantage of him financially. This is particularly characteristic of an eighth house Saturn. When investigated, it will often be found that on the sexual and emotional levels there was difficulty in expression, and there is no sweeter revenge for many people than to air their disappointment and frustration in the face of an unresponsive Saturnian partner through material demands.

The area into which this discussion takes us is a prickly one, and this is usual for Scorpio and the eighth house; however, although the previous statement may seem inordinately hard, it is ironic that in our society the prostitute, who is at least honest about the wares she sells, is despised and generally ends up in jail, while the wife who fundamentally plays the same role and buys her security with her body is glorified because society condones this mask. There are a great many women who trade their sexual favours for a legal tie which promises them financial security and a great many men who buy these favours in exchange for what have been euphemistically termed "a husband's rights".

There is much rubble which must be dug through where our present attitudes toward sex in relation to money are concerned for we are still following the feudal concepts of family financial structure. In spite of the efforts of more enlightened souls, it will take another generation before we can begin to understand that the real nature of sex has nothing to do with the physical world at all but is the reflection of emotional and mental energies—which are in turn the reflection of still more complex energies. Money and sex are still too complex for the average man to understand except in a literal way, and consequently, we have a tremendous amount of confusion to wade through before the alchemical union of two people into one is understood.

The three watery houses and signs represent three aspects of the feeling nature of man. The fourth house symbolises the nurturing forces which shape his early life. The eighth symbolises the creative and procreative forces which he wields and through which he contacts others. The twelfth symbolises the dissipating forces which eventually break down his sense of separateness and release him into group life.

The eighth house is a battleground, the primary purpose of which is self-understanding and self-mastery through constant crises. There is no greater battleground or stimulus to crisis than the energies which are released through the apparently wholly physical act of sex. The union which occurs on the level of the feeling nature produces a flow of energy which takes a man, for a brief moment, "out of himself"—it is virtually the only time that he can feel himself to be at one with another human being. It is this intimate emotional oneness to which the sexual aspect of the eighth house refers; there is a death of the individual awareness and the birth of a mutual awareness for which reason the Elizabethans called the sexual act "the little death". Unfortunately there are many people who are as frightened of the apparent emotional vulnerability inherent in this as they are of death itself. What they do not recognise is that the union takes place whether it is recognised or not, and on the feeling level it is not possible to totally shut out the partner; it is only possible to believe that he has been shut out.

To consider this point of view is to recognise the real responsibility involved in a sexual union. This has nothing to do with morality. We have had many centuries of moral teachings which have done absolutely nothing to help us understand the real nature of the mystery. The currents of this great creative force or "serpent power"—whose cousins we may see as the serpent in the garden, the ourobouros of alchemy, and the plumed serpent of the Aztecs—may be released in other ways, but these belong to the sphere of the occultist and the magician, and the average individual knows only one—physical sex. Once set in motion, these currents bind and alter both souls involved. All states of consciousness which involve the "death" of the personality—ranging from those induced by drugs to certain kinds of religious ecstasy and trances of varying sorts—come under the rulership of the eighth house for they all refer to this same energy which can separate the self from its vehicles. Physical death is only the last in a series of deaths which begin with birth.

We understand very little about both sex and death at the

present time, and this ignorance is more than slightly owed to the confusion of the Piscean era with its pronouncement of sex as evil and of death as the gateway to never ending heaven or hell. This kind of conditioning runs deep, as it has been with us for two thousand years, and even the more liberal-minded and scientifically inclined have the same collective heritage of fear, superstition, and fascination about this area of human experience. The individual with Saturn in the eighth house has a double burden on his hands for he must not only come to terms with Saturn—who is evasive enough on his own—but he must also be willing to make the descent into Pluto's realm if he is to find the treasure hard to attain. It may be said, however, and with no attempt at poetry, that the person who accomplishes this possesses the key to his own immortality.

In a great many cases with Saturn in Scorpio or in the eighth house, the individual's fears or feelings of inadequacy are in the area of sexual expression. This is undoubtedly a symbol for an even deeper fear; but here the symbol is powerful enough in its own right to create great pain in the person's life. The average man who has to deal with this situation will not, however, take kindly to being told this fact bluntly by an astrological consultant. People are as prickly about sex now, when it comes to overt discussion, as they were during Victoria's time. Moreover the man's inadequacy is not a physical one but rather an emotional one; this is a watery, not an earthy, house. Saturn in the eighth is often linked with impotence or frigidity, but these are also not physical problems, and the physician who attempts to cure these problems through hormones alone is committing a grave error. The difficulty here lies in the fear of submission, of violation, of the control of the partner, and of emotional rejection for it is the psychic rather than the physical exchange which contains the threat.

It is fairly common to find an individual with Saturn in the eighth who may be affectionate and loving but who, when the last outpost of separateness is passed in the bedroom, shies like a frightened horse and cannot perform. Or he may overcompensate for his inner fears by becoming the "perfect lover" on a purely physical level, and he may try to block the flow of energy and emotion to his partner so that he is, somehow, not really there. However subtle this mechanism is, it can be deeply frustrating and disturbing to the partner although it may not be recognised on a conscious level by either person. The individual may not be aware that anything is wrong except that somehow it is always faintly disappointing, and he is never able to achieve the satisfaction his fantasies tell him is possible. It takes an unusual degree of honesty to look directly at the subtle patterns which surround an eighth house Saturn for there is, at the same time as fear, the overcompensation of great value placed on performace in our present era. No wonder that these people have such trouble with money during and after marriage; they may easily find themselves under financial obligations concurrent with the amount of frustration they have unconsciously inflicted on their partners.

As with all Saturn positions, two extremes of behaviour are possible. The effects of overcompensation can help to produce the overtly promiscuous person who is not truly motivated by physical pleasure but who is trying particularly hard to be "sexy" because he or she is dimly aware of a fundamental problem in relating emotionally to another person. Here Saturn again tries to make an emotional value into a physical one with little success. This kind of behaviour is prevalent now because there is great emphasis on sexual freedom as the reaction to too much restriction in the past. Both are extremes which are part of the natural process of evolution but which are unpleasant in themselves for fear permeates them both.

It is naturally wise for the consultant astrologer to express diplomacy when dealing with eighth house matters for he may be inviting a punch in the mouth otherwise. But with this kind of eighth house Saturn, we are reminded of that wonderful Shakespearean line, "Methinks thou dost protest too much!" This is reminiscent of the fourth house Saturn who "adores" his family, who had a "wonderful" childhood, who had "no problems whatsoever" with either parent.

On the other hand the person with Saturn in the eighth may cloak his fears with the garment of strong religious or moral convictions of a particularly intolerant sort, thereby declaring as sinful that of which he is essentially afraid. In these cases Saturn is a prompter toward celibacy but for all the wrong reasons. The devil, unfortunately, is not vanquished by being told to go away; it is the light of consciousness that he cannot endure.

We may also find that rare individual who is honest enough with himself to understand that there is something within himself that needs development—as there is in everyone—and who makes the effort not only to discipline but to comprehend his sexual nature as well so that he can express it in the most positive way. In all cases, however, the fascination with death and with sex is very great although there may be fear or disgust at the same time.

It seems that a characteristic pattern of the person with an eighth house Saturn is to be let down emotionally by others and often in the most intimate and painful way; and it is in this pattern that a clue to the larger purpose of the placement may be found. There is frequently a denial of deep emotional contact in childhood, and as Saturn has some connection with the father, this placement often occurs where the father dies or is emotionally cold. Often the individual grows up in an environment where very little physical expression occurs or where the sexual problems existent between the parents have filled the atmosphere with hostility and fear. There is some link between the father and the sexual energies although this may be very subtle. Often it is not subtle, and beatings or assault occur. The effect, whatever the actual circumstance, is a feeling of isolation and loneliness and the awareness that no one can share or alleviate the scars. For Saturn in the eighth house carries deeper emotional scars than any other Saturian placement, and the wounds are slower to heal.

The emotional isolation with an eighth house Saturn is even more acute than with a fourth house Saturn for the emotional needs are far more intense and directed toward individuals. It is union rather than security which is sought and union of a particularly intense and transforming kind. The individual often feels that through another he can be reborn and can achieve awareness of his spiritual nature. The lesson with Saturn, of course, is that one must do it himself; the transformation and resurrection into higher consciousness, the deep knowledge and mastery of the unconscious, must come from within the man himself. There is often a fascination with all things occult or, at the very least, an interest in the depths of the mind, and it is in utilising this interest and in learning the real nature of the energies of creation that the individual becomes a magician. The secrets of the powers of the unconscious are his, and these are literally life-giving powers for the healing of himself and others.

Saturn in Pisces and the twelfth house

The twelfth house, as the last in the circle and lying hidden behind the Ascendant or outward behaviour, symbolises both endings and beginnings. It is the end because it represents the sacrifice which must ultimately be made of the conscious personality as a separation unit. From a more abtruse point of view it represents the beginning because it refers to those causes from the past which, operating from birth and below the level of consciousness, draw to us those situations which require that we lose ourselves and die to be reborn into group consciousness. From water all life comes, says the Koran, and this house, reflecting Pisces and Neptune, the ancient god of the waters, suggests that plane where life, undifferentiated and without individuality, first sprang and where, wise with the lessons of individual consciousness, it must eventually return. Even shorn of its more esoteric associations, the twelfth house refers to isolation and submission, and to the dissolution of the personality.

This is often called the house of karma, based on the idea that planets found here are in some way denied normal expression and are often operating as unconscious rather than conscious drives. It is also called the house of self-undoing because isolation, incarceration, helplessness, and bondage are often the lot of the person with a heavily active twelfth house—literal or symbolic—and it is his own actions which draw these conditions to him. Whether a long past is considered or not, the inference is certainly present that the ego, built through the efforts of the previous eleven houses and signs, must eventually be laid on the altar of sacrifice so that the man may become a functioning part of a larger whole and give of his wisdom and energy for the good of the group. For the man who refuses to comprehend this, it is the house of hospitals and prisons, for only through the loss of individual power can a man realise that he himself is nothing without a link to the rest of life.

This is always a difficult house, unless the path of service is pursued. Somehow the release of energy in this way alleviates much of the frustration and loneliness which accompanies twelfth house planets and makes the required sacrifices bearable. Great pain often occurs through the twelfth house for the loss of the will after so much careful building is a great blow to the man who has come to identify himself with his personal desires. Yet loss of will is the price which all planets pay when found in this house although the finding of real inner serenity is often gained in exchange.

As the last sign of the watery trigon, Pisces symbolises the completion and fulfillment of all emotional strivings—unity not with another person but with life itself. This is the mystical marriage, and it is most difficult for the average man, centered in his personality, to deal with. There is no battle required; only acquiescence and devotion. It is almost impossible to make any sense of the twelfth house from a purely mundane point of view, for even more than the eighth, this is a non-material house and pertains to matters which bring a man into closer touch with subjective reality. Any planet in the twelfth is subject to the dissolving and transmuting influence which blocks the ordinary personal expression of the planet and forces its energies inward and upward. That which occurs here occurs in secret like the gestation of a child. Only when the term is complete can this facet of the individual unfold like a newborn baby into external expression; and by then it is changed.

Saturn in the twelfth house, and to a lesser extent in Pisces, is difficult from the point of view of the personality because the Saturnian energies, geared initially toward self-protection and defense against the environment, are rendered ineffectual. This may in extreme situations be through hospitalisation or imprisonment for a period of time, and the man may learn through his own helplessness how ultimately impotent the personal will is against the forces of his own past which he himself has set in motion. The feeling that one is helpless and must submit to something larger and greater is frequent with this placement of Saturn although it may occur on a very subjective level. This is a cadent house and refers to states of mind, and Saturn here often generates a vague fear that someone or something, a misty or generalised fate or destiny, is going to destroy him or control him. He may isolate himself and attempt to shield himself from contact with others at the same time that he is weighed down by an oppressive loneliness and sense of powerlessness.

The sacrifice of one's material ambitions is often concurrent with a twelfth house Saturn, and this is also one of the commonest significators of the child who dedicates his life to the care of an ailing or helpless parent at the cost of his own development. This is often done not because it must be—there are always alternatives—but because there is an intense feeling of guilt, obligation, and an instinctual understanding that he must make some sacrifice or pay some debt. It is also often the reflection of a fear of confronting external life and a sense of impotence in being able to handle practical affairs.

Guilt looms large with this placement of Saturn although it is generalised rather than specific guilt. It may cause a man to seek penance through solitude, or there may be religious penance in the literal sense resulting in the monk or nun. It may be apparently involuntary penance as is the case with incarceration; but the man himself chooses this course although he may not consciously believe he will have to pay. It may result in sickness or withdrawal from conscious awareness through drugs, alcohol, or insanity. Or it may be much more subtle and less drastic, as in the case of the man who is always alone and always feels separation from the rest of humanity and the rest of life, no matter how many people he surrounds himself with.

Typical Saturnian ambivalence occurs with a twelfth house Saturn too, and there is both a compulsive fascination with and a great fear of losing one's identity and individuality. But whatever the specific mundane situation which is reflected, the individual is generally called upon at some point in his life to endure helplessness and aloneness and the sacrifice of his control. When this occurs on an inner level, the individual is frequently unable to communicate his feelings to others which only increases his sense of isolation. He does not understand what it is that he is trying to protect himself against, any more than he understands the abyss which draws him with such fascination. He only knows that he feels powerless and may overcompensate for this feeling by attempting to prove that he is totally master of his life. This may land him in hospital or in jail without his understanding the inner motives which have brought him there.

Saturn is representative in his disguised and baser form as the most personal kind of power, that which a person seizes for self-protection through manipulation of his environment. It is man's defense mechanism which is necessary for a long time while the unfolding consciousness needs defending; however, when Saturn is found in Pisces or in the twelfth house, the time has come for the scaffolding to be taken down for the inner structure is nearly complete, and stripping this away is initially like stripping off one's outer skin and exposing the raw and tender area beneath.

As opposite to the sixth house, the twelfth disorganises that which the sixth has put in order and offers chaos instead. This is not the chaos of sickness and madness, however; it only seems so to those who have built their conception of reality on a mundane base.

Understanding the meaning of this position takes us beyond the field of orthodox psychology which has certainly mastered the fourth house and some of the eighth but is lost when confronting the mysteries of the twelfth. Recognition of the urge for evolution, for meaning, for the spiritual side of life as a valid psychological drive in man is now becoming widespread however; and when it is understood that this is perhaps the most basic and most important instinct in man—although an instinct of the psyche rather than of the body—then it will not be such a painful experience for a man to sacrifice his personality to permit his total self expression. The real potential of Saturn in the twelfth house is unfortunately only available now to those of a mystical bent who are inclined toward the path of inner contemplation. To them it is the final sacrifice of the sense of separateness and is willingly undergone because it is the last door between man and his freedom. It depends in the end on one's perspective. Trying to hunt Saturn down through the mazes of the unconscious is difficult enough in the eighth house where there are still some personality links; but the twelfth is wholly of the soul, and analysis does not help understanding unless it is backed by a knowledge of man's innately spiritual nature. The gold available from a twelfth house Saturn is the power to serve, not to "do good"— which is not service at all—but to experience the sense of unity which the mystic is forever seeking and the sense of responsibility and detached love which accompanies this unity. This will, of course, make no sense to the earthy man and may offend more pragmatic astrologers; but the fact remains that the twelfth house has not yet been satisfactorily explained any more than has the nature of man. It may be that as scientific evidence piles up, slowly but surely, in demonstration of the occult teachings of the past, the interrelationships of all living things and their essential underlying oneness will be a fact on the objective plane as well as a subjective experience on the part of the mystic.

Saturn in the watery signs and houses is worthy of first place because it is in this area that he displays his greatest ambiguity and also his greatest emotional suffering. As man is only now beginning to learn how to think objectively as a group, and as the majority of people are still polarised in their feeling natures, Saturn in water is responsible for a great deal of the loneliness and isolation so apparent at the present time. It is of some help for the individual who has Saturn in a watery house or sign to recognise that his potential in terms of inner peace, understanding, and wisdom is as great as his potential for despair if he will only turn inward to the realm of the feelings and of the unconscious.

2 in the earthy signs and houses

The element of earth is related to the plane of matter in which we all consciously function and pertains to those areas of life where one's efforts, and mistakes, yield tangible results and require tangible tools. Earth is considered a simple element, and it is generally associated with money, resources, security, work, service, and achievement in one's profession. Earth may also be related to the psychological function of sensation; which means that through this function an individual's perception of reality is based on that which he experiences through his five senses and through the use of his concrete or rational mind. It may be assumed from this that there is little mystery about the kind of frustration which ensues from Saturn's placement in earth, and it is here also that the typically Capricornian qualities of perseverance, thrift, caution, and self-discipline are thought to provide the most obvious solution to Saturnian problems.

Earth is not, however, as simple as it is generally considered to be in our basic textbooks. This element has been the unfortunate victim of a body of popular opinion which suggests that matter, or the materialistic view of life, is in contradiction to, or exclusive of, spirit or the spiritualistic view of life. Those unfortunate souls who are predominantly earthy in chart makeup through Sun, Moon, Ascendant, or a stellium of earthy planets are considered in some vague and obscure fashion to be not quite as "evolved" as those coming under the other, more colourful, elements. Because the earthy temperament is concerned with the laws and workings of the physical plane and attempts to direct its creative energy and effort toward the understanding and control of that plane, this temperament is considered materialistic and therefore lacking in vision.

We may often obtain a good view of inner psychic reality from a study of man's myths and of the symbols he chooses to describe his various concepts of his gods. Through these symbols we express what we inwardly value as truth whether or not this is part of a prevailing popular conception of truth. We have chosen to place the birthdate of Jesus under Capricorn, the densest of the earth signs and the most ambitious in the worldly sense, although there is no historical evidence that this birthdate is appropriate. We have also chosen to place the birthdate of Mary at precisely fifteen degrees of Virgo, that most mundane and critical of signs. We also celebrate the birthdate of the Buddha under Taurus, that slowest and most inflexible of signs. The entire esoteric concept of initiation is connected with Capricorn specifically and the earth signs in general because the initiate has not earned his initiation until he is able to apply the higher consciousness he has discovered to the body and the environment in which he functions as a personality. Only when the physical world is made a fitting garment or symbol of the inner spirit is his task complete. The mysteries of the duality of spirit and matter have occupied the thoughts of occultists and mystics throughout the ages, and alchemy and astrology in the form we know them were both outgrowths of this attempt to understand spirit in terms of matter through the law of correspondences. The various myths and motifs which are connected with the symbol of Saturn, from Pan through Satan and Lucifer to the prima materia or "Mercurius Senex" of the alchemists, from the serpent in the Garden to the Hermit of the Tarot deck, should be sufficient to indicate that there is more to earth than meets the eye. And finally we must consider that we exist on the earth itself, and that we are now beyond doubt demonstrated to be intricately connected through the "etheric" or energy field around us to every other kingdom of nature. There is much that we do not understand about the nature of matter. It may be that when we are told in esoteric literature that earth is the final test of initiation for man, there is also an equally valid rational or scientific law which describes the same truth—but we do not possess it yet.

Saturn in the earthy signs and houses pertains, on the surface, to those problems and limitations which affect an individual through his bodily comfort, his ability to support and sustain himself, his capacity to find meaningful work which allows him a share in the ordering of his environment, and his ability to achieve responsibility or authority in those areas where he has shown competence and skill. This is the simplest interpretation of Saturn in earth, and it will generally be found that this interpretation is valid. It is unfortunate that we are given in the Old Testament the inference that man was driven to labour as a result of original sin for we no longer believe that work can be a creative act. Even God, according to the same document, worked for six days to create the world. There is a basic need in each man to feel himself useful, and this is connected with what is called "group consciousness"—the sensing of a unity which implies individual responsibility and the need for a contribution, according to ability, to the whole. This group consciousness has nothing to do with enforced contribution or with mass consciousness where the individual has no meaning in himself. There is also a basic need in man to know that he has earned through his labours something permanent which is his unique accomplishment or possession. By it he establishes a sense of his worth to the group. This "something permanent" may be actual material reward. It may also be more abstruse: standards, values, talent, honour, service. Commerce and trade are as valid a form of communication between people as the written and spoken word, and money, as well as being a symbol of emotional independence, may also be a symbol of individual worth and of skills and services which are offered to others. Consequently, when we look to mythology, we find that Mercury, among his many rulerships, was the god of merchants as well as being the divine messenger, and presided in his inimitably suave fashion over the business deal.

It is possible that Saturn in one of the earthy signs or houses offers an opportunity to learn about the deeper meaning of this element since the solution to the frustrations which he symbolises when placed in earth rarely comes about through the application of earthy tools. It would appear that the other three elements must be understood and integrated to form a tool effective enough to influence the apparent dead weight of earth and alleviate the pain of thwarted instinct.

Saturn in Taurus and
the second house

The second house is traditionally that of acquisition and possessions. From it one may assess the individual's capacity to earn a livelihood, his attitude toward those things which he defines as security, and the manner in which his income is likely to be derived. This is a fixed and earthy house, and the emotional need of a secure foundation is suggested, a desire rather than the outcome of desire. All of the houses connected with the fixed signs appear to have some bearing on one's values, on the desire nature, and on instinctual reactions of a habitual kind. They have little bearing on events or objects. If this group of houses is considered as the reflection of a man's desire nature, it would appear that greater depth of meaning exists in relation to the second house and that it is not merely the house of possessions. Possessions are merely a simple and tangible form of satisfying desire.

The urge to possess something outside oneself and make it a permanent possession appears to be a collective need whether the desired "something" is a person, a value, a state of consciousness, or an automobile. It is then the man's possession, in a deeper sense than physical ownership, because he values it. It is of worth to him, and therefore it has meaning. That which is desired through the second house only applies to material things if these have value; and although the majority of people at present place the highest value on these things, it has not always been the case nor will it necessarily continue to be so as the collective consciousness of man develops.

The second house may apply as much to relationships as it does to money in the bank since possession of a valued object is often closely connected with what we define as love. In the end, however, the possession of worth which is truly a permanent possession can only be a quality within the individual himself. There is nothing else in life which is permanent and unalterable except those attributes which we term spiritual. Everything else may be lost, destroyed, taken away, or devalued. It seems that the desire for values, not only tangible but mental, emotional, and spiritual as well, is more representative of the second house than possession.

It is the definition of value—a nebulous and relative term—which becomes important when planets are located in the second house for the meaning or expression of each planet then becomes a value. Of all the planets only Saturn appears to have an exclusively material value, but as we have seen, this is deceptive because his function is to demonstrate the relativity of all tangible values. Through Saturn everything on the material plane takes on new meaning because it is seen as a symbol for an inner quality or state of being. Security may be defined very differently when viewed in this way.

The simplest reading of Saturn in the second house is fear of poverty, and certainly this placement frequently accompanies a childhood spent in want where the luxuries of material life, and sometimes even the necessities, are lacking. This is Saturn on his most literal level where he denies a material quality necessary to the individual's well-being so that later in life there is a constant need to fill the gap. We have all come into contact with the self-made man who has struggled from the bottom of the heap by his own dogged efforts and has finally succeeded in accumulating some money in the bank, a house, an automobile or two, and other symbols which society has taught him to interpret as security. Saturn in his most unconscious form is eminently conventional in these matters, and Saturn in Taurus as well as in the second house has a penchant for accepting as values only those which society accepts and therefore makes apparently stable. Yet the self-made man with a second house Saturn is often so frightened of losing what he has so laboriously acquired that he may not be able fully to enjoy what he has. He may be terrified of loss and display the remarkable facility—because he thinks about it so much—of attracting loss through his own bad judgment. He is frightened of the responsibility of ownership because he knows the pain of losing that which he owns, yet he is compulsively drawn toward collecting more and more. No amount is sufficient in the end to make him feel fully secure, and indeed he is not fully secure because forces larger than he can overturn his life and leave him bankrupt. He has invested wholly material things with value because he has never had them before and pays the price of trying to make an inner quality tangible.

There is another kind of pattern with Saturn in the second house which is outwardly opposite yet inwardly the same. This is the person who may have been perfectly comfortable as a child on the material plane yet who is denied a different kind of possession, a sense of inner values and of personal worth. One cannot blame this, or any other characteristic, wholly on the attitude of the parents, however, for the individual has chosen his environment in the first place and moreover would not be sensitive to certain values and not others if a similar note were not resonated within his own inner structure. So we will often see a person who, literally or symbolically, will sell himself for security because he has no other sense of values and in the end does not value himself. He judges himself and others by how much he has, not by what he is.

This kind of individual is often difficult to understand; for some of the most unpleasant Saturnian manifestations may accompany Saturn in Taurus or in the second house—not because the position is a "bad" one but because it tends to concur with obvious, tangible characteristics which are not easily hidden. To an unconscious person with this placement, the end often justifies the means, and avarice and greed may be very evident. The inner strength and self-sustenance which Saturn in his more conscious expression symbolises here may be apparently quite absent from the man's temperament, and he may lean heavily on others financially—the apparent opposite of our previously mentioned self-made man who will often rather starve than owe anybody anything. But these two extremes are the same psychological state for they both embody fear and the characteristic ambivalence of wanting and needing desperately yet attempting to reject the desired object. These states are both, in the end, phases of development, however, for either way the dependency is upon external values rather than inner ones, and Saturn the taskmaster will surely, at some point in the life, accompany experiences which teach the individual to shift his level of evaluation. He attracts these experiences himself because it is the desire of the total self to develop a sense of reality about values which is the intention, on a more esoteric level, of a second house Saturn.

There is another common manifestation of Saturn in the second house, and this is the individual who has denied all involvement with material things. This is overcompensation at work in a different direction. Like the man with Saturn in the eighth house—another fixed house which deals fundamentally with values and emotional attitudes—who cloaks his fear of deeper emotional and sexual encounter with a moral or religious reason why it would be sinful to do so, the man with Saturn in the second house frequently considers money as evil. He has a dim awareness of the fact that greed is as much a part of his own psyche as it is of others, but he cannot express tolerance toward his own humanity and therefore becomes intolerant of the apparent greed of others. He is frequently not merely content to be austere in his own life style. Instead he feels that it is his responsibility to criticise others for not following the same path because he cannot put his guilt to rest but also cannot confront himself. This is classic unconscious projection of the casebook kind: what we hate in others is unconsciously living within us.

This pattern of projection is extremely common with Saturn for he is the dark shadow of the bright, differentiated conscious personality, and he certainly includes some of our nastier and less attractive human qualities. These, however, are qualities which are not inherently evil; they have simply been outgrown or are not part of our conscious plan for development at any given time. It is only our harsh judgment of ourselves, based on other people's morality, that causes us to push these qualities into the unconscious where they form the shadowy figure of the Dweller on the Threshold. Psychic energy does not vanish but simply takes another channel, and with Saturn it is often that of projection—we do not see others as they are; rather we see in certain of their behaviour characteristics the reflection of our own negative qualities.

The sinfulness of worldly goods has always been the prerogative of the devout adherents of orthodox Christianity which has always had a difficult time in reconciling the opposites in a harmonious and constructive way; however, with the advent of a new age and the consequent emergence of new symbols and a new burst of growth in spiritual and psychic directions, the old values and concepts of God warring with the Devil, Lord of Matter, have appeared in a curious modern form. These values, which when put badly and stripped of their glamour are often of the "if I can't have it then you shouldn't either" variety, are now being coupled with political idealogies which have very little connexion with the real distribution of resources and opportunities. It would appear that projection still runs rampant among us, and it is fashionable once again to consider worldly goods as being synonymous with evil. It is no longer fashionable to consider sexual expression in this light because of the advent of psychoanalysis; but we have no similar revelation in the realm of commerce and material wealth. This trend may, however, be seen as the first rough and uncut demonstration of a fundamentally positive change toward a new sense of values.

The earthy signs are custodians for many layers of meaning; for when seen from the more esoteric point of view, matter is an expression of spirit which contains in symbolic guise the blueprint for mind, emotion, and the inner purpose for which the vehicle has been created. This is a more ambiguous but possibly more productive way of looking at matter and may be applied to Taurus and the second house. Following this thread is unquestionably like plunging into a labyrinth for what eventually emerges is that the second house has nothing to do with objects at all. The "pearl of great price" appears to lie at the heart of the labyrinth, but the persistence of a Taurean is required to reach it. The placement to find this central and unalterable value whose definition cannot be properly articulated but whose reality, to the man who has subjectively experienced it, is not to be questioned.

Saturn in Virgo and
the sixth house

Work, health, servants, and employer-employee relationships are the traditional meanings assigned to the sixth house. From it one is said to gain insight into the individual's work habits, the kind of situations he is likely to attract in his work life, his attitudes toward routine and toward service, and his attitude toward his body as a vehicle of service. The state of one's health is denoted by this house, and any tendencies toward organic or functional illness are generally reflected by it. This is generally considered to be a "weak" house, as is the twelfth, because it is cadent and planets which are placed in it do not appear to express through the mode of events or external activity. The sixth house is in fact often overlooked or considered unimportant. It is possible that we possess very little real understanding of its meaning because we do not understand the nature of the physical body and its link with the mind and the feelings of the individual.

This house seems to be of great importance on an inner level, as is the twelfth house, for it seems to refer to a process of inner synthesis, purification, ordering, or gestation which precedes the external and objective expression of the person into the world of others. We are used to linking the first six signs and houses of the zodiac with one's personal development and the last six signs and houses with one's participation in group life. As a cadent house the sixth is the inner process of attunement or ordering which synthesises the qualities developed through previous effort and forges of them one integrated personality which can then be the vehicle of expression for the self. Work, when it is related to this house, then becomes not only a means of livelihood, or a means of justifying one's existence, but it also becomes a ritual or preparation or purification and assumes importance as a symbol—just as money is a symbol when considered against the deeper meaning of the second house. The body itself is a symbol if this point of view is logically extended, and the health of the body is related to the success or failure of the integration process which is necessary for planets placed in this house.

This may seem an abstruse definition for plain, hard-working Virgo and her plain, hard-working house. But if we look once more to mythology, we will find that the virgin goddesses of the ancients were virgin not in the sense of sexual innocence or naivete for these goddesses were also prostitutes and ruled over the mysteries of sexual union and of birth. Virginal meant whole, single, possessed by no man, and the servant or slave of no husband or lover. The virgin mother goddess was a female archetype who mated and gave birth but who would never be a wife or helpmeet for she was wholly herself, independent, self-contained, integrated, and dependent on no one for her meaning or expression. It was only later that these goddesses were given to solar deities and were deprived of their autonomy and their sexuality in one clean swoop of patriarchal social development. There may be in this symbolism another key to the meaning of Virgo and the sixth house, for they appear to be connected with wholeness, the synthesis or integration of the various warring components of the psyche. On a larger level the synthesis or integration of the individual with his physical environment is also suggested, prior to his being able to join with others in a cooperative relationship.

The mysteries of the power of the mind over the body are being tentatively explored in psychology and psychosomatic medicine, and the less orthodox schools of healing, such as hypnotherapy, are perhaps even more aware of the subtle but unquestionable link between one's state of mind—and this includes the feeling nature—and one's health. But we still understand very little of these matters, and as much as medical science has been able to accomplish since ancient times, the recent exploration of the energy field or "etheric double" which permeates and co-exists with the physical body suggests that we have only just begun to comprehend the full meaning of the physical vehicle. The ancient science of acupuncture and the esoteric doctrine of the chakras or energy centres are not so absurd or unprovable as they were once thought to be. What we have always believed to be physical illness now appears to be originated from an entirely different level. We have only recently become aware of the concept of the unconscious mind, and prior to the birth of psychology in this century—accelerated by the discovery of Pluto—it was left to the medieval alchemists to make some sense out of man's fantasies and dreams, and this they were never able to achieve fully because they lacked the methods of scientific research. Perhaps we must wait for the discovery of another planet before the sixth house and sign will yield their secrets to us.

Saturn in the sixth house seems to provide an opportunity—often through frustration, disappointment, and ill health—for a journey into the mysteries of the interconnexion between mind and body and the possibility of a conscious and deliberate synthesis of these two, the reward of which is good health and a new awareness of the meaning of the body and of the material environment. Few people, however, are aware of this opportunity because we are not made aware that there might be a deeper meaning to work and to health. More commonly Saturn placed in the sixth refers to a state of disease, of discomfort, or of frustration and limitation in one's work situation. The fundamental psychological need for rhythm and ritual, the careful ordering of external life as a symbol of the careful ordering of the inner life which should, and rarely does, parallel it, is often denied in childhood. This need is as valid and as real as the need for security or for achievement.

If Saturn's darker side is considered first, the lack of this ordered rhythm of both inner and outer life will often be felt later as an area of inadequacy and fear. A heavily structured discipline or routine in childhood is common with this placement, but the routine is often lacking in fundamental meaning because there is no effort at inner alignment. Chaos threatens perpetually to intrude on the inner level for there is little integration there, and an almost compulsive ordering of the outer environment frequently ensues. Saturn may exaggerate the natural love of work, routine, and order until the love becomes a fear of anything outside the known and well-trod path. There is often a deep inner anxiety over physical or mental disintegration, and this placement has been linked with mental as well as physical disorders. It is the outer form of order which Saturn clings to rather than the inner blending of the mind, the feelings, and the intuition through the medium of the body; consequently, he experiences frustration for once again he has attempted to make tangible something which is essentially an inner process.

The individual with Saturn in Virgo or in the sixth house may externalise his situation so that the adjustment and the frustration pertain to his work life for in the function of usefulness to the larger group, he expresses the function of his body and its intricate structure to his total psyche. Just as an organ in his physical body may be out of harmony, he likewise may, as an organ of his environment, be out of harmony with the larger structure. It is his task to integrate himself to his world and to his body for he stands at the midpoint of these two. His body must serve his inner purpose as he must serve the inner purpose of the group.

When the man is relatively unconscious, Saturn may be symbolic of discontent and resentment because he may be aware only of the fact that he is in a rut and that he is imprisoned by circumstances. He may feel that he is capable of better things and will chafe against the boredom of his endless routine. Yet the meaning of the routine escapes him because he does not truly understand the meaning of service. The inner serenity which can be achieved through an alignment with the group life by service is rarely achieved in this case. Only the monotony of the outer pattern, repeated over and over again, is apparent. Saturn in the sixth house may suggest that the individual will be drawn toward service, but his conception of service is generally a situation where one does menial tasks for others. It is said in esoteric teaching that service, rather than being "good works", is an innate quality of the inner man; it is a state of consciousness rather than a planned act. Service of this kind is the result of inner integration for once the body and feelings and mind of a man are in balance, he can then begin to become aware, intuitively, of the purpose and nature of his inner psyche. He is no longer occupied in reconciling the battling components of his nature, but through an inner attunement—achieved through a ritual ordering of his personality—he can listen to his real direction. This is the goal of meditation, and of yoga, and of certain kinds of ritual magic, all of which are given to the sixth house—although the meaning is rarely made clear. Service which is the result of inner balance is the potential result of Saturn in the sixth house when he is expressing in a conscious way, and this placement is common among physicians, surgeons, and those who tend to the mental and emotional ills of others because it is a fulfilment of the inner need of the group.

Service is often seen by the average individual with Saturn in the sixth house as an easy road because it does not require courage, initiative, or the braving of the unknown—qualities which Saturn placed here often has difficulty expressing. Yet he may resent being a servant because of the sameness of his situation and the anonymity of his role. One of the most common reflections of this placement is the individual who remains in a job which he dislikes intensely yet cannot leave. We may hear him complain about it bitterly and about those for whom he works; he may be underpayed and overworked, or at least believe that he is; yet he will generally find excuses for avoiding any confrontation or effort at improvement because if his circumstances are irritating and frustrating, at least they are safe and familiar. If he does attempt to help himself, he is frequently refused because he projects an attitude of self-doubt or because he lacks the skill or qualifications to earn him a better situation. He often misses the need for the development of a skill because this requires an inner purpose for the outer training, and he is uncomfortable when forced to consider inner purposes. He may very neatly lock himself into his own prison without realising that he still, and always, possesses the key.

There is real administrative or organising ability with Saturn in the sixth house and often real healing ability and a fine and subtle insight into the intricacies of the mind, but these must be brought into the light and polished into usefulness. They are rarely available without effort. The man generally finds that a confrontation with the shadowy side of his nature, which seeks to avoid the problem of responsibility to the life of the group, is necessary. Humility of a genuine kind, which is one of the more endearing Virgoan qualities, is rarely present by natural inclination when Saturn is in the sixth house; subservience is often expressed instead, and they are not the same thing. The unconscious man with Saturn in the sixth house is like a gardener who loves only the flower, the final result of the process of growth, without understanding that the flower has meaning only against the context of the slow and orderly sequence of growth of the entire plant. The plant does not grow to produce the flower for him; it is only accidental that he is even there to appreciate it for the plant responds to its own inner purpose. Therefore, when the flower dies, his joy is gone.

Saturn in the sixth house is commonly associated with ill health as well as with a fascination for the laws of health. There is no reasonable answer to the problem of inherited or congenital disease for if we seek a cause-and-effect principle, or even a purpose, we are confronted with the philosophical problem of the nature of the soul. There are often simpler principles at work in the case of psychosomatic illness, however, and this is common with a sixth house Saturn. The least glamourous cause of this kind of pattern is a desire for attention, and this is common enough; the individual who completely dominates his household and his family through the demands of his illness is very common. Also common is the desire to avoid that which is unpleasant, either work or the deeper need for ordering which the psyche calls for and which seems an impossible task. The hypochondriac with a sixth house Saturn is not an infrequent occurrence. This is Saturn's method of avoiding the problem of integration for illness is always a reflection of imbalance—even if we assign it a purely physical origin.

We may also see the opposite extreme of Saturn in the individual who is obsessed with being "healthy". This is a much clearer example of the need for ordering which is compressed into a tangible method of expression. But whatever the external manifestation, Saturn in the sixth house reflects an imperative need for inner integration which, if avoided, may produce illness and, if forced into a material channel, may produce inner frustration, moodiness, irritability, and depression. If an individual works consciously toward a practical understanding of his psyche, and of its relationship with his body, and of the relationship of this working unit to the environment of which he is a part, then Saturn in the sixth house can make of the mind and the body not two interrelated things but one thing, a finely balanced vehicle which is then available for the use of the inner man who is no longer confined by his material expression. Toward this end alchemy was directed, and today the process of individuation in analytical psychology is also directed toward this synthesis. It is reflected in the ancient alchemical injunction: "Thou wilt never make from others the One which thou seekest, except there first be made one thing of thyself."

Saturn in Capricorn and the tenth house

The tenth house is Saturn's own, and in Capricorn he is dignified so we may therefore expect a "purer" manifestation of Saturn both in an ordinary and a more esoteric sense. This certainly seems to be true from the mundane point of view as the tenth house is traditionally associated with achievement, honor, ambition, and authority, and the cusp of the tenth house by the quadrant systems— the midheaven—is symbolic of the image which one projects outward to society as well as the image which is held inwardly by the person of his "role" in life. It may be assumed that Saturn in the tenth house refers to limitations, delays, and difficulties in the achievement of one's goals and in the successful expression of the self outward to the group as well as intense ambition—frequently unconscious—and a determination to succeed whatever the cost.

This is the interpretation generally given to Saturn in his own house and sign, and it is generally true as far as it goes. Much information may be obtained from the tenth house about the person's role in society, the way in which he appears to the group, and the purpose he identifies with when he considers his deeper reason for being. Although the precise nature of one's profession is impossible to determine from a birth chart, the lines of least resistance or of likely expression are often suggested, and the tenth house with its occupants and its ruler is one of the best pointers if not to the actual work, then to the inner goal or meaning of that work from the point of view of both the individual and society.

So far so good, and this interpretation of the tenth house is familiar ground to most astrological students. The association of the tenth house to the mother or father is also important, although less frequently stressed, particularly in view of the ambiguity surrounding the fourth-tenth axis. Whichever parent is represented by this house, it would seem to be the one who has had the most to do with shaping the social attitudes and ethics of the individual for these standards are reflected by the tenth house with its connexion with structure, tradition, and exemplary behaviour. It is generally the mother who infuses the child with her social values, partially because it is she who spends the maximum amount of time with the child and has therefore greater access to his apparently unformed mind. For more subtle reasons than this I am inclined to assign the tenth house to the mother. It is no piece of new information that ambition runs later in life in direct proportion to the suppression of identity in early life. By ambition I do not mean the inner need to achieve, which is characteristic of the cardinal signs, but rather the need to prove this achievement to others, which is characteristic of the man who has never been considered an individual in his own right. One has only to look at the uniform history of those who have achieved prominence through personal ambition to recognise the familar pattern of family rejection and isolation. Of course suppression of the individuality does not create ambition by itself to this degree nor does it create success. It is, however, an important component to be reckoned with and follows the psychological law that if psychic energy is denied an outlet in its chosen direction, it will return with doubled force in another, compensatory direction. This is the psychological interpretation of the kind of ambition which is often found concurrent with a tenth house Saturn. The more esoteric interpretation would not contradict this but would suggest that the important factor is the achievement because this is needed to precipitate some kind of change in society, in response to a collective need or following the purpose of the soul or inner self. It is then necessary or reasonable to choose a childhood and a vehicle which will provide the right psychological effects and the subsequent ambition needed for the personality to make the achievement.

The psychological interpretation of this situation postulates a cause-and-effect principle over which the individual has little control. The second interpretation is rather abstruse and is of the nature of an arrangement, filled with purpose, by which the man himself, functioning as a total unit, chooses to fulfil a function needed by the group of which he is a part. It is possible that both these ideas are correct.

The concept of self-determination as it is postulated here is a very ancient one which places the responsibility of the choice of earth plane circumstances in the hands of the self. It is one worth considering with an open mind, whatever the labels are to describe the situation, because it sheds some light on the deepest meaning of Saturn himself. He may be seen, finally, as the instrument or opportunity through which the person comes to understand the nature of his free will. It is certainly evident that those with a prominent tenth house, and particularly with Saturn in this house, often have the role either thrust upon them or seek it assiduously— and these are probably the same thing—of effecting some kind of change in the structure of the group, or of holding authority, or serving as an example of achievement. The inner sense of purpose, drive, and responsibility is often very strong when Saturn is in the tenth house, particularly if he is conjuncting the midheaven. There is frequently a strong sense of fate with regard to the role in life. Often sacrifice is required and a long, arduous process of building and preparation, where the personality with its desire for recognition drives the man on until he has achieved some degree of notice or responsibility. It is generally only later that, as the integration occurs which allows him to understand himself and his inner motivations better, the larger reason begins to emerge as to why he has done all that work.

One of Saturn's main characteristics is his duplicity, and one of the characteristic duplicities of the tenth house is that all that an individual accomplishes through it—and this can be great—is apparently done for the satisfaction of his own personal ambition or for the fulfilment of a personal goal or ideal. If the individual identifies with this area of personal ambition, he is likely to see his accomplishment as a means of gaining control over his environment so that it cannot control him—a Saturnian self-defense mechanism on a large scale. When viewed in perspective and from a safe distance, however, it may often be seen that the man has really been working for others; for he will frequently immolate himself, deny himself any spontaneous enjoyment or relaxation, and sacrifice all to the achievement of his goals—goals which have a very brief life-span, being a reflection of the life-span of the individual. The effects may in the end be historical ones, and even in a small area the person who is expressing to the fullest his tenth house Saturn may create long-lasting changes in the structure or organisation of his particular corner of society. It is only when he realises the nature and meaning of his work on a deeper level, and when he begins to cooperate consciously with his own inner blueprint, that he can truly enjoy the fruits of his labour.

Saturn in the tenth house is generally considered to symbolise ambition, a slow climb to power with many setbacks and delays, and, if he is afflicted, a subsequent fall from power. The overused examples of Hitler and Napoleon are usually quoted to demonstrate this pattern, which certainly applies to them both— along with the emotionally impoverished childhood. There are, however, many people with Saturn in the tenth house who never attempt to conquer the world; many of these are women who have never attempted to conquer anything more vast than the kitchen sink. This does not negate the meaning generally given to Saturn in the tenth; but his penchant for overcompensation and for projection of values onto another person must be considered. We must also consider the fact that the chart can only map out a series of potential developments, but the individual must be able to meet the challenge of these developments if they are to express in his life.

It is of interest to consider the relation of the tenth house to the mother for the development of the potential of Saturn in the tenth often sticks here. She is usually the dominant parent when this placement of Saturn occurs although this may be because of the death or absence of the father rather than a temperamental bias. This dominance may be of an obvious kind and may be expressed in stern, authoritative behaviour which is lacking in warmth or empathy. There is often a preoccupation with rules of conduct, propriety, and what the neighbours think, and an emphasis on material rather than emotional values. The dominance of the mother may equally often be reflected in that kind of instinctual woman who carries an unconscious and powerful ego drive beneath an apparently passive exterior. Sometimes the mother is a burden because of ill-health or dies young. In all these situations the seed is sown for a powerful influence on the psychic level which must be dealt with by the individual before he is able to express his full potential. He must symbolically cut the emotional umbilical cord, which generally remains well into adulthood.

There is a rather disturbing frequency of tenth house Saturns among the charts of homosexual men. This does not of course imply that Saturn in the tenth house causes homosexuality, and we are moreover not dealing with a strictly cause-and-effect principle but rather with an arrangement of circumstances which contain a purposive direction; however, if we relate the tenth house to the mother, then it is conceivable that some difficulty in relating to women may be one of the by-products of the rather powerful mother figure suggested by a tenth house Saturn. Difficulty with women can, of course, express through many forms of behaviour only one of which is homosexuality.

Emotional rejection, or a suppression of the will or identity, by the mother, is common with this placement, and the man who has experienced this in childhood may find that he does not trust women later in life. A woman with a tenth house Saturn may have equally serious obstacles to overcome for women must learn from their mothers the means and ways of femininity, and if a mother's nature is symbolised by Saturn, it is unlikely that the feminine principle will be the primary thing expressed. It will more likely be power. To this a woman may react by becoming feminine in the socially acceptable way, saying the right things and cooking the right meals, and simultaneously attempting to live a frustrated need for self-expression through her husband or lover. Or she may become consciously aggressive herself and reject the feminine principle within her own psyche. In all of these cases the first job confronting the individual who seeks to understand the inner potential of Saturn in the tenth house is a coming to terms with the mother and a reevaluation of the male and female roles. Although the fourth and tenth houses are rarely considered when problems of a sexual nature are considered, they do in fact have great bearing, indirectly, on the area of masculine and feminine roles.

An intense self-consciousness and great sensitivity to public opinion are common reflections of Saturn in the tenth house, as well as a fear of failure and a propensity to attract situations which are publicly embarrassing in some way. These expressions are all connected with a basic sense of inadequacy. Dealing with Saturn in the tenth house, where he displays some purely Saturnian qualities in the most difficult sense before he begins to yield his gold, requires considerable self-honesty. It is, however, difficult to achieve objectivity in questions which deal with male and female roles and equally difficult to be detached when considering one's mother. A considerable amount of sentimentality must be waded through on the subject of motherhood and many centuries of rigid sexual roles which have taken their toll on the collective human psyche.

Sensitivity to one's image is the next step on the ladder, and Saturn is inclined in this area to focus on material values as he usually does. It is often terribly important for the individual to be important, and his definition of importance may be strongly coloured by material advantage and social status. There is often a fear of public humiliation, which inclines toward shunning the limelight, yet there is also an equally strong urge for exposure. In group situations this is a very self-conscious placement although in individual relationships this tendency may not be apparent. Saturn in the first house may be intensely self-conscious in a personal situation yet will deal well enough with a distant public. It is the image which is important with Saturn in the tenth. The person is likely to be conservative in his approach to social values because he does not wish to compromise his position. When this characteristic exists in combination with other, more adventurous factors, a considerable amount of inner friction may result.

When a broader perspective is taken of this most interesting placement of Saturn, it often happens that the sensitivity, the self-consciousness, the attention to public estimation, and the constant effort to demonstrate usefulness and value through achievement all conspire to prepare an individual in a very helpful way to dealing with the great responsibility of holding authority over others. He may find when he reaches the top that he has learned diplomacy and statesmanship along the way as well as a sense of compassion for those whom he is attempting to teach or structure.

Professionally the person with Saturn in the tenth house is generally successful, largely because he tries so hard and is so persistent. He does not work well under others because although he may for a time be able to present the smooth surface of humility which is such a gift of the Saturnian personality, his own ambition and love of success will eventually push him out on his own. His problem does not lie in the achievement of success once he has begun his climb. It is getting started in the first place which is the initial task and which involves his overcoming a fear of failure which may lead to inertia. The remainder of the task is to establish a definition of achievement which is not based on purely external values. It is difficult for a person intent on a mountain climb to comprehend the fact that his climb is meaningless, and the reward of the summit is illusory, unless his success serves as a demonstration to others that the summit can be achieved. It is usually the work of Saturn in the tenth house to give structure and form to some group idea. If an individual refuses to accept the offer of this opportunity and attempts to live his task through another person, he generally must accept the price of frustration and a sense of purposelessness. If he accepts the challenge of his own inner self, then he himself can become Saturn the teacher in his most beneficent form.

3 in the airy signs and houses

The element of air is related to the principle of the logical mind, and it is this principle which ultimately differentiates man from the lower kingdoms of nature and allows him to observe himself—that is, to become self-conscious. Because of this exclusively human attribute, it may be observed that the three airy signs form the only trigon which does not incorporate animal symbolism but is expressed through either a human or an inanimate symbol. The other three elements are represented by at least two bestial symbols each. Although Virgo, ruled by a mental planet, is linked with a human symbol, Taurus and Capricorn are represented by animals; and although Sagittarius is connected with a half-human symbol, Aries and Leo are also symbolised by animals. The watery trigon is portrayed completely by creatures from the animal kingdon and is the most instinctual of the elements, relating to the function of feeling. Although we do not yet understand precisely what the mind is from a scientific point of view, or where it is located, or by what laws it functions, we can get some idea of its nature by observation of its behaviour. And we can at least understand that it is mind that permits man to call himself man.

All three airy signs, the houses associated with them, and the planets that rule them deal with one aspect or another of mind and the human need to exchange information with others and with the environment. All living things exchange information with their environment, and this is a biological process common to unicellular creatures as well as to man. But only man analyses his information and is aware of it as information. The ancient symbol for man is the pentagram or five-pointed star, and the number five has always traditionally been associated with both man and with Mercury, the significator of mind. Following this line of thought, we can see a correlation with the fact that five divided into the circle of three hundred and sixty degrees yields the quintile aspect of seventy-two degrees, one which is associated with skill and the possession of an unusual mental capacity—the province of Mercury—and which is also associated with sexual ambiguity—also the province of Mercury who was an androgynous figure in mythology. All of these associations help to illuminate the nature of the airy trigon.

The faculty of detachment, or of dissociation from the ordinary vehicles of life, is apparent only in the element of air. Each is logical, but it is dependent for its function on the matter in which the person is immersed. Water and fire are irrational elements and evaluate and experience life through the feeling nature and the intuition respectively. It would appear that thought is the basis of all manifestation, an idea which is familiar enough to the esotericist but which can only be demonstrated in an empiric way through the behaviour of man who must first conceive of a thing before he can attach emotional value to it and work to produce it in tangible form. We know very little about the real power of thought but are beginning to discover through research that thought, if concentrated, has the power to effect physical changes and may be communicated without benefit of physical implements—a phenomenon we call telepathy. We know as little about the real nature of telepathy as we do about the other "psi" phenomena which appear to be linked to the creative powers of the human mind. The dim outline of a picture is slowly emerging which suggests that mind is an attribute which is very close to our theological definitions of the attributes of deity.

If we consider that the airy signs are connected with the enormous potential of the human mind in its creative aspect, a rather sad fact presents itself: the great majority of people are not able to utilise the potential of this element for they have not yet developed the capacity to think. A person can be born with a natal chart which shows a predominance of planets in air, but this does not necessitate his being able to express these planets in a manner which partakes of the divine nature of the creative mind. What we consider ideas are frequently opinions, and these are not the same thing; this is particularly true of ideas which become ideologies. The faculty of detachment is not often to be met; instead, we may perceive a coldness which is the result of fear, rather than true detachment, or a rigid control of the feeling nature which is based on a terror of its potency. Of all the kingdoms of nature only man aspires to intellectual creativity, and even many men do not aspire so high but limit themselves to physical and emotional concerns. For the man who is trying to polarise himself mentally, and who is attempting to learn the nature of his mental equipment, frustration is far more subtle and less observable than the frustration of physical or emotional expression. If we consider the idea that Saturn always offers an opportunity to develop the function or quality associated with the element in which he is placed—and this refers to either sign or house—then we may consider that Saturn in the airy signs and houses brings about, through frustration of the creative mind and a blocking of the capacity to utilise it as a tool for communication and relating, a finer and stronger capacity for the use of thought as a creative act and as a tool for the integration of the psyche.

Saturn is dignified in Aquarius and exalted in Libra and is at least reasonably comfortable in Gemini. Seriousness, concentration, and stability are considered fitting attributes for the mind, and Saturn in air certainly offers these possibilities. The "scientific mind"—in spite of its dangerous penchant for narrowness and prejudice—is at present fashionable in our society and is responsible for the major technological advances of this century. We tend to place great emphasis on logic and tend to look askance upon the intuitive or mystical approach to life, for the last two thousand years of history have demonstrated amply the dangers of the devotional path. This is one of the more extreme qualities of Saturn in air for when he is unconscious, he is a personification of the objective and scientific intellect in its most separative aspect. Yet these qualities are not truly those of air; they are rather the qualities which result when air is not permitted its natural circulation and synthesis to and fro between minds and between people. The great difficulty with Saturn in air is that he may be accepted in this kind of sterile guise because it is currently considered the apex of normality. He may not be permitted to finish his task of destroying and rebuilding the values of a particular area of life, and the finer uses of his placement in air may never be expressed. Instead there is an ever-present sense of loneliness and isolation, a fear of the irrational elements within oneself, and a fine capacity for concentration and thoroughness which masks a sense of intellectual inadequacy or a feeling of social isolation.

Saturn's primary manner of expression in the unconscious man is through loneliness, fear, and frustration. This may be expressed through the limitations of matter, as is the case with earth, or through denial of the needs of the feeling nature, as is the case with water. When he is placed in air, he is related to mental isolation, and the person with Saturn in an airy sign or house must often struggle with loneliness because he finds it difficult to communicate with others. His thoughts are often of a deep and inquiring kind for his isolation will frequently lead him to question his values; and he is often inept at the kind of light and superficial relating which is commonly attributed to airy personalities. His task is to explore the potentials of the mind so that he can become its master, and this does not permit him easy comradeship with others. We will rarely hear him complain of his loneliness for it is not of the feeling nature, and he does not often express the "neurotic" personality which accompanies emotional frustration. Nor is he unhappy in the ordinary sense of the word for we usually apply this to disappointments of the feelings or the desire nature. He will generally suffer his isolation in silence.

Obviously the understanding and control of the mind are gifts which can only be developed when there is a reasonable degree of mental activity expressed, and a man who has Saturn placed in air must first begin to use his mind before he can begin to make of it a beam of light to shine into the darker areas of his psyche. The presence of Saturn in air on the birth chart, however, would appear to suggest that these stages in growth are fully capable of achievement by the person who must deal with an airy Saturn.

Saturn in Gemini and
the third house

The third house symbolises the sphere of the intellectual, of education, communication, and movement. It offers some indication of the kind of mind a man possesses, the manner in which he goes about developing it, how he communicates, and the subjects which provide food for his intellectual nourishment. Gemini seeks information for its own sake rather than for a material end and is simply curious about life and the diversity of its manifestations. As the first airy sign, it is the intellectual flexing its own muscles. Unlike its opposite sign, Sagittarius, which seeks to correlate the diverse fragments of life and find among them a common meaning which reflects a larger concept, Gemini is content to revel in diversity. The third house reflects this aspect of the mind and this tendency to perceive, analyse, differentiate, label, and then move on. In order to acquire the information necessary for this kind of relation to life, communication must be established so that knowledge can flow back and forth and new interpretations can be given to old material.

Saturn in the third house, when he is functioning in an unconscious way, has a tendency to block this breathing in and breathing out; he places strain on the faculty of easy communication and often produces a fear of that which is new, unexplored, and irrational. The flight of the mind is grounded by the demand for empiric information, for that which has been tried and proven safe. From this we may see some reason for the connexion often suggested between Saturn's associations with Gemini, the third house, and Mercury, and diseases of the lungs, particularly asthma, an illness which medical science recognises as psychosomatic or functional in nature. There appears to be a symbolic relationship between the biological phenomenon of breathing, whereby oxygen is brought into the body, and the psychological need for intake of information about the environment. Both appear to be equally necessary for survival, the former for bodily survival, the latter for psychic survival.

There are various external situations which are often associated with a third house Saturn, but they all tend to reflect this symbolic inability to breathe freely with the intellect. The individual who as a child is denied education, or given a narrow and restrictive education, is common, and this often mars his capacity to approach life with fresh mental interest later because his creative mental faculties have never been stimulated. Equally frequent is the only child who is denied companionship and communication with others of his own age and finds that later in life he has lost the faculty for spontaneous communication. Often there is fear behind the apparent paralysis of the mind which sometimes occurs. The child may be considered stupid because he is silent, or he may have been constantly criticised for his speech and has learned to keep his thoughts to himself; and later on, when there is no longer a disapproving parent or teacher to criticise, he finds that he has lost the capacity to share his innermost thoughts. Speech defects and difficulties also occur frequently with Saturn in the third house. These are often functional and are based on fear and insecurity, such as stuttering or stammering. Also common is the individual who simply cannot communicate easily, particularly about those personal and ordinary matters which are the traditional province of the third house. He may display unusual mental gifts, concentration, and depth of thought, but he finds it most painful to participate in the "small talk" which serves as a symbolic gesture of common humanity. To the man with Saturn in the third house, speech must contain items of serious interest, and he may display an unusually pedantic quality in his speech and his writing, for Saturn dislikes superficiality.

With all of these various expressions the common thread remains, and it is connected with the frustration of the mind and of communication. There is inevitably a feeling of isolation with this placement because the mind is generally deep and by nature serious, and there is usually some fear of being humiliated or of sounding silly or foolish to others. There is frequently a feeling of inadequacy about the mental equipment although Saturn in the third house is often a brilliant scholar. The brilliance, however, is rarely from intuition but rather from many long hours of painful concentration and self-discipline. Information must be concrete and provable to be of use to Saturn, and this tendency to crystallisation of knowledge is antithetical to the light and purposeless meanderings of the third house. To Mercury all information is of use, even if it is not the truth.

The phenomenon of overcompensation may also be observed with Saturn in the third house. Often the individual may be one of those who "talks a blue streak", and this tendency to loquaciousness—apparently in contradiction to the ordinary reading of Saturn here—is also apparent with Mercury-Saturn configurations and with Mercury in Capricorn as well. Inevitably the subject of conversation will range in every field except those which truly mean something to the individual. He will say many things but will rarely say what he actually feels. He is no closer to communicating than is the more taciturn individual with the same placement. Saturn in the third house has a reputation for tact, diplomacy, and a canny mind, and this tendency to circumlocution is very useful to a statesman or politician; it is often one of the greatest gifts of a third house Saturn. But this does not ease the isolation of the individual; it only increases it for he cannot truly express himself.

The more silent type of third house Saturn is a more typical expression. His field of interest may often be an earthbound and occasionally a narrow one although he will generally be careful, thorough and methodical in his thinking. Sometimes one may meet a kind of thick-headed, obstinate, almost deliberate stupidity with Saturn in the third house, and it is difficult to imagine that this creature and the brilliant mental gymnastics of the accomplished statesman may reflect a similar inner sense of fear and inability to share personal thoughts and feelings. But Saturn is rarely stupid. He may tend to cling to that which is pragmatically provable because he feels uneasy in lighter and more irrational realms. Saturn in the third house often underrates his intellectual capacities and may raise a shield of rather stubborn or dogmatic opinions to protect himself against the onslaught of those he considers more clever than himself.

When this placement is seen from the point of view of the opportunity offered, the sense of isolation and impatience with superficial ideas and attitudes may become an inner striving for truth, insofar as this is capable of perception by the human mind. The individual is turned inward by his circumstances and his fears so that he seeks reasons for things and begins to explore their structure and meaning. The inquiring mind dedicated to the intellectual under-standing of those things which are shrouded in mystery, or belong to the realm of the irrational, is characteristic of the man with Saturn in the third house who has accepted his apparent isolation in the face of the more meaningful contribution he is able to make to the sphere of knowledge. Saturn only becomes dogmatic when the man is afraid of the unknown and of his own lack of knowledge and of intellectual training. The suggestion with Saturn's placement in the third house is that the knowledge must be acquired through experience and personal observation, and that the training must be taken from life itself. No other education will suffice because to the person with this placement, Saturn's inner strength and independence must be applied to the development of the mind.

There is often a connexion drawn between accidents—particularly those occuring during travel—and the third house. As this house is linked with mental and physical motion and coordination, it is often called the house of short journeys, both of the body and the mind. It is of some value to explore this idea of accidents and of what is called the accident-prone tendency as it is often suggested by afflicted planets, particularly Saturn, in the third house.

It is possible to assume a completely empiric attitude to this question and to accept the idea that by some mysterious law, or by the hand of fate, Saturn in the third house precipitates accidents—and that if one has an accident, that is one's fate. This same attitude may be applied to many of the darker expressions of Saturn's placements, and this inevitably poses questions which can only be answered philosophically rather than empirically; however, this sort of blind passivity in the face of a totally predestined future is in direct antithesis to any constructive interpretation of Saturn or, for that matter, with any other factor on the natal chart. If we are indeed circumscribed by the boundaries of fate or our "karma", we cannot know where this boundary lies in the individual's case until we attempt to pass it. It is very possible that the boundary varies from person to person.

It is apparent that in many instances Saturn in the third house is concurrent with a fear of those things which are new, untried, irrational, or uncontrollable and which require a genuine sharing of minds on a personal level. Psychology has recognised for a long time that many apparently accidental injuries and illnesses are in reality a kind of arrangement, constructed by the unconscious mind of the individual, to avoid a situation which looms in the future or to achieve attention or power within the personal environment. This kind of situation occurs with some frequency in the case of Saturn in the sixth house where it is often expressed through illness or hypochondria. It is often expressed as an accident-prone tendency with Saturn in the third house, and it will usually be found in these cases that if the individual's inner life is examined with some care, the motive for the incapacitation will emerge with clarity. This does not mean that all accidents stem from this kind of "arrangement". But many do. Sometimes a few weeks in a bed, although physically uncomfortable, is preferable to confronting a situation which requires change or a new outlook.

It is inconceivable to many people that a man could deliberately injure himself or make himself sick because he does not wish to deal with a problem in his life. It is not the conscious personality which decides such things but the forces of the unconscious, which are fully capable under certain exceptional conditions of even destroying the man, physically or psychically—the latter being termed insanity. We know very little about the amount of power contained in the darker portions of the psyche, but we are learning that it merits our respect and our careful handling. Saturn is frequently responsible for the repression of fears and resentments because he is symbolic of the shadow, and the ordinary man does not wish to consider that the qualities he despises the most may exist within his own psyche; nor will he readily admit that his judgment may be in error and that these qualities can be positive, constructive, and of use to him.

The acceptance of responsibility necessary for a comprehension of Saturn is not the *mea culpa* which condemns, but a recognition that the human mind may have more power over the arrangement of one's outer circumstances than we care to admit and that there is much that we do not know about ourselves. When this attitude is related to accident-proneness and to Saturn in the third house, it is possible to avoid the necessity of an accident if the unpleasant situation precipitating it is recognised. Even if one considers the reality of karmic obligations, it is unlikely that anything occurs to a human being which is not necessary for his growth or the growth of the group, and the orderly beauty of life as it is reflected by the horoscope scarcely implies that random and senseless suffering is part of that order. Saturn always strives for the truth; it is man's fear of this motivation within himself that brings about the catastrophe, for the relentless search for reality as symbolised by Saturn threatens his most cherished illusions.

Saturn in Libra and
the seventh house

Libra is the sign of Saturn's exaltation, and as the concepts of exaltations and falls have stubbornly held their ground in modern astrological interpretation, it is possible that there is a deep and meaningful significance to them and that Saturn's placement in Libra is worthy of a close and careful look.

The seventh house is traditionally that of marriage and the marriage partner as well as that of open enemies. The characteristics which are valued in others, and which are sought in a partner, are symbolised by this house as well as the characteristics which are possessed by our enemies and through which we are vulnerable to opposition. In the seventh house the perfect match is represented, the attributes which, when added to the components of the personality of the individual, will round him out and make him whole. The situations which the person is likely to attract in marriage are also represented here and some indication of what kind of partner the person himself is likely to be.

We have for a long time accepted a rather superficial interpreation for Libra and its mundane house, and the psychological mechanism of projection is most clearly and obviously displayed by the traditional meaning assigned to this house of the "other." For the other is in the end within oneself, and it is a balance between the male and female halves of the man's own psyche which stands behind his balance with a marriage partner. We seek in others what we are not able to express consciously ourselves; and we also hate in others what we are not able to express. No perfect match with another can create inner wholeness. Marriage as it is reflected by the seventh house is a reality only in proportion to the inner integration of the individual; otherwise, it is a charade and although this view is apparently a cynical or depressive one, it is possible that it is in fact hopeful because it suggests the possibility of something better than what we see around us. The basic psychological mechanism of projection of the unconscious, transexual half of the psyche—termed by Jung the anima in men and the animus in women—is intimately connected with the qualities of the marriage partner as they are evidenced by the seventh house.

When Saturn is in the seventh house, the opportunity for an inner integration or balancing of opposites is offered, for it is unlikely that the individual will find the qualities he seeks happily expressed by a partner. It is more likely that he will attract to himself situations which involve some degree of pain, isolation, rejection, and disappointment until he begins to reorient himself toward an inner search. This placement is analagous to the coniunctio or mystical marriage of alchemy, which in psychological terms suggests an inner integration which results in a new centre for the psyche and new balance and meaning in life. In alchemical symbolism this marriage is always accompanied by darkness and death previous to the distillation of the elixir, and the darkness which often accompanies a seventh house Saturn is matched only by the brilliance of the gold which is also promised.

The most basic interpretation of Saturn in the seventh house is sorrow, difficulty, or constriction in marriage or other close relationships. Generally these sorrows appear to be the hand of external fate and often do not seem to be connected with any fault in the individual himself. Saturn in this house is frequently in his most elaborate disguise because his action is so completely externalised. It always seems to be the other person's fault. This is characteristic of seventh house planets, and good or bad luck, happiness or unhappiness, appear to come through the agency of the partner or the opponent. We are accustomed to interpreting this house as a symbol of the effects of others upon us without considering that these effects are the direct result of our own inner needs and conflicts projected outward upon others. It is not wholly the partner's shortcomings that are responsible when Saturn in the seventh house does not foster a union of unmitigated bliss.

The restrictions of a seventh house Saturn are often of a very obvious sort. Commonly isolation or aloneness is one sort of restriction. We may also see the older, more serious partner who, although stable and faithful and perhaps financially solvent as well, dampens and constricts the individual's expression because he does not understand or appreciate his partner's thoughts and dreams. The partner may be ailing or dependent in some way through illness or monetary obligations, thereby becoming a responsibility rather than a companion. Sometimes he is possessive and demanding, or he may be a disappointment simply because he is incompatible, or abandons the individual, or causes hurt through emotional or physical infidelity. In situations of this kind we are accustomed to assuming that it is the person's bad luck in the choice of a mate. Everything is usually all right at the beginning. It all seems to happen later, after the knot is tied. We may then hear the familiar cry, "I never realised when I met him..."

There is much that we know about others at the first moment of contact for we are as sensitive to the subliminal signals given in a thousand subtle ways by our fellows as the lower kingdoms of nature are to the subtle signals of their environment. But these are intuitive realisations, and they are not often welcome if the inner needs contradict the conscious ideal of what a mate should be. It is invariably the inner needs which are expressed, and which are answered, for like attracts like. The fact that someone later seems to be different is not due to bad luck but to a deliberate inner choice which was made at the very beginning. Once again it is wise to assume some responsibility where Saturn is concerned for the awareness of these inner needs and the honest sharing of them is very likely a prerequisite for happy and productive union when Saturn is found in the seventh house. Although it may at first seem difficult to understand why an individual would choose, consciously or unconsciously, a partner who will hurt, disappoint, or limit him, it is not so difficult to understand that a man may be at war with himself and be compelled by unconscious motives of which he is unaware. His choice of a partner is often a reflection of this war.

The consistent thread which runs through the many expressions of Saturn in the seventh house seems to be the successful avoidance of a relationship which might involve real union on all levels instead of merely the physical or emotional. The dangers of dependency or vulnerability are carefully sidestepped by Saturn's action although the man may be unaware that he is doing this on a conscious level. Seen from the viewpoint of the detached observer, relationships formed with a Saturnian influence are often "safe" in that the partner is himself dependent, weak, needful, and unable to form any kind of threat or support to the individual. The partner may be cold or unfaithful or incapable of establishing a meaningful relationship himself, and this is a neat mechanism for avoiding the effort and responsibility of a fully conscious union while having a scapegoat on whom the failure of the union may be blamed. Saturn in the seventh house does not necessarily describe the failure of marriage because of the failure of the partner; but it often appears this way to the conscious eye of the individual who must project his own inaccessability onto someone else.

From the point of view of the personality, this mechanism appears to be a depressing one for it would appear that there is something lying deep within the individual's psyche which will not permit him happiness in union. This is true but is only depressing when seen out of context. What is really implied is that happiness in union is not possible unless the union is based upon values other than the ordinary superficial ones of appearance, financial status, emotional dependency, and social pressure; for these causes carry with them inevitably the seeds of failure if Saturn is in the seventh house. He often places great emphasis on the formal structure of marriage while managing to avoid the inner exchange of which the formal structure is the symbol. Saturn in the seventh house tends to symbolise a rather painful arrangement because of the ensuing loneliness. But in the end the thing which is sought is inner integration, an inner marriage, and inner wholeness rather than dependency upon another person for the centre of one's psychic life. From the point of view of the self, the total psyche rather than of the personality, Saturn placed here offers a great opportunity. There is no suggestion of the necessity of a lonely life; there is rather the inner push to understand the deeper levels of union, the psychic fact of which marriage is a symbol, and the kind of true relationship which stems from two people who have centres of their own and are therefore free consciously to choose.

Patterns of hurt and rejection are common with Saturn in

the seventh house. There is often much talk of giving for Saturn often plays the martyr; yet it is frequently found that the individual who complains the most about having given so much with so little reward has in reality given little that does not have a condition attached. He is frightened of being alone yet he is equally frightened that he will be hurt; so he tries to follow both these impulses and establishes relationships into which his inner self does not enter. Often Saturn will overcompensate, and instead of being the one who is consistently abandoned, he will play the Don Juan figure—of either sex—and give the impression of being hard, callous, and unfeeling. This is very rarely the true inner nature of Saturn, but it is one of his most frequent masks. He is more likely morbidly sensitive underneath his armour so he will seek safety rather than the possible pain of a union which might end in his rejection. Sacrificing love for safety, which he often calls duty, he may believe that he has made an advantageous choice and then finds he cannot extricate himself when the enormity of his sacrifice becomes clear to him. The man with Saturn in the seventh house who attempts to make partnership a material affair generally finds that he must pay a higher price than he intended. This is often the case when Saturn's inclination toward truth and dispelling of illusory values is blocked. It is not necessary to postulate the idea of hell after death when one has glimpsed the inner hell of loneliness which is often the companion of this attempt to distort Saturn's energies.

Saturn in an angular house suggests that events, and direct contacts with others, are involved in the working out of the process of inner discovery. In the seventh this is apparent in that the marriage partner becomes either a source of suffering or a source of great opportunity for mutual growth. This choice is free to the individual, but he must first realise that he has a choice; if he does not, it is not his bad karma which has brought him suffering but simply ignorance.

Saturn in Aquarius and
the eleventh house

It has been said of Aquarius that everything may be seen in the shop window but nothing is to be found in the shop, and it is easy enough to draw this conclusion when confronted with the textbook descriptions of the sign and the association of the eleventh house with hopes and wishes, clubs, and societies. The immense depth and wisdom which are revealed by a study of astrology are not so apparent in this rather incomplete interpretation of the eleventh house and sign. With Saturn and Uranus as its rulers, Aquarius is perhaps entitled to a more complex meaning, and it is possible that the eleventh house is also more complicated and more abstruse than it is traditionally considered.

The tenth house is both the high point of achievement for the individual and his place of burial for it symbolises his deepest immersion in the material world and demands of him the sacrifices of his private and personal desires in order to obtain his goal. If the circle of the twelve houses is seen as a cycle of progressively more complex steps in the unfoldment of the individual's outer life, the tenth house, which belongs to Saturn, may be considered the end of the climb of the personality. In the remaining two houses, both of which are connected with "higher octave" planets and therefore with states of consciousness that are collective or transpersonal rather than personal in nature, the individual loses himself in the group and shoulders his responsibility as a cell in the larger body of humanity. His tests have been met, he has developed personal integration to the point where his mind, emotions, and body function as a disciplined and finely balanced tool to serve his inner purposes, and he is now free to join in the larger task of group integration and development. The passage from Saturn to Uranus marks the transition from the supremacy of the personal will to the development of group consciousness. Group consciousness is not mass consciousness for with the former the contribution is voluntary and the worth of the individual is not lost. This may appear to be a rather esoterically inclined interpretation of what is apparently a superficial house and sign. But if we are ever to make any sense of Saturn and his houses and signs from any viewpoint other than a fatalistic one, or are ever to understand the real nature and extent of the individual's free will and purpose, it is possible that in the esoteric tradition of Saturn some information may be found which helps us to lead freer lives.

People who are strongly Aquarian or Piscean in temperament, yet who have not yet developed a purpose which permits them participation in a larger expression, are often lost creatures, and it is perhaps more difficult for this kind of temperament now because the idea of group consciousness is not yet a reality. It is reasonably common to find the average Taurean personality concerned with his security for this is his natural outlet of expression—or for the average Libran to concern himself with his personal relationships, or the

Geminian with his education. But the Aquarian and Piscean temperaments have no personal concerns. And if they are not yet sensitive to the more universal concerns which are the natural expression of these signs, they are left with no concerns at all. It is small wonder that so many alcoholics and drug addicts are strongly Piscean or Neptunian by temperament and that so many of the mentally ill must cope with Aquarian or Uranian energies. To balance this, it must be considered that we owe some of our greatest scientific and psychological discoveries to the Uranian type and some of our greatest poetry, music, and spiritual vision to the Neptunian. It is somewhat easier to understand the great potential and the great failure of these two types in light of the urge toward group involvement and contribution which motivates them both.

If we then look past the level of clubs and societies when considering the eleventh house and apply the idea of group consciousness and the nature of one's responsibility and contribution in this area as a possible additional meaning for this house, more insight may be gained into the meaning of Saturn's placement here.

The more ordinary meaning of the eleventh house is often in evidence with its connotation of friendships and social acceptance, and Saturn in the eleventh may display his usual aloofness and isolation and thereby mark the individual as a "lone wolf", one who somehow does not fit into the group. He may find difficulty in making casual friendships and in functioning at the more superficial social level which, in our present society, is considered of such value. He may feel himself to be an outsider and will often behave as one, and his separateness is deeper than a mere inability to conform to popular standards of behaviour. The group which is presented to him as the "acceptable" one—those people whom he meets through family, business, religion, or interests—rarely receives him warmly, and he rarely feels himself to be a part of any artificially structured social unit. He is looking for another kind of group, a deeper group, but he rarely understands that the bounds which link this more abstruse group are of an inner, not an outer, nature.

Saturn is often painfully self-conscious and hopelessly inept at the social graces, but he is always the enemy of superficiality when he is expressing his true nature. His presence in the eleventh house is made doubly difficult because the nature of our present ideas about friendship and group activities can be eminently superficial. Saturn may often feel awkward and uncomfortable as he often indicates an introverted and shy tendency. Thus the usual effect of Saturn in the eleventh house is a deep, although often concealed, feeling of loneliness. He may want badly to feel himself a significant part of a larger whole, to be released from the burden of self-consciousness and "differentness". Yet he is often unable to express his need and will sometimes not even admit it to himself.

We consider man to be a gregarious animal, a communal creature rather than a solitary one, and the man who spends long periods alone or rejects the opportunity for social intercourse is somewhat suspect to the average individual. We are brought up to believe that there is something neurotic or unwholesome about aloneness, yet it is probably far more painful to carry the sense of separateness into a crowd than to be physically alone yet experience a sense of belonging. The man with Saturn in the eleventh house is often compulsively driven to be alone, and he may draw back from friendships because he is afraid he will not be accepted. It is frequently necessary for him to balance this fear and sense of inadequacy with a need to glamourise his uniqueness so that out of pride his separateness is demonstrated to be a virtue rather than a shortcoming. It is probably neither a virtue nor a lack, but the unconscious man with Saturn in the eleventh house is not aware that he has more choices than this. So one of the most typical reactions of an eleventh house Saturn may be demonstrated: he must be superior, he can have no equals. Just as Saturn in Leo finds it painfully difficult to express his uniqueness in an open way, Saturn in Aquarius often finds it painfully difficult to express his ordinariness, his similarity with every other human being—although it is this ordinariness, this blending with the group, which he desires the most. Saturn in the eleventh house is often interpreted as giving few and faithful friends; and it is the quality, rather than the quantity, which is important.

Overcompensation is often expressed by this Saturnian placement, and it is common to find the individual who crams his life full of social activities so that he scarcely has time to be alone. He will often fill his time so that he rarely needs to have personal confrontations, and it is often so important to him that he demonstrate his belonging that he will subdue his own individuality in order to cater to the standards and ideas of the group. So Saturn in the eleventh house may become a follower rather than the leader which he essentially needs to be. His own ideals, his wishes, and his dreams are worthless when compared to the final and inexorable word of the great They. Saturn in the eleventh house may sometimes symbolise this kind of social butterfly in the same way that Saturn in the third house may suggest a chatterer and Saturn in the seventh a perpetual Don Juan. But this butterfly often has wings of lead. He remains as essentially isolated and apart, as if he were alone, because inwardly he seeks a deeper and more meaningful sharing. But the work involved in achieving that deeper level of interchange would lead him into himself and into a search for a different set of social values as well as a deeper understanding of society itself and its purpose.

The opportunity which is offered by Saturn in the eleventh is not easily utilised without the kind of broad view of human oneness and gradual evolution and unfoldment which marks the truly progressive mind. This has little to do directly with political involvement although this area is a natural adjunct to the kind of vision which is often found in the Aquarian temperament. But Saturn has little to do with theories; he offers his wisdom through the more difficult but more meaningful channel of personal experience and realisation; and the understanding of the psychology of the group and the direction in which man's consciousness is slowly striving is an understanding which can be the inner illumination of the individual who has Saturn in Aquarius or in the eleventh house. Esoteric literature speaks repeatedly of "the Plan" for man, and this plan must remain in the realm of the theoretical and the visionary for the majority of people. To the discerning eye of an eleventh house Saturn, it is possible that the reality and nature of this plan may become visible if he seeks long enough and deeply enough the inner group which means so much to him.

If he permits his vision to be narrow, Saturn will rarely find the solution to his isolation, and we may then observe the fulfilment of the prophecy of hard luck through friends which is said to accompany this placement. For one who sets himself apart to such a degree, and who feels such mistrust of others is bound to attract something similar in return from his fellows. Like forever attracts like, and the bristly defensiveness which may often be seen in an eleventh house Saturn—even in those who have polished the surface of social charm until it shines but who cannot permit deeper friendships—usually attracts defensiveness back.

Each individual contains the potential of the higher or more universal meaning of the eleventh house to unfold along with the

more personal. Few people are conscious of this potential because a
more careful investigation of values and a more inclusive interest in
humanity is generally a prerequisite for its unfoldment; however, the
eleventh house is present on every birth chart, and the challenge of
finding meaningful expression for the urges which are symbolised is
present in every life. This becomes more urgent a task for the person
who has Saturn in the eleventh house, or in Aquarius, because as with
any other Saturnian position, second choice is not acceptable, and
with this placement the sense of commitment to and participation in
group life must be real.

4 *in the fiery signs and houses*

The element of fire is related to the function of the intuition and is often linked with spirit, energy, and the initial source of life and consciousness. This rather exalted conception of fire may be considered too lofty for our more personalised examples of Arien aggression, Leonian pride and autocracy, and Sagittarian irresponsibility. However unsavoury our individual examples may be, all three fire signs tend to possess an innate consciousness of their individuality and often have limitless vitality, self-confidence, and enthusiasm which stems not from any mundane accomplishment but from an intuitive perception of the worth of the self. Earth expresses confidence when it has acquired mastery over matter, and water expresses confidence when it has established meaningful emotional bonds. Air expresses confidence through the exchange and development of ideas. But the fiery temperament needs no further justification than its existence for the innate belief that life is essentially meaningful and that man deserves the best from it.

The sense of inner purpose or meaning, which we tend to call the urge for self-expression without fully understanding what self we are speaking of, underlies the behaviour and outlook of all three fiery signs and houses. Physical man's primary need is food and sustenance, but the symbolism of fire suggests that something must purposefully decide to express as physical man in the first place. It is this "something" or self which the fiery individual knows himself to be; and the needs of the body are to him secondary—as is literally demonstrated in the second house.

Fire is not a difficult element to understand if we consider the concept of a total self which possesses will and purpose and of which the conscious personality is only a fragment. This is both a psychological and an esoteric postulate although psychology politely avoids the use of the word "soul" except in a limited sense. We may see the expression of this fiery self in a more personal and human way through the urge to explore and conquer as it is displayed by Aries, the urge to create and to love as it is displayed by Leo, and the urge to expand and understand as it is displayed by Sagittarius. In each of these signs there is a deep sense of purpose and an innate acceptance of the fact that the ordinary arenas of life—body, feelings, and mind—exist solely for the self-expressive urges of the creative self. All the world is to the fiery trigon indeed a stage to be explored, acted upon, understood, and loved, and, when necessary, destroyed so that new forms may be built. For there is value only in the meaning, and it is the meaning which is always sought in every experience.

Naturally there is a side to this energy which is not appealing to other kinds of temperaments, particularly the earthy temperament which expresses great accuracy of observation and appreciation of form but is often unable to find the meaning for the form. Fire may appear to be egotistical and self-aggrandising, and fiery individuals often are. This kind of man may intuitively know that he is a god, but he is inclined to forget that everybody else is as well. Most of the shortcomings of this type of temperament stem from the man's insensitivity to the finer details of life, and the feelings of other people are frequently part of these finer details. For this reason Jung places intuition and sensation at opposite ends of the axis of perception for one relates to the purpose of a thing or an experience and the other relates to the appearance of that thing or experience. Fire perpetually seeks purpose and generally finds it although he often lacks appreciation of the myriad of beautiful forms in which the purpose is couched. He is naturally first concerned with the purpose of his own life.

Saturn in the fiery signs or houses tends to suggest a barrier between the conscious personality and the intuitive perception of the self as it ordinarily is experienced by fire. This often precipitates a loss of the sense of one's innate purpose and significance in the broader context of life. Saturn in fire may appear to produce problems which are more philosophical than real in nature, but it should be remembered that Saturn in any element brings out the importance of understanding and experiencing the meaning and sphere of that element. To the person with Saturn in a fiery sign or house, the consciousness of the self is a tremendously important issue although he may not verbalise his need in such terminology. Often compulsive self-centredness is a by-product of this frustration of and search for meaning and purpose. But it is not that there is too much ego in the colloquial sense of this term. The individual is not selfish in the way that we popularly refer in our tirades to those people who do not do what we want. There is in fact too little Ego, and this loss of contact with the centre of the psyche tends to rob the individual of his confidence in life. He will often mask this loss with an exaggerated sense of his own importance for he has nothing else. Saturn is in his fall in Aries and in detriment in Leo for he does not initially get on well with the element of fire.

It is easy enough to see Saturn in the role of the Lord of Karma, but to perceive him merely as an instrument of suffering and the payment of debts is only a possible part of the picture. If he is seen as a motive, leading to a process which results in growth, then it is easier to comprehend the reason for his apparent restrictions in any area of life. The sense of despair and feeling of insignificance which often accompanies Saturn's placement in fire may be viewed as bad karma or the penalty for too many lives of self-aggrandisement or power, but this interpretation is not of much use for the person who experiences the crushing feeling of purposelessness. If it is instead seen as a challenge, where the individual can through effort and the development of the intuitive faculty begin to apprehend his true nature and his true role in relation to the group and to life in general, accompanied by the destruction or elimination of those values which are no longer of use or which are based on illusion, then he can make use of his opportunity and develop that aspect of his temperament which, symbolically, will yield the alchemical gold.

The Sun is exalted in the sign of Saturn's fall for the conscious personality is strengthened by its contact with the larger self. The Sun is in dignity in the sign of Saturn's detriment, and Saturn is exalted in the sign of the Sun's fall. These two opponents, who sometimes take the guise of God and the Devil, perpetually circle each other about the ring whether they are in actual aspect on the birth chart or not. They are two faces of the same basic principle, and in the individual's psychology they are related to the conscious personality and the shadow or unconscious personality. The Sun's face looks outward to the world while Saturn's two faces look both toward the Sun and downward toward the darkness of the collective unconscious of the race. Saturn placed in the fiery signs or houses suggests another facet of this perpetual conflict which is not really a conflict, for Mars and Jupiter, the two fiery planets, are in the end more specialised suns.

Saturn's effects in the fiery signs and houses may aptly be described as "spiritual constipation" which is observable in ordinary life as a lack of spontanaeity and self-expression, lack of vitality and inner confidence, and a feeling of purposelessness. The three basic qualities of will or purpose, love, and intelligence which are esoterically considered as the attributes of deity may also be considered basic attributes of man's psyche. Jung called the factor of love Eros and the factor of intelligent activity Logos; and he believed that the will was a third factor which could be utilised to direct the energies of the other two. We have here a rough psychological analogy to the Trinity, both Christian and Hindu, which latter expresses these same attributes as Brahma the Creator, Vishnu the Preserver, and Shiva the Destroyer. In Aries, Leo, and Sagittarius we see yet another symbolic correlation to these three basic kinds of energy for these three fiery signs are the simplest representations of the astrological qualities. It may then be suggested that Saturn in Aries or the first house is connected with the understanding and development of the will or sense of purposeful activity; Saturn in Leo or the fifth house is connected with the understanding and development of creativity or sense of purposeful love; and Saturn in Sagittarius or the ninth house is connected with the understanding and development of intuitive perception and wisdom. These may appear to be abstruse definitions of Saturn in fire, but they are a fitting introduction to a symbol which suggests the opportunity for the development of an intuitive understanding of the purpose of one's life.

Saturn in Aries and
the first house

The first house is usually considered to describe the physical body of the individual, the personality with which he relates to his external environment, and on perhaps a deeper level the kinds of experiences which he is likely to attract during his life and which help him to shape and develop a certain set of conscious tools with which to govern his life. There is a two-way flow of energy through the first house of the chart because it is—as has often been suggested—a kind of lens through which the experiences of the environment pass to reach the individual and through which his own qualities must pass to reach the environment. Whatever factors are present within the individual birth chart, they must pass through the conditioning qualities of the first house and in particular the Ascendant before they can be recognised by others or expressed in a tangible fashion. All four angles of the chart are related to this inward and outward flow of the reality of the inner person into the outside world, but the most personal and most obvious of these four points of release is the Ascendant. The entire first house relates to the physical presentation of the individual in a conscious and deliberate manner. Whatever a man innately is, he must express it through a body and according to a body type—which gives the term "body" a larger framework. The Ascendant and the first house are often equated with the Jungian idea of the "persona" which, if it is to be a positive and effective medium through which a man may present himself to the world, must be in reasonable accord with the more hidden, unconscious aspects of his psyche.

The idea of the "persona" offers a considerable amount of insight into the function of the Ascendant which is often maligned by being considered merely a superficial mask which has little relation to the inner reality of the person. Like the masks of the ancient Greek tragedy, the persona is the person's statement of himself to the world; through this cultivated component of the psyche he declares his role according to the manner in which he has developed over the years. The persona, like the Ascendant, does not come into full conscious flowering until a certain level of maturity has been reached. Ideally this role should be a synthesis of what is best in him, and most useful, and should be worn lightly so that the man does not make the mistake of identifying with his presentation. It is very much what he would ideally like to be, or what he is developing into, rather than what he automatically is at any given time. The first house is the most unformed part of the birth chart for it, even more than the rest of the chart, is in a process of becoming.

According to the strength or weakness of this presentation, and according to whether or not it is crystallised and rigid or flexible and lightly worn, the man is able to stand at a precarious balance point between his outer environment and the world of his unconscious motivations. If he pulls too much toward one, the other reacts; he is required by the tension of the pull to stand at the centre. If he begins to identify with the role which he has chosen, he crystallises into it and is then at the mercy of the hidden and more treacherous aspects of his own psyche. If he ignores the outer world and attempts to withdraw into his own darkness, he is at the mercy of the environment and is dominated by it. From this viewpoint the importance of the Ascendant may be inferred for it would appear that its development needs always to be in delicate balance with the direction of the chart internally in order for the man to be in balance within himself.

Some idea of the effects of Saturn in the first house of the natal chart may be seen if this psychological adjunct to the traditional astrological interpretation is considered. Saturn's traditional associations with crystallisation and identification with mundane values suggests that one of the most frequent psychic effects of this position, if left unconscious, is a crystallisation of and identification with one's mask, with a consequent inner vulnerability to moods and effects and a great difficulty in expressing the inner person to the outer world. The mask becomes a prison and cannot be torn away; and behind it the man slowly suffocates.

One of the main qualities which appears to accompany Saturn in Aries or in the first house is a lack of self-assertion of a positive kind. There is often a need to enforce one's will and to control the immediate environment; but rather than being the spontaneous and self-confident assertion of the individual, this is more of a defensive maneuvre which sometimes attempts to attack first because it is fearful of attack. Sometimes the need for control is expressed in a subtle and indirect way so that situations are manipulated without any real evidence of aggressiveness. This is the characteristic coupling of need and fear which is so often found with Saturn. The natural shyness and stiff awkwardness of Saturn is expressed more obviously with this placement than with any other, although the individual often learns during life to cultivate a smooth, cool and polished surface.

Saturn conjuncting the ascendant is frequently concurrent with a difficult birth, usually physically but sometimes psychologically as well, and this curious coincidence occurs too often to be a real coincidence. It is, moreover, reasonable to assume that the natural reluctance of the person with Saturn in the first house to expose himself to the outside world might even extend to birth. It is common with a first house Saturn for the individual to learn from childhood that it is costly to get too involved with life, and there is a basic weakness in the persona which causes him to identify both too much and too little with the outward shell of his personality. He is therefore vulnerable to attack and control from the outside and generally knows it; and much of his life may be spent in devising ways of protecting himself so that the extent of his vulnerability is not discovered. The person with Saturn in the first house is often high in suspicion and low in self-confidence, and he looks out at others from behind an intangible but often very powerful barrier that effectively isolates him from the real impact of life. He may sometimes be burdened with chronic ill-health, particularly as a child when he has not yet learned other means of successful withdrawal from the arena. He often has little faith in himself, but the self with which he identifies is the mask rather than the total psyche; from the deliberate withdrawal from the roots of his own psychic life stems the curious lifelessness and dryness which is so often observable in the person with this placement of Saturn.

Saturn is considered to be in his fall in Aries, and from this one might deduce that this is a difficult position for him and one which is not easily carried. Possibly the most difficult side of it is the tendency to be cut off from both the flow of outer life and the flow of inner life so that the individual is stranded in a very small and very arid area of his psyche, difficult to reach, and unable to touch the mainspring of purpose and meaning which would enable him to face the outer world with courage. But I am inclined to believe that planets in their fall, and Saturn in particular, can offer to the persistent and perceptive person a much greater key to the meaning of the planet and therefore to the development in life of the function which it symbolises. This is because a planet in its fall must generally struggle, and it is this struggle which if carefully tended, yields insight and eventual expansion of the field of consciousness. This is particularly true of Saturn, who when placed in the sign of his fall is often stripped of the courage and confidence—the natural gift of the Arien—which is required to tackle the problems of living head-on. Yet the thing he wants the most is the joy of being free, of being first, of exploring unknown regions and meeting unknown challenges and revelling in the innate realisation that his existence is guarantee enough of his purpose. It is the person with Saturn in Aries or in the first house who with effort has the greatest possibility of achieving this kind of freedom.

Saturn may overcompensate with this placement as much as with any other. Consequently there are usually two distinct kinds of reaction to this struggle between the desire to challenge and experience life to the fullest and the fear of being hurt, dominated, and crushed by the forces of a hostile environment. The man who perpetually effaces himself to avoid a struggle and who backs away from those situations which might call for strength, aggressiveness, or direct confrontation, expresses one kind of unconscious Saturnian reaction. He often has no "temper" and rarely displays anger, but this can be very hard on the physical body because the natural tendency toward irritability is turned inward against oneself. This position is often connected with symptoms of a psychosomatic kind such as migraine headaches which are often linked with unexpressed anger and frustration. The self-effacement of this expression of Saturn is not truly humility but is rather a fear of entering the fight because of the inner certainty of losing it. There is often great emphasis on being "unselfish", a favourite keynote of Saturn in Aries or in the first house. But to be unselfish one must first have a self to give away, and the difficulty with this placement is that, in the beginning, until the individual comes to terms with his fear, there is no real acceptance of or expression of the self in the first place.

Saturn in the first house often feels that he is never able to have what he wants, that life is forever thwarting his desires. This is largely because he does not ask for what he wants, or if he does ask, then it is with the concurrent feeling that he does not actually deserve a reply. The will and the use of the will are often frightening to this kind of individual because he is afraid of his own will and consequently projects what he terms wilfulness or selfishness onto others. As he comes to terms with this shadowy and powerful aspect of his own personality—for the person with Saturn placed here has a powerful and controlled will if he chooses to recognise and utilise it— he generally finds that along with his frustration he has also learned control over his desire nature and has shaped his personality into a disciplined tool. Although Saturn is in his fall in Aries, Mars is exalted in Capricorn, and the energy is similar with both these positions; the controlled and directed will, coupled with a sense of purpose, is one of the more positive qualities offered by Saturn in the first house.

At the opposite end of the spectrum the more aggressive manifestation of Saturn in the first house often appears, and this individual may be at first glance rarely distinguishable from the truly fiery type of temperament. No one is more outgoing than he is, no one more prepared to take charge or seize control of a situation either through sheer force or more subtle calculation. His philosophy is that the best defence is offence because it has not yet occurred to him that it is possible to control oneself without the necessity of controlling everybody else as well. On closer expression this kind of individual is often found to be as shy and awkward as his more self-effacing brother. He may find it as difficult to participate fully in life and to experience the sense of richness and fullness which is so characteristic of the fiery personality.

The use of the will is something available to every human being, but it grows in proportion to one's self-knowledge and self-mastery. The natural fear that the majority of people feel about the unpredictability of life is connected largely with the unconsciousness of the majority of people about the resources and richness of the human psyche. Most men feel inadequate when confronted with their own powerlessness. The man who has achieved a degree of psychic integration is far better equipped to cope with life because he is generally aware of the purpose of his own life in a broad sense, and also more aware of the energies which he can utilise from within himself to carve out a piece of life for himself. Saturn in Aries or in the first house tends first to emphasise the fear of powerlessness because it suggests a clinging to the more superficial features of the personality and a consequent loss of contact with the richer inner person. Eventually this fear can prod the individual into a deeper exploration of what he considers to be his identity. Saturn in the house of the identity is closely connected with this search which can help to yield greater knowledge, greater integration, and the greater and more productive use of the will.

Saturn in Leo and the fifth house

Under the general umbrella of the fifth house are usually included pleasures and amusements, love affairs, children, creativity and self-expression, and speculation and investments. This is a rather large mouthful for one mundane house. As this house is the reflection of the Sun, the symbol for the conscious ego, it might be easier to approach it as the expression of the individual's "selfness", those areas where he can be uniquely and wholly himself, where he can permeate his feelings, desires, ideas, and activities with his own essence, and where he is completely unimpeded and uncoloured by the necessity for compromise. This is the house of the individual identity, and through the activities of the fifth house one begins to apprehend, through creative self-expression, the meaning of his own identity. Leo and the fifth house have a great deal to do with the recognition of the self both by others and by the individual himself. We interpret it also as the house of love, but it might more aptly be called the house of romance because this also is an area where the individual may express—or project—his own identity without interference, and through the experience of love of this kind he may get a glimpse of his own inner centre. Love in all its meanings is perhaps as much an archetype as is the archetype of the Self, and neither one is discernible on the birth chart; only the ways in which they are likely to be approached and expressed are evident, and they are both connected with the fifth house.

This house, like the first and the ninth, is also connected with the faculty of the intuition and with the individual's intuitive perception of the purpose and completeness of his total psyche. Expressing through Aries, the individual intuits purpose through his interaction with the environment; expressing through Leo, he intuits his wholeness through reflecting upon himself as he appears in his own creations. This kind of reflection can lead, in the end, to the experience of the "I" as a complete and unique idea, but this experience is not approached through the intellect. Otherwise it becomes a meaningless set of concepts which only serve to throw up more barriers between the individual and his experience of himself. Through an act of creative expression he may intuitively catch himself being himself, and the importance of this psychological experience should not be underestimated. It is one of the motives behind creativity.

It is usual to find the Leonian personality described as egotistical and self-centred. But it might be more correct to say that rather than being self-centred, he is seeking the self at the centre, and in consequence everything that he does is of dramatic importance to him because somewhere in all of it he senses the possibility of the direct encounter, the direct experience. Rather than criticising him for his tendency to exaggerate his own importance, it is perhaps more helpful to realise that no individual can be of any value to himself or to others until he first discovers who and what that self is. Through the fifth house the individual begins to glimpse himself through those expressions which contain within them a piece of his own unique identity. This is not necessarily limited to creativity in the artistic sense although this is perhaps a more direct form of self-expression. Every individual has some area of life where he is seeking to understand his own significance through completely unimpeded self-expression whether this is in an artistic field, an intellectual one, an emotional one, or the creation of a living child.

From this it may be inferred that the conventional attitude toward the bearing of children is sometimes in need of some further reflection. Often the first half of the creative process is accomplished—the child is born—but the second half, the half in which the education and self-recognition of the creator begins, is frequently neglected because this act requires humility of a kind which is usually absent from the parent-child relationship. Children are, in our society, very much a means of living out vicariously those qualities and expressions which are unconscious or have not been permitted to unfold in the life of the parent. Rather than helping to provide a means of self-realisation, they are seen as empty vessels which can be moulded, shaped, and filled with any content we choose. An act of creativity can always lead to greater self-awareness when we consider who it is that is doing the creating, but it always involves a gamble because of the possibility of pride distorting the perception. In any painting or piece of music, there is a fragment of the consciousness of the creator; and in the end it is for the greater consciousness of his psyche that he creates, not for his audience, although his audience may be a part of the alchemical transformation by which he achieves divinity. This may seem abstruse, but we are fond of tossing about concepts such as God's love for his children and the artist's quest for immortality without having the vaguest idea what we are talking about. It is worth some meditation upon the idea of the creative act, and its psychic significance, in order to get fuller understanding of the meaning of Saturn in the fifth house.

When Saturn is in Leo or in the fifth house, there is a temporary barrier between the person and his self-realisation, composed primarily of those shadowy attributes which he will not permit into consciousness. The creative flow is often blocked, or if it is not blocked, then the experience of self-realisation which is the natural result may be blocked. The perfect circle of outpouring and inner transformation is interrupted, and the man often pours his energy out and thinks that he receives nothing back because his own sense of inadequacy prevents him from realising that it has nothing to do with the audience. This applies not only to creative expression but to romantic love as well. Usually the person with a fifth house Saturn cannot easily find himself among his creations because he has had a minimum of recognition from anyone else. This is the classic indication of the unloved child, the child who may be ignored or treated as merely an extension of his parents, where his own identity and significance has somehow been swallowed up in the trappings of what passes for parent-child love. Children with Saturn in the fifth house are often loved in the sense that their parents love the idea of the child, but they are rarely loved for the unique quality of "selfness" which is at the base of the individuality. Later in life, because these children have never experienced the recognition of self by anybody else, they are hard-pressed to recognise it themselves and often find it difficult to make contact with their own inner significance. The child with Saturn in Leo or in the fifth house must often pay the later price of intense feelings of inadequacy and insignificance no matter how many gifts or abilities he may possess.

This placement of Saturn often concurs with a reluctance or inability to have children, or the children may bring burdens, responsibilities, or pain. This is the traditional interpretation of a fifth house Saturn. He may deny himself love in the sense that, not loving himself or being able to understand his own value, he is afraid that no one else will find him lovable either. Caught in his own feelings of inferiority, he may be jealous and resentful of others, ensuring the fact of his rejection by them. There is often a stiffness and lack of spontaneity about Saturn in the fifth house; one has the feeling that the individual is always watching himself watching himself and is rarely able to relax. He strains and pushes in the hope, unconsciously, of getting some glimpse of what he truly is mirrored in the loving eyes of others, but he generally consistently fails when he attempts it in this way. Because he pushes so hard, he often alienates those who otherwise might have helped him. His disappointments may come through many channels, but behind the heartbreak which is often associated with this position lies the individual's inability to love himself, to recognise his own significance, and to find an inner centre which can give his life stability and meaning.

Saturn in the fifth house has a reputation for being cold and heartless, but this kind of face is characteristic of Saturn and should not be taken literally. The heart of stone is apparent in many people who are concerned with protecting their own vulnerability with a veneer of callousness. Usually beneath this veneer is a small child who cannot understand his own importance. There is often an intense selfishness exhibited by Saturn in the fifth house and a desperate need to feel important, admired, envied, and popular. Envy is most typical of this position for the individual who cannot find his own centre is often deeply resentful of what he thinks are the meaningful lives of others. To the individual with a fifth house Saturn, everyone else's grass often seems greener. Usually he is most envious of those who seem to attract love, friendship, and affection without having to make the strenuous effort at skill, superiority, and dazzle which is typical of the fifth house Saturn. No one seeks popularity as assiduously as he does, whether this is conscious or not, and no one is so crushed and heartbroken when he is not accepted. Saturn is awkward in the Sun's sign, and the challenge offered to the person with this placement is a difficult one for he needs to find his inner centre and identify with that rather than the trappings with which he usually surrounds himself. Without these trappings the person usually feels naked and vulnerable. The opportunity offered, however, is an important one, for if he succeeds in finding this centre and manages to shift the focus of his personality from the ego to this more meaningful self, he can begin to recapture the naive joy which is apparent only in a child, the joy which comes from an innate trust in life and in the existence of love in the universe. Having once found the secret of his own identity, he can never lose it again, and that natural integrity and brightness which is one of the most endearing of Leonian qualities becomes his permanent expression. He is no longer dependent on whether others recognise him or not for he has at last recognised himself. This experience of contacting the self always seems to evoke the same response in those people who have experienced it: they seem to recapture some of the spontaneous joy, vitality, and innate honesty of the heroes of folklore and fairytale, regardless of the inhibiting aspects of their outer lives. This joy is not unconscious however, for the process is a conscious one and is not a regression. Somehow the duality of conscious sophistication, or fine discrimination, and unconscious integrity, or the sense of trust, are fused within the personality. This is a great challenge and an important opportunity and if taken, certainly balances the pain and loneliness which are usually the initial gifts of Saturn in the fifth house.

There is often an interesting blend of inflation and an intense and often crippling shyness apparent with Saturn in the fifth house.

The individual both overrates and underrates himself but rarely perceives himself clearly; consequently, he cannot see others clearly because he is always projecting his own evaluations onto them and usually does badly in affairs of the heart because of this. He often cannot express overt affection easily yet at the same time cannot bear to be ignored. Loyalty and honour may become of exaggerated importance to him for he often tries to crystallise and solidify the love of others through emphasis on the forms and codes of behaviour which love sometimes takes as its outer expression. It is not so much love in the affectional sense as recognition that he seeks, and it is easy to see why this placement is often associated with those in the entertainment professions. Leo himself does not need this feedback from others; he simply is, and that is enough. Saturn in Leo cannot see the "I" and must seek it in the applause of the crowd.

With this placement of Saturn the psyche seems to be directed toward a realisation of itself, toward a process of individuation as Jung calls it, and will often not permit the conscious personality to find any solace in the usual activities which supply an identity for most people. Thus children, who often provide a sense of purpose and significance to their parents, are a disappointment, or there is no possibility of having them. Romantic love rarely turns out to be the ideal which is expected because the eyes of the lover somehow never reflect that missing flash which will convince the person of his own value. Creative expression never quite seems fulfilling and usually misses the mark. The individual usually is driven, in the end, to seek himself within himself because no other means are left available to him. It is he himself who has set it up in this way, but to recognise the underlying purpose behind these disappointments is the beginning of wisdom and the final taking of the opportunity.

There may be as much overcompensation here as with any other Saturnian placement. Many people with Saturn in the fifth house work very hard at never taking life seriously although no one is more sensitive, touchy, and serious in matters of affection than the fifth house Saturn. His fears of rejection and insignificance usually lead him to lace the idea of love heavily with concepts such as loyalty, duty, fidelity, and responsibility although these may be unconscious lacings. He needs structures so that he may be guaranteed a sufficient amount of enduring love. Unfortunately no matter how many structures he erects, he usually still cannot trust, and the disguise of frivolity rarely deceives anyone after a while although he may continue to deceive himself. The heaviness and needfulness of this placement usually shows through, and because of this the person is often deeply hurt.

If the person does not work with his fifth house Saturn, this is a rather unhappy position; any coupling of Saturn and the Sun carries weight with it, whether this coupling occurs by sign, aspect, or house interchange. All these contacts are connected with the discovery of the self, and this is painful because it involves the tearing away of the veil. We are taught in early childhood that we are many things—our feelings, or beliefs, or bank accounts, or children, or talents, or loved ones—anything and everything except ourselves. The person with Saturn in the fifth house often demands so much from others that he is left lonely and heartbroken. He is capable of much love and devotion but does not dare to express it without asking for a guarantee back; only when he recognises this unconscious process of barter can he begin to free himself of it. We are familiar with the exaggerated display of megalomania which was expressed by Hitler and which was in part connected with his prominent Saturn in Leo at the midheaven of the birth chart. What is often not recognised is that the ordinary man with Saturn in Leo or in the fifth house, who has no aspirations to conquer the world, may nevertheless have a small share of this desperate need for importance and recognition, coupled with an acute shyness which leads him to wait in the wings when what he wants most is to be at the centre of the stage with all eyes focussed, adoring, upon him. Failing this, he may become a petty tyrant in the home, a hypochondriac, a domestic dictator.

The person with Saturn in the fifth house is sometimes not easy to love because he is like a jug with no bottom and absorbs affection and attention endlessly without being satisfied; however, if he begins to understand that his path is inward toward the self, he may begin to see what kind of opportunity is offered to him. For the individual whose heart has been unlocked, every moment contains joy and significance, and although this may sound like the classic mystic's vision, it is also an empiric psychological fact and may be precipitated by certain psychological techniques, coupled with insight and patience. Having once seen this vision the individual needs nothing else to complete himself for the self is whole. We may observe this motif in many myths and fairytales for this is the treasure hard to obtain, the jewel guarded by the dragon or hidden in the beautiful princess' ring. It is the finding of this jewel which seems to be the special task of the person with Saturn in Leo or in the fifth house for nothing else will suffice.

Saturn in Sagittarius and
the ninth house

The ninth house is considered to be the house of long journeys, both those made by the physical body and those which increase consciousness and broaden the perspective of the mind. In this basic interpretation, which is traditional, the duality of the Gemini-Sagittarius axis and the third and ninth houses may be clearly seen; for third house movement, related to Mercury, deals with the gathering of information, while ninth house movement, related to Jupiter, pertains to the discovery of meaning which emerges when the information is finally put into perspective. These are, as has often been suggested, the two aspects of that perceptive function which we term the mind.

The ninth house is also the house of law by traditional definition, and just as there are two kinds of journeys—those of the body and those of the mind—there are also two kinds of laws. Man-made laws deal with the structuring of society so that it develops along the most positive lines and offers the maximum of protection to its members. Spiritual laws are not very well understood because they can only be apprehended by their reflection in human behaviour; they might in psychological terms be called archetypes in the specific sense that Jung means this word. These laws are simply inherent in life rather than a product of life; in fact they are perhaps, in a more esoteric sense, the reason for life. Unfortunately all we know of these laws, apart from the discoveries of modern psychology is that interpretation given by theology which calls these archetypal patterns the Will of God and then attempts to interpret this Will according to a particular dogma or ideology. The entire subject of law, whether it is the instinctual patterning of nature, the intellectual and moral structuring of man, or a less tangible and more ambiguous patterning of life in general, is at best an abstruse subject and not one to be defined in a few paragraphs; it is likely that there is no proper definition. The realm of the ninth house, however, is an abstruse and subtle realm because it is connected with the intuition and with the intuitive perception of the laws of living and being and consciousness;

and an understanding of this house, which requires the exercise of the intuition, can provide the key not only to the over-all patterns of humanity but to the meaning behind a single life. Although a cadent house, and therefore considered by tradition to be "weak", the cadent houses are the birthplaces of thought and the expression of a meaningful life as it is manifested through the midheaven and the tenth house has its seeds in the level of consciousness indicated by the ninth.

This house is steeped in a symbolic perspective which suggests in an interesting manner the meaning of dualism as it is expressed by Sagittarius. From the perspective of the Sagittarian temperament, nothing is taken at face value whether it is a person, a thing, or an experience; it is always a symbol for a broader, more basic experience or archetype, and this perpetual dual awareness of seeing the larger reflected in the smaller, of searching for cosmic meaning in the least of things, is a basic quality of Jupiter, of Sagittarius, and of the ninth house. Jupiter is a symbol for the intuition as Jung describes this function of consciousness—the means of perception whereby the instrinsic meaning of a person, a thing, or an experience is seen instantaneously, without analysis, against the broad framework of the meaning of life as a whole. This is a more modern way of interpreting the ancient Hermetic axiom of "As above, so below"—an expression which is worn through misuse but which still yields increasingly complex meanings with each successive look.

Understandably, as the ninth house is connected with the intuition and the perception of meaning, the broad areas of religion and philosophy are usually associated with it, and on the individual birth chart the ninth house will generally suggest the quality and amount of involvement which the individual is likely to have with what is loosely termed "the Path"—toward individuation or broader consciousness, in a psychological sense, or toward initiation, in an esoteric sense. It is probable that these two are connected in spite of the difference in terminology and viewpoint; and once again the duality of the ninth house is evidenced, for the two worlds of psychology and esotericism, ordinarily considered poles apart, are brought together under the umbrella of the search for meaning.

Through the medium of this house and sign, Saturn tends to have a pronounced effect in colouring the individual's overall view of life and his capacity to find meaning in his own life. Whether we assign Saturn a psychological meaning and associate him with the shadow or "trickster" archetype of the unconscious or whether we assign him an esoteric meaning and call him Lucifer, the behavioural patterns which seem to be concurrent with Saturn in the ninth house follow the usual path of constriction, overcompensation, disillusionment and pain, searching, and eventual inner realisation and control. The kind of pain which usually accompanies this placement is loss of faith, and the search is generally for a new framework of spiritual and moral values by which the life may be given structure and meaning. The opportunity which Saturn offers here seems to be connected with a potential for direct intuitive perception of the wholeness and meaning of the psyche, and this perception often comes through what depth psychology now calls a peak experience. This kind of experience is the goal of the individuation process as Jung structured it and is also the goal of many later developments in the field of depth psychology; it is also, under a different name, the goal of the discipline of certain schools of meditation and yoga. Whatever the experience is and whether it comes in one brief and overwhelming flash or is pieced together over a period of time by an increased flow of the intuitive function, Saturn in the ninth house is connected with the possibility of this kind of experience. This does not mean that only those individuals who have Saturn in Sagittarius or in the ninth house are likely to experience this influx of intuitive perception; however, it is possible that those individuals who have these placements, or have Saturn and Jupiter in aspect, find that it is more necessary for their psychological growth to pursue this kind of perception. It might be said that the psyche aims toward this more urgently because Saturn in the ninth house suggests that the more superficial values and theological offerings will not suffice. The man with Saturn in the ninth house is driven toward a direct experience of what we choose to call God.

As usual Saturn may disguise himself, and one of his favourite presentations when he is in the ninth house is the individual who believes in nothing. This kind of rather compulsive agnosticism or atheism is rarely the outgrowth of logical analysis and a naturally pragmatic or earthy temperament; it is usually linked with fear and a rebellion against an inner urge toward things of a more abstract nature. Sometimes this kind of orientation is linked with an early upbringing of a dogmatic nature and a subsequent disillusionment. Saturn in the ninth house is often connected with a finely tuned sense of justice and a great sensitivity to the plight of humanity as a group, but there is often a tendency toward depression and lack of hope with this placement, particularly hope in the individual's own future. He may find it difficult to make contact with the flow of his over-all self through the intuition and is consequently left with a sense of futility and often with a fear of the future. The man with a ninth house Saturn often finds through hard experience that faith in someone else's interpretation of life and of justice does not suffice, and it is often difficult for him to accept any authority, temporal or spiritual, other than himself because he has been severely disillusioned by such authority in the past. This is the first stage of the process of disillusionment and rebuilding connected with Saturn in the ninth house; if the individual persists in his growth, the development of his intuitive perception into the world of meaning guarantees him a much more direct and meaningful authority—himself.

There appears to be a definite link between Saturn in the ninth house and an early exposure to religious teachings of a dogmatic kind. Generally this exposure ends in disillusionment later in life. The individual will often follow the characteristic pattern of attempting to crystallise values of an essentially inner and subjective nature into the formal ritual, structure, and uniformity of orthodox religious ceremony. This becomes his spiritual security, and he relies on this structure for his sense of meaning rather than on any real perception of his own. The higher authority—whether a church or a father—offers a formula by which the rules given form the structure of life, and the individual is expected to cling without question to these rules rather than initiating an inner search whereby he can apprehend the laws of life by his own inner authority. Someone else's sincere but often narrow vision becomes his opinion, and he is trapped within the prison of his own narrow-mindedness. Generally these opinions in the end fail him for they do not stand up to his own life experiences. He is thrown back on his own resources and must begin again to build a different kind of framework for his beliefs.

Saturn appears to have affinity with certain of our western religions, or at least with particular aspects or interpretations of them—in particular Catholicism, Mormonism, and Judaism. It is not that these paths are to be criticised, for the outer form of religion is created by man in response to an inner need and perception and any form created is necessary for a period of time. These paths become problems when they begin to crystallise; and this is often due to their interpretation by well-meaning but unimaginative individuals. What Saturn in the ninth house suggests is not that there is anything fundamentally wrong with one's religion but rather that there is some degree of crystallisation in the interpretation; the form has outlived its usefulness. Saturnian orientation in a religion inclines toward much emphasis on law, structure, guilt, punishment, and the unknowable Will of God with little emphasis on life, quality, inner meaning, or individual growth. It is often the parental interpretation which is the problem. A childhood steeped in the Saturnian kind of morality and belief can be a fruitful source of guilt. It can help to create in the individual a doubt in his own right to decide for himself the inner or spiritual meaning of his life. This is destructive because it stifles growth. This is often the goad which drives the person with a ninth house Saturn deep into the realm of philosophy or psychology so that some kind of solution can be found for the riddle of one's existence. The prison of a ninth house Saturn is a subtle one, but it is built through loss of hope and faith and an inability to establish the meaningful subjective contact upon which real vision is built. By the denial of this basic need for hope, Saturn suggests the necessity of the individual's finding the needed experience firsthand, without the help of dogma, of groups, guides, or gurus. Nothing except direct experience will suffice. It is in this direction that the opportunity of a ninth house Saturn lies.

The entire spectrum of Saturnian camouflage may be observed with Saturn in the ninth house, ranging from the complete skepticism of the rational thinker through the narrow vision of the fanatic to the disciplines and probings of the practical occultist and finally to the muddled and well-meaning gullibility of the man who is willing to believe anything as long as it will give him back his faith. Behind all these costumes stands the inner urge toward a direct spiritual experience and a direct personal acquisition of knowledge which will throw light on the more ambiguous areas of human existence. This is quite a long way from "conflict with the law", and yet the phrase applies. It is perhaps descriptive of the man who is engaged in a struggle between his own inner convictions and the beliefs and formal trappings which have been handed to him by his environment. This kind of struggle between inner values and outer opinions always applies to Saturn's placement on the birth chart, and in this position the struggle lies in the realm of the ideas which, when coloured by emotional values, become translated into ideals. The

Sagittarian temperament must have an ideal by which he can live; without the dream or the vision at the end of the climb, he cannot find the necessary one-pointedness even to begin. The same situation is true of the person with an emphasised ninth house, and it is particularly true in a specific way of the person with Saturn in the ninth. He also must have an ideal by which to live, but he must also understand the idea behind it, which lies beyond the plane of emotional aspiration and is more purely a product of the intuition. Without this kind of direct understanding he loses hope and plunges into the kind of depression which is so typical of this Saturnian placement; or he may seek to escape by one of the various expressions of overcompensation.

Saturn in the ninth house is often referred to as concurrent with a profound and penetrating mind. The more conscious individual will generally express this quality to a greater or lesser degree. He generally arrives at this point, however, by the long circuitous route, and it is only after he has experienced the opposites that he can be truly free of the crystallising effect that Saturn has on the mind. He has the possibility of finding some very valuable answers to some very broad questions; but he must find them himself without help. Saturn will tolerate no one else's authority. The man with a ninth house Saturn usually finds that he has to be his own priest, pope, and saviour because all moral and ethical values lie within him. It is the fine tightrope between the opposites which he generally is required to walk with an acute sensitivity to the fact that all moral and ethical values are, in the end, relative and yet that the universe is intrinsically moral in an altogether different sense. While realising that all ideals and concepts are relative because they are only a part of the whole, the responsibility still lies on his shoulders to act in a fashion which serves the growth of the whole. This is a tightrope in a very literal sense. On one side lies the grey purposeless which usually exists side by side with the relinquishment of one's dreams; on the other lies an incessant struggle with anything which symbolises authority. At the end of the rope, successfully crossed, lies a kind of freedom which usually is experienced with the quality that the Sagittarian expresses most easily: joy.

5 aspects on the birth chart

The older view of the astrological aspects is that those obtained by the division of the three hundred and sixty degree circle by three, the number of harmony and perfection, or its derivatives are "good" aspects and those obtained by the division of the circle by two, the number of imbalance or separateness, or its derivatives are "bad". Older textbooks speak of planets being "badly afflicted" or "evilly aspected", particularly if they were squared or conjuncted or opposed by Saturn. This attitude has been largely replaced by the more mature view that no energy is inherently good or bad, that all of the psychological functions represented by the planets have their place, and that the use and expression of these functions or energies can yield constructive or destructive results depending upon one's relative frame of reference. All aspects on the natal chart serve a purpose or have a place in the shaping of the psyche as a whole, and although some aspects require more effort at integration and are generative of more inner disquiet, it is generally these very aspects which promote growth and the development of greater consciousness. Beauty is in the eyes of the beholder and so is a "good" aspect; some individuals feel that the pinnacle of achievement in life is happiness, comfort, and security while others welcome the inner friction which drives them on to greater challenges and greater growth. In the end it is the fact that two planets contact at all that is the important thing since any contact provides an opportunity for greater integration. In the older view of the universe, which coloured medieval astrology and still colours the viewpoints of many people, God wars with the Devil for dominion on earth, and man is helplessly caught between the overwhelming pull of these two great external powers. In psychological parlance God and the Devil live within the individual and not in the world outside him, and rather than being eternal enemies they are more aptly described as two faces of one psychic fact which we call the ego. In astrological terms these two faces may be connected with the Sun and Saturn.

The nature of an aspect does not alter the intrinsic energy of the two planets involved. It simply indicates whether their contact is easily integrated into the whole of the psyche or whether some conscious effort at adjustment is required. It is the contact which is important. Every factor on a birth chart is in delicate balance with every other factor, and the key to the individual's understanding of himself appears to lie in his capacity to find an effective use for all his random bits and pieces so that they function as the whole unit necessary for the fulfillment of his purpose in life. Nothing is superfluous and nothing is "bad" or "unfortunate"; what is generally unfortunate is the individual's ignorance of the value of his total self and his consequent tendency to chop up the whole into bits and pieces most of which he discards and thinks himself rid of because he does not approve of them. This is generally true of a man's attitude toward the position of his Saturn for this often corresponds to memories and qualities of which he would rather not be reminded, these are, more often than not, projected onto others so that life, rather than his own psyche, is the culprit when things do not go well for him. With most Saturnian aspects, especially the squares, Saturn is externalised, and something in the environment becomes the guilty party, the cause of the friction and inner disquiet associated with square aspects. The more strenuous the efforts are to get rid of him, the faster he comes back.

So Saturn remains Saturn regardless of whether he conjuncts, squares, trines, parallels, or even quintiles another planet. Because he is Saturn he is never easy to deal with because his function is that of promoting growth and it is only frustration and pain which at present are sufficient goads to get a human being moving. Each Saturnian aspect on the birth chart may be seen as a heavy cross to be borne, an "affliction" which dooms the individual to frustration and limitation and loss, and which must dutifully be endured because it cannot be changed. Or the Saturnian aspects may, alternately, be seen as opportunities, and each planet touched by Saturn may be considered to have offered the possibility of a deeper, richer, and more purposeful expression of its meaning. This kind of expression always requires a reevaluation, a closer look at values, and a careful weeding out of those things which are values imposed by others. It is generally a painful process because any planet aspected by Saturn cannot follow the easy path. It is generally those individuals who have a "badly afflicted" Saturn who have a greater possibility of finding meaning and purpose for their lives because they are bound to searching for values which are built on an internal rather than an external reality. It is impossible to explain to the person who skims over an experience how much richer that experience can be if it is taken whole; however, for the man who wishes to have a whole life, and to know that he is alive, there is nothing more useful to be found on the birth chart than aspects to Saturn.

Saturn in aspect
to the Sun

The Sun and Saturn may be seen as polar opposites in a psychological sense, together forming a unit which we call the individuality. In mythology these two functions of the ego and its shadow are often represented as the hero and his trusted companion, such as Theseus and Pirithous; they are also the hero and his long-standing enemy, who is also himself, such as Parsifal and the Red Knight whose armour Parsifal later dons. The functions which the Sun and Saturn symbolise need to be integrated within the conscious awareness of the individual if he is to make any real steps in growth. But the human intellect is not accustomed to seeing opposites as having the same meaning, and it is often difficult for the average person to understand that his darker side, symbolised by Saturn, is the pathway by which he may find the bright light of his full potential, symbolised by the Sun.

In Gnostic teaching Jesus and Satanael were the twin sons of God, each having an equally important and necessary role in the structure and unfoldment of the universe. They were symbols of the light and dark aspects of life and of the psyche but had not yet come to mean the principles of human good and human evil in the petty sense in which we now understand these principles. The Sun is always symbolically pitted against Saturn on the birth chart, whether they are actually in aspect or not. It is for the individual to discover that they are the two faces of himself; but to perceive them in this way requires standing at the centre and not wholly in the light of the conscious ego. This is another way of looking at a birth chart; it is simply a shifting of viewpoint. The relationship of the Sun—by house, sign, and aspect—and Saturn, taken as opposites and complements, is often suggestive of the broad path of development of the individual with the necessary crises or points of reorientation which he is likely to meet as a part of his development. When the Sun and Saturn actually form an aspect, this process of integration is accelerated and rendered more urgent at the same time that it becomes more difficult. The psyche as a whole seems bent on achieving a kind of completeness and self-determination which is not so imperative when there is no Sun-Saturn contact. Sun-Saturn contacts seem to be the mark of the individual who has the opportunity to shape an integrated and finely edged tool out of his personality components and to put this tool to work as a servant of the perfected will.

The Sun-Saturn individual often deals with life by pitting himself against it, because he usually finds at a fairly early age that those things which are of value to him must be worked for. No matter how extroverted or apparently carefree a personality the individual possesses, there is usually a quality of controlled and disciplined energy about Sun-Saturn contacts; there is a careful deliberation and a concern for self-protection which suggests that these people feel they must guard themselves against life so that life does not deal them a blow which will flatten them. The Sun-Saturn person is often more acutely aware of responsibility than other people, perhaps more so than is healthy for his self-expression. But it is often the case with him that he has never really had the chance to be a child, and so he has never learned that naive trust in life's bounty which permits the relaxation of effort. The echoes of this intense self-determination may also be seen in the placement of the Sun in Saturn's sign, or Saturn in the Sun's sign, or the Sun in the tenth house, or Saturn in the fifth. These are all subtly different in interpretation, but there is about all these positions the quality of self-determination. The individual must make something of his life and find his identity by the efforts of his own hands and brain. That which is accepted from others inevitably disappoints him.

The Sun-Saturn individual is frequently very successful although he rarely achieves this success on his own before Saturn has completed his return by transit around the houses of the birth chart and the necessary practical experience has been acquired. But Sun-Saturn people are also often extreme failures, and the aspect is common in the charts of alcoholics—particularly the opposition. When the contact is a close one, the individual usually is either intensely ambitious or professes to have no ambitions. This latter expression is typical of Saturn and is often a means by which the person tries to save himself the pain of admitting his ambitions and failing to see them realised. He may surmount great environmental obstacles to achieve his goals, or he may succumb to these obstacles and may even unconsciously amplify them to justify his failure. Whichever expression he chooses, the Sun-Saturn person may be handed certain advantages, but in the end he must work for that which he truly values. He is always offered the opportunity to become truly master of his fate. The goals which he achieves are rarely sufficient to satisfy him; it is the strength and self-confidence which he acquires in getting there that is important and the emergence of an integrated and well-defined conscious identity. If he does not take the opportunity offered, his failure is much deeper than a mere material failure, and it is often difficult for him to live with for any length of time.

Early environmental conditions are often difficult with these contacts, even the harmonious aspects. The relationship with the father is immediately implicated, and there is the suggestion that some disappointment is experienced through him. There is often outright coldness or rejection from the father or the emphasis on duty, form, and material values. Sometimes the father is loving and kind but weak and is a disappointment because he cannot assume the strong and protective role necessary for the child's psychological balance. He may be a material failure or a burden because of ill-health. Both ends of the spectrum are possible, along with all the shades in the middle, for the outward expression of any Saturnian aspect is always ambiguous. The meaning generally is the same: the male half of the psyche, the ego or conscious identity, must be created fresh by the individual because he cannot inherit or acquire his identity through his own father.

This association of Sun-Saturn contacts with a failure in the father-child relationship has important implications in the sphere of personal relationships. It is a particularly significant contact for women because a woman's relationship with men and with the masculine half of her own psyche is affected by the disappointment and failure of her relationship with her father. She may develop hostility toward men, openly and consciously expressed; or she may carry this hostility inwardly and unconsciously, finding that she can express only the instinctual, feeling side of her nature and must live her masculine decisiveness and will out through a partner who becomes the father she did not properly have. The psychological patterns are often very subtle with these contacts, but they usually suggest a point of friction which needs to be examined and understood and which compels the person's attention inward to the world of the unconscious and of inner values. Handled with insight and care, Sun-Saturn contacts on the chart of a woman are suggestive of an opportunity to explore the realm of conscious initiative and creative endeavour, permitting a wholeness which is usually not developed in a woman's psyche.

For a man with a Sun-Saturn contact, there is often the need to prove himself to himself and to his father for he often feels the failure of the relationship as an indication of personal inadequacy. This is one of the spurs to ambition which is such a characteristic feature of these contacts. The nature of the real struggle is often externalised, and the man must prove himself successful in a sometimes compulsive fashion; but it is not really material success that he seeks. It is a sense of importance and of self-worth, an acceptance of his own masculinity—not in a sexual way, but in a more general way—which will permit him to rely on his own inner centre. The usual symbols of importance and identity which the majority of men accept with clear conscience do not suffice for the Sun-Saturn individual; he must develop his own definition of worth and must experience his own capacity to control, direct, and master his life. It is ironic that the extremes of inherited money and position and poverty and lack of opportunity can both be expressed by Sun-Saturn contacts. But in both cases the values and the identity must be earned by the individual himself if they are to be real to him.

The person with a strong Sun-Saturn contact often experiences a kind of guilt if he is too happy or if he relaxes too much. There is sometimes a deep inner feeling of the need for self-denial, and this is occasionally exaggerated so that the individual brings ruin down on his own head through poor judgment, through functional illness, or through an act of martyrdom of one kind or another just at the point where his dreams threaten to become fulfilled. Sometimes this self-imposed psychological hair shirt is concurrent with a childhood permeated with strict religious training, for the Sun-Saturn tendency toward an unsympathetic environment is sometimes expressed as an unsympathetic deity of the kind that Job encountered. Sun-Saturn people often find themselves attracted to the more Saturnian religious symbols for man has indeed interpreted God in his own image, and the Sun-Saturn person's God has a Sun-Saturn quality. This expression of Sun-Saturn contacts is an interesting one, but it is fundamentally the same in its inner meaning as the more typical expression where the material environment or the father is the villain of the piece. Whether it is a man's conception of deity, of his father, of his capacity for success, or of his role as a man, the presence of a Sun-Saturn contact suggests that he will get no outside help in his path toward discovery of his own identity.

There are many ways in which Sun-Saturn aspects may be expressed for the Sun is a very personal symbol of a mode of self-expression and each individual has a different mode. But the contact is in reality a simple and basic one because of the complementary nature of these two planets. Any combination of complementary bodies, such as Sun-Saturn, Venus-Mars, Sun-Moon, suggests an almost archetypal simplicity where the integration of the two functions becomes a psychic necessity for the individual. This is true of Sun-Saturn contacts in the sphere of the conscious identity.

Saturn in aspect
to the Moon

Moon-Saturn contacts have a poor reputation traditionally, although the classical Saturnian virtues of thrift and caution are usually linked with them. They are said to indicate a personality which is often sensitive to the point of morbidity, restriction and inhibition, withdrawal and difficulty in emotional expression, shyness, and lack of imagination. These qualities, which are generally associated with the afflictions of Saturn to the Moon, are fairly awe-inspiring for what is a common enough contact, and although this description is accurate enough about many Moon-Saturn personalities, the contact may also be seen from a different and less depressive point of view. Thrift and caution are, in the final analysis, fairly uninteresting compensations for the unpleasant qualities usually linked with Moon-Saturn aspects.

The Moon has a variety of possible interpretations which is fitting for her fluid and changeable nature. From a psychological point of view alone there are many avenues of meaning all of which are applicable to the Moon's symbolism. There is some general agreement that she is, among other things, a symbol for the feminine half of the human psyche—the feeling nature, the sensual nature, the mother, the unconscious or dark aspect of a man's psyche. The archetype of the great lunar goddess in ancient mythology, who was also goddess of fertility and of the earth, still carries power today in the conscious expression of woman and the unconscious of man, and the language of symbolism and dreams, of moods and fantasy, is also linked with the Moon. She is also, on a more prosaic level, a symbol of one's childhood and of the roots from which the individual's character grows; she often describes in a clear and concise manner on the birth chart the nature of the atmosphere of early home life and the relationship with one's mother. In terms of behaviour the Moon appears to be related to an individual's instinctive habit patterns, his natural unconscious manner of expression. The Moon is the line of least resistance, and her qualities by sign and house and aspect are expressed most obviously in intimate emotional relationships and in those situations where instinct rather than conscious deliberation governs a man's actions.

There is an old esoteric teaching that the sign in which the Moon is placed in the present life corresponds to the sign in which the Sun was placed in the last life. This is rather simple and not very helpful for literal interpretation; we have not yet ascertained in a definitive way the validity of the concept of rebirth and have no real information on the astrological patterns which might be associated with it. But there is some value in interpreting this teaching in a symbolic sense because the Moon represents a link with one's childhood and one's heredity and roots and usually suggests an area where the need for security and a sense of continuity with the past is obviously expressed. In some ways the Moon symbolises what the parents have been and where the longing is greatest for an emotional rapport and instinctual closeness which will replace the comfort of the ancient umbilical tie.

There is the suggestion with Moon-Saturn contacts, including the "soft" aspects, that the experiences of childhood have been structured and defined along Saturnian lines and that there has been rather a lot of emphasis on duty and on the appropriate forms of behaviour. Sometimes Moon-Saturn contacts are concurrent with a childhood which is difficult because of financial reasons; sometimes there is an abundance of material comfort but little warmth or spontanaeity of emotional expression. The mother is frequently undemonstrative, or a disappointment in some way. Many Moon-Saturn people carry a well-defined stamp of emotional close-

fistedness which infers a long past of learning to control the feelings—
beginning at an age where feelings, freely expressed, are the only
outlet a child possesses for communication. There is often a brooding
loneliness about this contact, and even with the apparent stability and
steadfastness which are typical of the easier aspects, there is an
aloofness and isolation which is not easily broken. There is frequently
a cool and apparently efficient exterior presented although the
efficiency is questionable if the aspects are close because there is often
compulsive defensiveness which interferes with the practical
instincts. Moon-Saturn contacts often concur with the sort of
personality which likes to present itself as practical, but this is usually
a substitution of values of the kind which Saturn is so good at; the
practicality is usually developed because the individual cannot
express himself in any other way. Often a deep loneliness and
needfulness is present with Moon-Saturn, particularly for the
security of emotional bonds which only a family with its sense of
blood relationships and continuity can provide. There is a need for
roots, for tradition, and for the physical structure of a family unit.
Usually this emphasis on the structure carries an inherent disappointment with it for the family, when the Moon is closely aspected to
Saturn, can often offer nothing except structure.

The early home life is of primary importance in the shaping
of the Moon-Saturn personality characteristics. Both of these planets
are related to the vertical axis of the chart with its associations of
parental influence, and both planets are also connected with aspects
of the unconscious and of behaviour patterns which are built up over
past experience. Both parents are represented by this contact and not
in the kindest of fashions. The suggestion of a "business before
pleasure" attitude is strong. Sometimes there is the atmosphere of a
strict morality, linked with religious viewpoints; this contact is
common among people who have been subjected to the more
dogmatic religious systems with their emphasis on a harsh and duty-
conscious deity. The parents, often through no fault of their own, are
a burden or a disappointment to the child.

What this kind of pattern does psychologically varies
depending upon whether the individual is a man or a woman; it also
varies because the bias of the rest of the chart may suggest the usual
wide spectrum of apparent expressions of Saturn, ranging from the
close and withdrawn emotional temperament one might expect, to the
apparently effusive and sentimental temperament which Saturn so

easily demonstrates as compensation. But whatever his external manifestation, Saturn always inclines toward the development of strength through isolation, and the individual with Moon-Saturn is usually cut off from both his literal roots and his psychic roots and must develop his own sense of continuity and emotional security. He cannot retreat to the pleasant memories of childhood because they are frequently unpleasant, and he also cannot depend upon others emotionally to provide a nest in which he can bury himself so that he does not have to grow. When he relies on his instincts, they usually let him down, and he often finds at some point in his life that he must burn his bridges behind him if he is to develop into a mature human being. The structure of the family and the rules of good behaviour which served him in the past as a reason for being are no longer satisfactory, and the individual is given an opportunity to develop the conscious decision-making aspect of his nature more fully, symbolised by the Sun, because the line of least resistance is blocked. It might be said that when Moon-Saturn contacts are present on the birth chart, it is time for the individual to begin to become a conscious, thinking entity; the total structure of his psyche will usually not permit him to fall back on his feeling nature for his direction or his behaviour.

The Moon on a man's chart has some bearing on his choice in a female partner since this is affected by the temperament of his mother and the kind of relationship he had with her. As a symbol of his own female side, the Moon usually suggests those qualities which are likely to be projected upon a wife or lover; the Moon is one of the keys to the attributes which personalise the "anima" figure in a man's unconscious psyche. Moon-Saturn contacts suggest that some difficulties are to be expected both in a man's relationship with his own unconscious and in his relationships with women as the living symbol of his female self. The feeling side of his nature is likely to be forcibly clamped down, and in place of feelings—which are likely to be a rather powerful and not always wholesome energy—the man may express sentiment of a kind which is peculiarly characteristic of Moon-Saturn contacts and which is always well-behaved. The feeling nature is not consistently well-behaved any more than the Moon is consistently full or new; it is the totality of feeling experience which is symbolised by the Moon, and it is this totality which is such a threat to the Moon-Saturn man. Because the feeling nature is rarely permitted acknowledgment let alone expression, the Moon-Saturn man is likely to attract women of a particularly instinctual and dominant nature into his life, and the voracious lunar goddess, flanked by her bestial symbols, which has been denied integration in his own psyche, will usually appear as a woman in his personal life. Just as he is inwardly at the mercy of his moods and feelings—one of the typical characteristics of Moon-Saturn—he is also at the mercy of his women through the vulnerability and childishness of his feeling nature. The medieval astrologers stated that the Moon's application to Saturn on a man's birth chart boded no good in terms of marriage, and it is possible that in some ways they were correct.

One of the most important opportunities offered by this contact on a man's chart is the possibility of coming to terms with his feeling nature because he generally suffers disappointment through women and consequently finds it useless to attempt to project his feeling nature onto them and live this side of his psyche out vicariously. He must experience it himself, and it is through this means that a man can in the end free himself finally from the grip and control of his own past. He becomes what is called "twice-born" through this confrontation with and understanding of his feeling nature, and it is possible for him to become closer to a whole person than the ordinary man whose female half is always expressed through the women in his life. Moon-Saturn contacts are important on a man's chart although all too often the man will attempt to sidestep the challenge and bury himself in practical affairs which take his mind off the loneliness and vulnerability which constantly nag at him from within. Saturn's gift of independence usually follows on the heels of failure or disappointment because only failure appears to be sufficient to cause a person to question himself or to develop the necessary inner wisdom and strength. With Moon-Saturn contacts he offers the possibility of true emotional independence—a quality or experience which is relatively rare. The security of family ties is an illusory one, and it is often very dangerous to assume that one has the right, because of blood ties, to command emotional support from others. Parents can die, partners can leave, and children can grow up; and the person with Moon-Saturn is generally courting pain and disappointment if he seeks to bind these external things to himself by emotional need. As he builds his own inner stability and taps the resources of his creative and intuitive side, he generally finds that he does not have to demand the affection of others. This is offered to him freely, because he has something to offer in return—a whole person.

Moon-Saturn contacts are often associated with ill-health in the charts of women, and this appears to be true as far as it goes. There is often a propensity, especially with the conjunction, toward chronic illness of one kind or another. This illness, however, is frequently functional rather than organic and is sometimes of the kind which Freud, in the days of the infancy of psychology—which is still in its childhood—called "hysterical". Emotions which are not able to be expressed freely through ordinary channels are often short-circuited and take their toll on the body. Moon-Saturn illnesses are often a symbol of the frustrated feelings of a person who, because of background, a sense of duty, and a fear of rejection or humiliation, will not express herself in an open and spontaneous way. Sometimes it is emotional disappointment which is expressed through the physical body. But in many cases it is the feeling nature, rather than the body, which is the source of the difficulty.

The Moon is particularly important on a woman's chart because the feeling nature is often the most developed function of consciousness and is the channel by which the woman usually expresses herself. It is often the Sun, as a symbol of maleness, which is unconscious in a woman's psyche, and the directed will and desire for recognition and self-expression are often projected upon the partner and lived out through him. In the same way a man will often live out his unrecognised feelings through his more emotionally expressive partner. A Moon-Saturn contact is often suggestive of difficulty in expression through this more important channel of feeling; this can cut a woman off from her own femininity and from acceptance of herself as a woman. This is sometimes connected with the relationship to the mother in childhood, which may be productive of feelings of rejection, isolation, and inadequacy. A woman with Moon-Saturn must generally create her own psychic "space" and needs to discover her femininity apart from its associations with her mother's image and role. In one way or another Moon-Saturn contacts in the charts of women often suggest what Jung called a "mother-complex", and although this term has been misused and overused in many ways, nevertheless the mother, or the woman's image of the mother, is a formidable energy which must be dealt with carefully. The two extremes of the overly instinctual woman, who has no function other than childbearer and cook, and the overly aggressive woman, who resents the biological bias of her own body, are both related to this idea of the mother-complex and to the aspects of the Moon and Saturn.

For women as well as men the opportunity is offered of

emotional freedom when the Moon is in aspect to Saturn. Although this means different things to women and men, nevertheless the opportunity is basically the same. There are few women who are truly themselves as independent individuals; there are many who are attempting to overcompensate with apparent freedom but few who have come fully to terms in a conscious way with their own femaleness and with the mother who stands pyschologically as a symbol of that femaleness. It is the experience and understanding of this mystery which is possible for a woman with a Moon-Saturn contact. This is a far more important offering than thrift or caution in terms of the development of the whole psyche.

Saturn in aspect
to Mercury

Mercury in aspect to Saturn is traditionally considered to concur with profundity of thought, a shrewd, careful and thorough mind, canniness in business matters, and on the more negative side, a tendency to depression and gloominess, narrowness and rigidity of viewpoint, and a propensity for prevarication or evasiveness. There seems to be some association of Mercury-Saturn contacts, particularly the "hard" aspects, with speech difficulties such as stammering or stuttering and also with defects of hearing. The close conjunctions, squares, and oppositions of Mercury and Saturn are also said to have some connexion with dullness or lack of intelligence. In general, however, Mercury-Saturn contacts are considered to be reasonably easy to deal with although not particularly important unless other planets are involved in the configuration or unless one or the other planet is on an angle.

It is possible that Mercury-Saturn contacts assume major importance only at a particular stage of an individual's development—that is, when he learns how to reason. Not everyone makes use of this capacity. Mercury-Saturn contacts are not productive of the kind of stress and emotional frustration which is more typical of Mars, Venus, or the Moon in aspect to Saturn. Mercury, being symbolic of cold reason and common sense and being inclined toward matters of business or commerce as well as intellectual pursuits, tends to blend agreeably with Saturn regardless of the nature of the aspect. It is fairly obvious why a combination of these two planets should be associated with tact, shrewdness, and diplomacy.

There are many people, however, who labour under the less agreeable side of these aspects, and this seems to be more in evidence with the more intellectual type of temperament. Frequently there is much frustration felt in the area of communication and feelings of inadequacy about one's mental capacities. These feelings, if amplified enough, are often at the root of physical expressions such as stammering; the ease with which this difficulty in speech is helped through such therapeutic methods as hypnotherapy strongly points to the psychological origin of the difficulty. Like Saturn in the third house, Mercury-Saturn contacts often suggest the appearance of dullness when the situation is actually one of fear and inhibition. The curious expression of the chronic and uncontrollable liar is also one of the less attractive facets of Mercury-Saturn. But Saturn remains true to form here in that there must be present a reasonable degree of intelligence, sensitivity, and complexity of character in order for such distortion or overcompensation to exist. Often it is the person who experiences the more difficult face of Mercury-Saturn who in the end is able to make use of the opportunity for mental development and illumination which Saturn offers.

Mercury is a highly important planet symbolising a highly important function because he represents the instrument of communication of the birth chart's potential to the environment and likewise the instrument of assimilating data from the environment. In spite of the fact that many esoteric schools of a devotional nature teach us that the mind is the "slayer of the real", it appears that man can make no sense either of his experiences or of himself unless he develops the faculty of understanding and discrimination. Otherwise he is a creature of instinct and is no different from the animals. No matter how strong, able, gifted, or developed an individual may be, he cannot communicate his gifts to others, nor can he absorb understanding from them, if he has not developed the use of the mind. The well-worn maxim that energy follows thought is nevertheless a valid one, and all things begin on the plane of thought as a basic idea before they become reality on the mundane plane. This is not so abstruse a concept as it seems. Mercury symbolises the concrete mind, and without him there can be no comprehension of the meaning of an experience because there is no way out of the sea of emotional involvement which cloaks the experience. There is also no self-understanding because Mercury symbolises the power of analysis and discrimination. He rules two signs and therefore governs two houses of the birth chart; it is a mistake to underestimate his importance. In the average individual who is developing his mental nature, it is the information available from the environment which helps to shape one's ideas and orientation. When this source of information is closed off, as it often is when Saturn aspects Mercury, the individual must then rely on his inner perception and on his own experience to develop his attitudes and ideas about life. This often takes a long time but can be a more valid means of understanding life because it is first-hand.

Mercury-Saturn aspects suggest a feeling of mental inadequacy or uncertainty, and this is often aggravated in childhood by the parental attitude of assuming that a child cannot think for himself because he is a child and that any independent thought or idea which conflicts with the wider opinions of his elders needs to be stifled. While the child will usually withdraw from this kind of experience, he will also often pay the price later by mistrusting his own mental competence. Often the Mercury-Saturn person will do poorly in school not because he is stupid, or unoriginal, but because he often believes that he is stupid and will in turn work so slowly, in such fear of making an error, that his intelligence is underestimated by those around him. Mercury-Saturn may equally often become pedantic and incline toward overcompensation by placing great emphasis on intellectual accomplishment; but it is usually laboured accomplishment without the natural ease and grace of the Mercurial temperament. The individual may in childhood have difficulty in articulating, because of shyness and fear, which may in turn be interpreted as lack of interest. He may express the characteristic Saturnian taciturnity, masking a sensitive and deeply thoughtful temperament with habitual silence. There is the likelihood typical of difficult Saturnian aspects, of a "vicious circle" perpetuating itself since his fear aggravates his frustration and incompetence which in turn aggravates his fear.

Mercury-Saturn contacts frequently are connected with either an incomplete or interrupted education or an exaggerated academic career. The practical lessons of everyday life, where there is no competition with faster or more fluent minds, is often more appealing to the Mercury-Saturn temperament, and there is often a compensatory development of great facility at earthy matters. Sometimes the individual is pragmatic and unimaginative, largely because the realm of abstract thought is frightening to him. He may feel inept when confronted with a more carefully educated or intellectual type of temperament, often becoming cynical and sardonic as a defense against what he unconsciously fears as a more competent mind. It is generally difficult for Mercury-Saturn to learn anything in any way except by his own effort whether he is the more taciturn type or is compensating by a more loquacious temperament. He will rarely trust a piece of information unless he has actually experienced it and made sure that he understands it thoroughly. This tendency is acceptable by our present standards because it is in line with the scientific method although Mercury-Saturn is inclined to lose the meaning of an experience by his insistence on pinning the experience to a board. The subtle and tenuous bridge which leads from the intellect to the intuitive perception of meaning behind an idea or a fact is blocked by Saturn, and often the most difficult side of Mercury-Saturn is the loss of real meaning and genuine understanding. Facts are comprehended and learning may be impeccable; but the life behind the structure is lost.

The presence of a strong Mercury-Saturn contact on the birth chart seems to suggest the opportunity for self-education in a deeper sense than simple accumulation of practical knowledge through experience. Saturn symbolises that motivation within an individual which seeks the bare bones of meaning buried within the layers of form, and this urge for discovery of the intrinsic truth or meaning of any experience is directed into the realm of knowledge under the influence of Mercury-Saturn contacts. Understanding an idea, a feeling, or a thing in the ordinary sense generally means identifying and categorising that idea, feeling, or thing; it is then assigned to its proper mental compartment in the contents of consciousness, labelled correctly for future use. A quick observation inward at the mechanics of this process of assimilating information usually reveals this rapid network of association and compartmentalisation of experience which occurs constantly throughout the day and throughout the life of a human being. Experiences have meaning to the average individual according to a framework of pre-established associations. It is by this means that the thinking individual evaluates life.

This framework is generally drawn not from one's own experience, which must necessarily be limited, but rather from other people's experiences which we then adopt as our own. The meaning of an experience in itself is lost; it is only what the experience evokes within the group that gives it its identity. It is the emotional associations which colour ideas, when the webs of illusion are stripped away and we are able to perceive the mechanism at work. The ideas of many people are opinions rather than ideas, and Mercury becomes a mere accumulator of other people's values rather than a creative instrument in his own right. Most people have opinions, and these are easily acquired and freely given; but few people know how to think creatively or to build an original framework of associations based not on emotional value judgments but on the intrinsic meaning of each unique, separate experience. This is real freedom of thought which forges the bridge between the intellectual and intuitive faculties—the only instruments we now possess to give us a glimpse of the totality of the human psyche. The person with a strong Mercury-Saturn aspect labours slowly accumulating what to him is truth because he cannot acquire it in the ordinary way; the free-flowing channels of communication of opinions are closed to him to a greater or lesser degree, and he is forced to build his own framework. He may be earthbound and apparently unimaginative, but he generally has a keen sense of illusion, and the sensitivity he experiences toward the delicate relativity of truth may send him violently into the opposite behaviour pattern so that he becomes a compulsive liar. Whether he consciously seeks a framework of knowledge which is sound and real or whether he gives up in despair because the effort is too great and becomes adept at the manipulation of opinion which is the gift of the good politician, he must probably endure the constant chastisement of Saturn, who reminds him that nothing is true and nothing is false but that there is a fine tightrope between these opposites which leads eventually to the opening up of the intuitive faculty.

Mercury-Saturn contacts are subtle and worth further investigation because they provide an opportunity for a completely different use of the mind. Rather than a tool for categorisation, the one-pointed mind, trained in concentration and the power to perceive meaning behind form, can be directed inward to explore the darker recesses of the psyche. It is the only means by which we can begin to apprehend this aspect of ourselves although the mind, as it is developed in this way, is not an instrument of evaluation; it is a detached observer. It is only when the mind is full of opinions that Mercury becomes the slayer of the real. Perception of the relativity of values bears its own kind of pain, and although it is not personal in the way that emotional frustration is personal, this is an important contact for the person who is beginning to be mentally rather than emotionally polarised. When there are no longer any familiar landmarks for what defines truth and what defines falsehood, the individual must search more deeply within himself to determine what is true or false for him alone. In the acceptance of this responsibility lies a great deal of freedom.

Saturn in aspect
to Venus

Saturnian contacts to Venus, when they occur in the charts of those who are not predisposed toward introspection or self-understanding, are some of the most painful contacts to deal with. This is particularly true for the charts of women. In both men's and women's charts one of the traditional interpretations, which seems to be accurate enough, is that of failure or sorrow in marriage and in love with a subsequent residue of disillusionment, bitterness, fear, and a great sensitivity to rejection which colours all successive romantic encounters with a certain aloofness and mistrust. It is probable that the initial failure—and there is generally one very painful one—is not the only key to the patterns of behaviour which are so typical of Venus-Saturn but that an additional and more important key may be found in childhood, in the individual's relationship to his parents and particularly to the parent of the opposite sex. This is not a new concept but has been suggested before in reference to Venus-Saturn configurations. Saturn's associations with the parents bring this element into all Saturnian contacts with the personal planets.

Venus seems to have importance in relation to one's capacity to be happy in the conventional sense, to be at peace or in harmony with oneself and with the environment. More than any other aspect Venus-Saturn appears to strike at a person's happiness, and the usual feeling with the aspect, even if its more drastic forms are not expressed, is a nagging discontent and the feeling that one will never be able to be happy or take pleasure in life. This contact, even the "harmonious" aspects of trine or sextile, strikes also at a woman's basic attitude toward her own femininity and her worth as a woman and affects a man's basic attitude toward women. Although it may be argued by the more esoterically inclined that personal relationships are of minor importance on the spiritual path, nevertheless loneliness and rejection, in the case of people with Venus-Saturn contacts, can ruin the entire life, and the importance of relationships as they are symbolised by the descendant of the chart is not to be underestimated. This is one of the cardinal points of the birth chart and of the individual's life. While the setting for Sun-Saturn contacts is a broader and more abstract stage, where the issues of one's significance to oneself and one's role in life are at stake, the setting for Venus-Saturn contacts is the sphere of intimate relationships, and it is often in the private recesses of the bedroom that the final effects of these aspects take their toll. In fine balance to the great unhappiness and isolation which often accompany Venus-Saturn aspects, there is also as great a potential for a deep and meaningful and permanent relationship based on complete understanding and on free choice rather than mutual need. The mysteries of union are within the grasp of the person with this contact for although he stands to lose much— and usually must spend a good portion of his life without a companion or without true companionship—he also holds the key to a relationship which is lasting and real. Libra is the sign of Saturn's exaltation, and Venus-Saturn contacts are similar and perhaps even more clear in their inference that relationships are the path to self-knowledge and self-development.

The connexion of Venus-Saturn contacts to sexual inhibitions, particularly the varying degrees of sexual defensiveness which we term frigidity, is rarely mentioned since "sorrow in love" is somehow expected to imply this often sorrowful area of experience as well. But Venus-Saturn contacts cannot be consciously utilised in a constructive way unless an effort is made at honesty with oneself. As with all Saturnian aspects we must consider the workings of the unconscious with its tendency to hold compensatory or opposite attitudes and feelings in relation to the conscious personality and efforts of the individual. Regardless of how badly the person with Venus-Saturn wants to express sexually and emotionally, there is usually an equally intense unconscious fear which makes defense necessary at all costs.

Venus-Saturn combinations imply a certain amount of emotional pain and rejection in the early home life. This may be of an obvious kind, such as the home where nobody touches each other or expresses any overt display of affection or warmth. It may also be of a more subtle kind, where much material display is offered, many gifts given, and great effort made to provide the physical comforts but where there is no real recognition of or love of the child in a straightforward way. It is common with these aspects to find parents who love their child because he is their child but do not actually like the child when it comes to a real appreciation of his individuality. This kind of "love" is very frequent in connexion with Venus-Saturn contacts. It is particularly common among parents who have children because it is the accepted thing to do but who do not themselves, unconsciously, want the responsibility. There are many similar and equally complex patterns which may be found with Venus-Saturn, but they generally involve a lack of real love in the home and often imply unconscious rivalry or hostility from one or both parents. The child is usually better off away from his parents as soon as he is old enough to stand alone, regardless of how much guilt and havoc this may create in the home. The longer he remains in the family fold, the greater his sense of inadequacy will be later in life.

The capacity for expression and receipt of affection, symbolised by Venus, is often cramped and twisted because there is so little genuine affection in childhood; and the individual often finds that he cannot untwist himself later in male-female relationships because he has grown so accustomed to his defenses. There is usually a deep and almost compulsive need to be loved which accompanies Venus-Saturn contacts along with the characteristic Saturnian coolness and defensiveness. It may be said of people with this contact that there is often a feeling of being unloved, and in consequence they find it difficult to express love themselves—except in that slightly demanding, sometimes possessive, discontented yet painfully sensitive and vulnerable manner which is more often seen in children of about three or four years of age. In some fashion the affectional nature has been frozen and remains in a childlike and awkward state while the rest of the temperament, including the defense mechanism, grows up around it. There is often much sophistication in people with Venus-Saturn contacts because their search for happiness may take them into some strange by-ways in pursuit of a love which does not bring pain. But the emotional nature in this area remains essentially that of a child.

We have all encountered those children who because of their fear of being unwanted can only express their need for affection through destructive actions, or an attempt to inflict pain, or sulking and weeping; if we transfer this rather extreme picture to the adult body and mind of the Venus-Saturn individual, and include the skill at portraying surface coolness which he has usually developed, we will hold the key to his peculiar and often misunderstood emotional nature. Of course not all people with Venus-Saturn contacts behave in this fasion. But there is a touch of this quality present although it may be beautifully masked or outweighed by more self-expressive factors. It is particularly rare to find men who express the real vulnerability of the contact since it is far less acceptable in our society for a man to admit that he is afraid of being unloved. So he will very likely affect the traditional Venus-Saturn exterior: coldness which can extend to heartlessness, callousness to the emotional hurts of others, a suspicious and jealous nature which expects, constantly and in spite of reassurance, to be eventually betrayed, and yet a very deep and unshakeable loyalty to someone who may be abusive, dependent, or the least deserving of objects. If we remember that these are people whose emotional growth, in the realm of relationships, has been stunted in childhood, it should be possible to see past the reputation this aspect holds for being incapable of love and understand that what we are pleased to call love is often the expression of need and of sentiment and that this expression, to be convincing, must be observed and experienced in childhood. The Venus-Saturn individual is often awkward when confronted with the world of sentiment; it makes him acutely uncomfortable because he is not used to it. For him love is often linked with sacrifice, and he will either avoid it entirely or make of himself—or his partner—the sacrifice which he believes is required.

In a woman's horoscope Venus, besides being the symbol of the affectional nature, is also symbolic of femininity itself—not the maternal aspect of femininity, which is the province of the Moon, but the ideal companion who expresses beauty, harmony, grace, and charm. Venus is the archetype of the hetaira or courtesan rather than of the mother, and these two faces—Venus and the Moon—together symbolise the female principle on a personal level. Venus-Saturn contacts usually affect a woman's confidence in herself as a woman—not only by society's definition of womanhood but by her own inner definition as well. It is usual to find Venus-Saturn women in the competitive world of business, and this type of woman often excels in her profession. She may be driven to achievement not only because she has a genuine love of work, responsibility, and creative self-expression but also because she may feel that she cannot properly function in any feminine capacity. Only the masculine world is left to her then. Venus-Saturn contacts in their unconscious form do not appear to be analogous to the truly liberated woman who has found her own centre; they appear to be more concurrent with the woman who is frightened of being a woman because she thinks she will fail at it. These two creatures are often apparently similar, but the typical Venus-Saturn woman carries deep feelings of inferiority and unattractiveness—regardless of how physically appealing she may be. It is common also to find Venus-Saturn women in the performing arts, as models, and even as the modern equivalent of the hetaira, with perhaps less glamour. For these women it is terribly important to be loved, admired, and thought beautiful. This is hardly liberation; it is closer to an enslavement to fear. It is no wonder that Venus-Saturn aspects have the reputation of making a woman unpopular with her own sex. As she despises and fears this sex within herself, she attracts resentment and fear from other women.

The prostitute symbolises one extreme of Venus-Saturn, and this is perhaps the most difficult expression for a woman because of the loneliness of this way of life. The woman at the opposite end of the spectrum—the celibate "spinster"—is not so opposite as she first seems to be, for both these women have found a way to avoid the pain of a deep emotional involvement without having to admit to themselves that this is the basis of the behaviour pattern. To love in the sense that Saturn requires it costs something, for this kind of love can entertain no illusions and cannot be based on the satisfaction of a personal need. Many people with Venus-Saturn aspects are afraid to pay the price, although the opportunity is given them to develop this deeper side of the affectional nature and to learn about the more meaningful aspects of relationships. These two extremes also bear some resemblance to the more typical Venus-Saturn woman who plays the role of the modern housewife; for she has sold her soul and her dreams in exchange for the security and safety of a house, an automobile, and the guarantee of maintenance payments if the marriage fails. She will often choose a partner not because she loves him, or because the relationship seems a valid one, but because he is safe and cannot hurt her or reach her more vulnerable feelings. No punishment is meted out by the angry gods to these women who have escaped from paying Saturn's dues. The endless frustration and isolation of a meaningless life is payment enough.

We may find Saturn overcompensating on occasion, and this kind of pattern is equally frustrating because it is just as isolating. It is

common to find a person with Venus-Saturn following a pattern of
relationships where the partner is a burden, emotionally or mentally
or physically "inferior" in one way or another. Venus-Saturn women
are often burdened with husbands or lovers whom they despise or
who are in some fashion a source of unhappiness; yet they will not let
go and will offer any one of a hundred excuses for maintaining the
relationship with such men. Martyrdom of a self-imposed kind is a
common Venus-Saturn manifestation; and the familiar cry, "I've
given so much to him, and all he does is abuse me" must have first
been given by a woman with Venus in aspect to Saturn. It is in
situations such as these that the deceptiveness of these contacts is
evident for it is as difficult to see one's motives clearly with a
psychological pattern of this kind as it is to see the bottom of a murky
lake. It takes courage to tackle this aspect and make something
constructive of it; but it can be so unpleasant in its manifestations that
it often has the knack of bringing out a person's latent source of
courage. Most important is the acceptance of responsibility for, as
with all Saturnian contacts, the "sorrow in love" is not the cruel hand
of blind fate at work but the natural response to an unconscious
pattern.

It may seem that in light of the psychological convolutions
which generally accompany Venus-Saturn contacts, there is little
positive to be said for them. But the rule seems generally to be, at least
with Saturn, that his benefits are in direct proportion to the amount
of pain he can engender. The individual with a Venus-Saturn aspect,
particularly with the conjunction, square, or opposition, has his work
cut out for him. This can unquestionably be a very distressing aspect,
particularly to a person who is sensitive or romantic by nature. If he is
willing to take an honest look at the motives within himself which
have helped to create the patterns of disappointment which he
experiences, he can learn a tremendous amount not only about
himself but about the nature of love and the nature of relationships.
This knowledge, which eventually develops into wisdom, can help
him to establish a fully conscious and free relationship with a
minimum of unconscious projection and a maximum of honesty.
Only the person who has truly loved in freedom, from the heart and
not from the solar plexus, can appreciate the nature of the gift offered
by Saturn aspecting Venus. It is a question of first learning to love
oneself.

The man with a Venus-Saturn contact may not have quite as

difficult a time as his female counterpart, but with men these aspects often are symbolic of a general mistrust of women. There is often the fulfilment of the usual pattern of the "safe" partner, and a great deal is often made of something which is referred to as duty but which is closer to martyrdom. Sometimes there is great resentment or hostility toward women, with fear behind the resentment, and this kind of man will generally dislike a woman who expresses any degree of intelligence or individuality because he maintins his security by keeping his women under control. This is one of the aspects which can incline toward the proverbial "male chauvinist pig" so despised by the Women's Liberation Movement; ironically, however, this movement in its more extreme forms is populated by women with the same Venus-Saturn contacts. With infinite gentleness and patience the universe informs us yet again that like attracts like.

Venus-Saturn contacts are highly important for several reasons, and it is worth the exploration of their nuances and subtleties to get a clearer idea of the amount of power they wield. There is an unmistakable stamp which often accompanies people who have the aspect on the natal chart, and although Venus is a personal planet without much power in the orthodox sense, the entire personality is often shaped by the presence of a strong Venus-Saturn contact. There is an inference in all of this which suggests that Venus is perhaps more important a planet than we give her credit for being and that she has deeper meaning than ornamentation and affection. Esoteric doctrine tells us that Venus is the twin sister or alter ego of the earth and that in the coming centuries she will have greater power both astrologically and symbolically. There is obviously no way to demonstrate at this point whether this piece of esotericism is of value. But in spite of our more modern declarations to the contrary, meaningful relationships—whether we call them marriage or not—are of major importance in the life and growth of the individual psyche both because of the actual experience and because of the inner reality which it symbolises. We have only to look briefly at mythology and folklore, and also at the alchemical "coniunctio" or marriage of Sun and Moon, to glimpse the enormouse psychic importance of the marriage rite as a symbol of union and integration. Even those who for religious reasons eschew relationships must find a suitable psychological substitute; so the nun becomes the Bride of Christ, and the priest offers service to Mother Church. It is in the area of relationships that human beings are the most vulnerable, and consequently it is here that they can make the greatest steps in growth and self-understanding. Saturn, as we know, is in exaltation in Libra, and some of this opportunity is reflected when he is in the seventh house or aspects Venus. The path of building a relationship based on love and on free choice is as valid, and as difficult, a path as the most abstruse of esoteric disciplines.

Saturn in aspect to Mars

(handwritten: ♃ Mars trine Sat)

Saturn-Mars contacts have always had a poor reputation, and among medieval and many modern astrologers, they are an index to cruelty or sadism. Hitler's prominent square from Saturn in Leo at the midheaven to Mars in Taurus in the seventh house is forever being offered as an example of the kind of temperament resulting from this configuration. More reasonable analyses have appeared recently which describe the lighter or more positive side of these aspects, and it has been pointed out that Mars-Saturn is often externalised and can indicate cruelty suffered at the hands of others. But in general the contacts are still considered to denote a harshness and ruthlessness in the individual on some level, mental as often as physical. If we substitute the term "projection" for the older concept of "externalisation", then cruelty demonstrated by others to the person with Mars-Saturn is still a part of his own psyche; otherwise he would not have attracted it into his life. Even the harmonious aspects between these planets have a reputation for a cold and selfish temperament although they are also associated with good organising power and control of the will. As is fitting for the combination of the greater with the lesser malefic, Mars-Saturn is linked with recklessness, a tendency to accidents, violence, and conflict with authority as well as a penchant for attracting enmity and ill-will. There is certainly enough evidence to suggest that Mars-Saturn does express in this rather colourful fashion with many people; however, it does not have to, nor is the only alternative projection so that we can blame someone else for the damage. Like any other Saturnian aspect this one is full of fear, and also like any other Saturnian aspect an opportunity is offered to develop more significant values and greater understanding.

Mars-Saturn aspects are more difficult when they are found in men's charts just as Venus-Saturn contacts are usually more of a problem for women. This seems to be reasonable if we consider that

Mars and Venus are the traditional symbols for male and female sexuality and that Mars on a woman's chart, being representative of her maleness, is likely to be projected onto a man rather than integrated into her conscious expression. Venus on a man's chart, as a symbol of his femaleness, is also likely to be projected onto the women in his life. Mars for a man, however, is the symbol of his sexuality, and he will generally identify with the qualities symbolised by the placement of Mars when he is considering his role as a man, particularly his sexual role. The effects of Saturn on Mars, when this identification is considered, will often be evident in his acceptance of himself as a man and in his confidence in himself as lover, aggressor, conqueror, and leader; it is in these areas that the frustration is felt. Although the Sun is the symbol for the great creative principle, Mars is a more personal and physical symbol for that same principle. And although society has effectively distorted the concept of maleness into a flat, two-dimensional, and often farcical advertising tool, nevertheless the quality of maleness as a psychic fact remains valid, whether it exists in a man, a woman, or an inanimate object. When Mars is aspected to Saturn, it is this basic principle of maleness which is usually denied full expression. When this occurs on a man's chart, he often unconsciously feels himself to be somewhat less than a man until he is able to overcome his sense of inadequacy and learns to understand the deeper meaning of his own masculinity.

The characteristic cruelty and ruthlessness of Mars-Saturn, when seen from this point of view, becomes understandable as overcompensation. They are still highly unpleasant qualities, but whether or not they are morally reprehensible is not the issue for the individual who expresses himself in this way is usually compulsive about it and cannot help himself. Intense inner frustration and a feeling of weakness and powerlessness are two of the more difficult side-effects of Mars-Saturn contacts, and it often becomes necessary for the individual to impose his will on others in a forceful way because he is so afraid that he will be imposed upon and controlled himself. This may be a violent imposition of the will, or it may be far more subtle and be demonstrated on the plane of the mind through manipulation. It may also be expressed as emotional domination. Mars-Saturn contacts can easily suggest this kind of exaggerated maleness in the worst sense of the word.

Mars-Saturn aspects appear to concur equally frequently with the opposite extreme of behaviour where the individual is inordinately passive and unwilling to fight for his own rights. This kind of person will usually give in under insistent pressure from other people and is generally taken advantage of because he cannot assert himself. When this expression of Mars-Saturn occurs in a man's behaviour, he is usually governed by his women and is generally a favourite with female relatives because he possesses that amiable charm which cannot say no. He usually carries within him a deep sense of frustration, anger, and injustice, and this may be expressed, finally, in an inexplicable outbreak of anger or violence—"But I just don't understand it, he seemed like such a *nice* man". Or the frustration may fester within him and be turned against himself, producing illness and a tendency toward self-destructiveness of varying kinds.

There appears to be some connexion with the parents here as with all Saturnian contacts, and the key to many of the Mars-Saturn behaviour patterns lies in the individual's childhood. Early frustration of the will by one or both parents is common, and there is also sometimes brutality shown by the father, who may often symbolise the kind of mindless "Do it because I say so" authority which, later in life, becomes the target for Mars-Saturn hostility. Powerlessness and curtailment of freedom often occur through strict discipline, early responsibility, rigid religious training, or subtly directed emotional control resulting in guilt. There is also often a stifling or punishment of early sexual curiosity.

Actual physical maltreatment in childhood sometimes occurs with Mars-Saturn aspects and as often with women as with men. Sexual inhibitions and difficulties later in life are often the price paid for this kind of childhood experience. The concept of the will becomes exaggeratedly important because the individual often feels that he has no will, or that his will is ineffectual, because it has been thwarted so often. He may either continue to allow himself to be controlled from without, or he may fight back with unusual harshness because his self-respect is at stake. Mars-Saturn people frequently hold to the attitude that the best defence is offence, and this attitude is generally based on hard experience. But whether a person with this contact is boastful or timid, he will generally suffer from deep and painful feelings of inadequacy about his will and his capacity to function as a man. He may abuse women or treat them primarily as sexual conquests because this helps him to feel more confident; but he rarely experiences the feeling of inner confidence which stems from the knowledge that he is in control. The Mars-Saturn person rarely feels that he has any control over himself or over his life.

Mars-Saturn contacts usually extract a price in the area of sexual expression, and this seems to apply to both men and women. The sexual act often becomes a symbol for asserting dominance and is consequently devoid of pleasure or companionship in a deeper sense; and there is often frustration as a result. Mars-Saturn aspects when they express in this fashion infer, as do Venus-Saturn contacts, that what we term sex has little to do with the physical body for the sexual inhibitions which are connected with both these aspects are emotional in origin and have no real biological basis. These inhibitions are generally due to fear—of rejection, of domination, of failure. Just as Venus-Saturn aspects have some connexion with frigidity, Mars-Saturn aspects have some bearing on impotence. In many ways these aspects are interchangeable and are concurrent with similar patterns; for like the Sun and Moon, Venus and Mars are two sides of the same psychic unity.

Aspects between Mars and Saturn, particularly the "hard" aspects, tend to be rendered more difficult to work with because of the emphasis on sexual role-playing which has been with us for so many aeons and which has reached a new height of superficiality through the importance of glamour in our culture. The collective psyche of man is gradually beginning to grow beyond the sharp lines of demarcation which once were valid, but this slow and steady growth has not been evenly paralleled by social custom. The man with a strong Mars-Saturn contact is generally not comfortable with the cool and aggressive role which is demanded of him; because of the Saturnian influence he is driven inward to explore the deeper levels and meanings of his biological and psychological maleness so that he can come to a better understanding of the balance which is appropriate for him between the man and woman in his own psyche. This kind of introspective direction is not, however, acceptable for a modern man; he is generally considered neurotic if he admits to this sort of search. Denied both outlets for expression of his will and his sense of purpose, it is no wonder that he is likely to display the edginess and explosiveness associated with Mars-Saturn contacts. Saturn offers the opportunity for a deeper understanding of the nature of the personal will and of the nature of power and control. But social convention may prevent a person from seeing this opportunity. He generally cannot accept the superficial costume which has been laid out for him because he knows its uselessness when put to the test. But he must find new values about his own sexuality to replace those which have failed him. Finding it difficult to express himself outward into the world, he needs to turn inward into himself—the woman's world of the inner psyche—to understand that it is not really his failure but can in the end be his great success because he no longer will need to dominate others to prove to himself that he is a man.

Saturn in aspect
to Jupiter

Marc Edmund Jones has referred to the Jupiter-Saturn square as a symbol of the "last chance lifetime". The contact between these two planets, which are neither wholly personal nor wholly transpersonal, may suggest an attitude of fatalism or, at the very least, a sharp dichotomy between intuitive perception and practical observation which tends to muddle the issue of free choice for the individual. Saturn and Jupiter may be viewed as a pair of opposites which together form one unit of psychic experience, one archetype or basic facet of human nature. The idea begins to emerge, however, that any planet may be considered a polar opposite to Saturn, and it is in testing this idea out as a reasonable hypothesis that the truly chameleon-like quality of Saturn is shown most clearly. In a sense he may be said to relate to any planet in the role of devil's advocate.

It is usually interesting to consider the mythological associations of a planet because in myth may be found the bare bones of human experience without the personalised overlay of a particular cultural trend or social standard. Jupiter is in some ways a surrogate sun, specialised in that he symbolises the creative solar energy directed into mental channels. It is Jupiter who rules Olympus in myth, while the solar symbol, more or less dimmed since his final heyday during the reign of the Egyptian Pharoah Akhnaton, is relegated to the less important figures of Helios and Apollo, gods of smaller stature. These changes in emphasis from the more ancient sun-worshipping religions to the specialised figure of Jupiter, king of gods and men, is very likely a reflection of a change in emphasis in the collective unconscious of man. The shifting values of man's psyche are always reflected in his mythology. The transition from a broader and more impersonal energy ruling life to a more humanised god-archetype who integrates aspects of both deity and humanity is an important one. Jupiter is a solar deity of a kind, a patriarchal sky-god emerging from the collective psyche of a fundamentally patriarchal society. It might be more accurate to say that both Jupiter and the Sun are symbols of this archetype of the divine man, the heavenly figure who is representative of the highest achievement that man is able to reach. Only Jupiter is a more reachable figure.

In myth Jupiter conquers his father Saturn and imprisons him in Tartaros under the guardianship of Jupiter's brother, Pluto. In time he is himself threatened by the same fate, through a prophecy, at the hands of one of his own sons; but this son is prophesied to be half-human. As far as our Greek and Roman predecessors were concerned, Jupiter remained unconquered during their time, having succeeded in avoiding his father's fate. It appears, however, that the prophecy has in the end proven itself true; for in the last two thousand years of the Piscean Age, the archetype of the sky-god has developed into the half-human, half-divine figure of Christ.

In its most basic interpretation Jupiter-Saturn contacts symbolise a choice between the faith which stems from an intuitive recognition of purpose in life, and the fear which stems from identification with and consequent control by the forces of one's environment. The squares and oppositions are associated with a kind of see-saw temperament which swings between the extremes of hopefulness and despair, and after the aspects of Venus to Saturn these are the favourite choice of suicides. Almost evenly matched in size and weight from both the astronomical and astrological point of view, each planet tends to illuminate the sharpest contours of the other, and there is often a dipping back and forth between a blind optimism untempered with discipline or practical understanding, and a blind pessimism which sees no possible hope of future happiness or meaning. In the individual who is unaware that he can do anything to change the pattern, Jupiter's profligacy and Saturn's meanness may alternate in phases within the personality. And although the sphere of these planets is not a personal one in the sense that the Moon, Mercury, Venus, and Mars are personal planets, the effects of Jupiter-Saturn contacts are usually felt strongly in the personal life because it is one's basic outlook on life, one's inner philosophy, which is affected. It is the outlook which conditions actions and serves as the motive behind conscious behaviour.

Jupiter-Saturn aspects are also traditionally associated with the sphere of monetary success or failure, but although they will very likely affect this area of life, the effect is more a by-product than a direct influence. The usual interpretation of Jupiter in sextile or trine to Saturn includes a supposed penchant for material well-being, and the individual with Jupiter afflicted by Saturn is often portrayed as being barely able to keep the wolf from the door. Bad judgment in business and loss through speculation are also often associated with the afflictions of Jupiter and Saturn, and from these interpretations, and Jupiter's persistant reputation as the "greater benefic", one can easily draw the conclusion that it is the material sphere which is affected by Jupiter-Saturn contacts.

Jupiter is, however, a mental planet, connected with a house which is mental rather than material in meaning. He has nothing to do with materiality except insofar as the Jupiterian type generally believes that he deserves the best from life and therefore usually attracts it. Saturn moreover may wear an earthy face and may often be found climbing the mountain of personal ambition, but the psychological function or archetype of which he is the symbol appears to be connected more with dissociating from identification with materiality than with succeeding on the mundane plane. The combination of these planets appears to be connected with the opportunity for development of a different and more subjective set of values in the area of one's broad philosophy of life and in the intuitive perception of life's meaning. Fear of failure because of an inability to make the intuitive contact with one's basic self is often responsible for the frequent tendency of many Jupiter-Saturn people to accept far less from life than their abilities and intelligence merit and to sacrifice their higher aspirations for the banality of a life of low aims and a regular paycheck. But it is the basic outlook, rather than bad luck, which sometimes dogs the Jupiter-Saturn individual from one material failure to the next.

Jupiter's function in a psychological sense seems to be connected with the intuition and the faculty of creative imagination or visualisation. It is this intuitive faculty which responds to the meaning of a symbol and which makes us capable of apprehending the basic meaning or "soul" of an experience or a person without prior analysis. The direct experience of the inner world of meaning establishes the quality which we term faith; it is not built on any deductive reasoning nor on any practical experience, and it is not—contrary to the usual definition of the word—belief in the sense that it

is a wish for something to be true. The man who has genuine faith has it because he knows, in an intuitive and non-rational way, that there is meaning and purpose to his experience and that it will unfold according to a pattern which contains intrinsic wisdom and purpose. The Jupiterian type may not be intellectual in the sense of possessing careful logic, but he usually possesses the qualities of faith and devotion which serve him as a lamp through the darkest of experiences.

The contact of Jupiter with Saturn appears to suggest the psychological necessity of transforming this faith into practical living so that the individual can live out what he intuitively senses to be the purpose of his life. The initial stages of this process are difficult, and they are often not seen as the opportunity they actually are. The demands of practical living are often seen as contradictory to, rather than the logical fulfilment of, the intuitive vision, and the necessities of self-defense and self-interest often lead the individual to abandon his faith. One expression of Jupiter-Saturn is the individual who has sold all to Saturn—or to the devil—and who abandons his quest because the realities of food, shelter, position in society, and the protection of his more vulnerable feelings seem to him to be of greater, or at least more imminent, importance. When this kind of outlook is left untended, it is a rather depressive one because the individual has usually lost all joy by the middle of life and finds himself in a sea of purposeless routines which give him no satis-faction. He lives to eat and eats to live, and although he may be very successful in the material sense, he has, in a rather literal way, sold his soul for it. Saturn's function in the psyche is opposed to such a bargain, and the sense of futility which is usually experienced is the common payment. Suppressing a function such as Jupiter symbolises is costly because in psychological terms it is relegated to the realm of the unconscious where it gathers power and eventually bursts loose in an irrational and compulsive behaviour pattern. For this reason the Jupiter-Saturn individual who has chosen this manner of expression is usually confronted with spells of irrational gullibility and superstition, which are often coupled with bad judgment as well, based on "hunches" that go wrong. He is also prone to fits of deep depression because of the lack of meaning in his life. It is apparent why the more extreme expressions of Jupiter-Saturn are linked with a depressive and suicidal temperament.

The opposite expression of Jupiter-Saturn contacts is also

interesting. Often an individual will swing through both extremes during his slow process of unfoldment of the potential of the aspect. In attempting to escape from Saturn's demand for real effort and actual demonstration and experience of what is intuitively glimpsed, the individual may become that familiar Jupiter-Saturn type who is forever trying to scrape together the last few pennies to pay for one more day's dinner and who is also forever expecting the big break through some flash of good luck which somehow never comes. This is not really a Jupiter type but rather a Jupiter-Saturn type who has not yet realised the potential of the aspect in both a subjective and an objective direction. The true Jupiterian usually experiences the good luck. The Jupiter-Saturn individual often does not and must be bailed out by his friends with fair frequency. Usually the inner voice of Saturnian demand is heard eventually, but it is in this expression of Jupiter-Saturn that we may understand with more clarity the reputation of dishonesty which the aspects have occasionally earned. Dishonesty is a concept as ambiguous as immorality, and one has only to consider the honesty of many business dealings in comparison to the dishonesty of the starving man who grabs an apple on his way out of the market to glimpse the quicksand of shifting values which lie behind this commonly used word. The dishonesty of Jupiter-Saturn contacts is relative and connected with the individual's outlook. Usually it is simply the naivete of someone who persists in believing that he is going to get something for nothing.

Jupiter-Saturn contacts actually have a great deal to do with one's personal morality. This is dangerous ground to work with, particularly since the morality covered by this contact is not limited to the area of sexual behaviour; it is much broader in scope and is connected with larger concepts like honesty and dishonesty, selfishness and selflessness, and numerous other opposites which have been the problem of religion to sort out during the Piscean era. It might be said that the opportunity offered by these aspects is in the direction of a personal and direct understanding of the nature of good and evil as these apply to individual behaviour and outlook and consequently to conscious decisions. The issue of good and evil is not an important one to many people; the realm of moral or ethical concepts does not pose a problem either because they seem to be perfectly clear or because they are considered unimportant. For the individual with Jupiter and Saturn in aspect, these issues are usually important ones in the life because there is an insistent urge within the psyche to come to terms with the idea of a mode of right action. The individual usually attracts situations in his life where he must in some way resolve the conflict of the two opposing viewpoints which bicker within his consciousness. He is given the opportunity to integrate these two viewpoints and understand them as one so that he can live with his good and his evil and comprehend the necessity and function of them both. This kind of integration has a way of freeing a person from the grip of illusion and disillusionment so that he is able to accept himself and life as they come with an inner sense of peace and a practical efficiency which permits him a materially productive life as well. This is no small accomplishment.

Saturn in aspect
to Uranus

The outer or "higher octave" planets need to be considered first as a group because they have certain qualities in common. They appear to have some connexion with what Jung terms the collective unconscious or with what modern depth psychology now calls the transpersonal unconscious. In other words, they bring the individual into contact with energies which are not wholly personal in nature but which belong to the larger psychic unity of the group. In an esoteric sense they may be considered symbols of urges toward development which are related to soul consciousness rather than personality consciousness, which is another and equally valid way of saying the same thing. This does not mean that the outer planets do not affect the individual in a distinctly individual way. It simply means that his experiences through these planets, or through the functions of the psyche which they symbolise, are likely to have a much broader significance, a more basic or archetypal quality, and are more likely to stimulate major steps in growth and major crises which shape the entire life and expand the level of awareness of the whole rather than the more specifically personal areas suggested by the planets within Saturn's orbit.

The common consensus about the outer planets is that they signify the trends of the group or the generation to which the individual belongs, and that only in rare cases, where they strongly aspect the Sun or Moon, or conjunct the angles, do they infuse any personal qualities into the character. On the charts of many people they are considered to be "dumb notes", relatively inactive points which when they are stimulated by a transit, a progressed planet, or someone else's natal chart, are likely to be "malefic" in nature because they seem to behave in a fated or uncontrollable fashion through external circumstances which are often destructive to material or emotional security. This description applies as far as it goes for these planets are certainly disruptive; however, as soon as we are able to understand that what is disruptive or negative to the comfort and happiness of the body, the feelings, or the intellect may be highly constructive and fulfilling for the total psyche, then we may begin to come closer to the meaning of these three planets.

Uranus, Neptune, and Pluto certainly represent uncontrollable energies if we are talking about the control by the small conscious ego of the entire collective psyche of man. The question of "controlling" a planet is one of those pieces of presumption which is easy for the individual to discuss who has never turned inward to glimpse the kind of power inherent in the unconscious. One may visualise a man standing on a small island surrounded by a turbulent ocean, attempting to command the forces of nature; his voice cannot even be heard above the tempest. He is a laughable figure until we realise that discussing the "control" of the planets is in a similar direction. These energies are not inimical or malefic in nature; they serve the purposes of the total self or psyche and are only inimical when the conscious man decides to pit himself against the direction in which his inner self is attempting to unfold. Rather than thinking about controlling Uranus, Neptune, and Pluto, it is perhaps wiser to consider understanding them so that we may consciously cooperate with the unconscious urge toward wholeness and more inclusive consciousness of which these planets are a symbol.

The function of the Destroyer has always had a place in mythology, although we do not understand it now except in its most literal and petty sense. In the Hindu pantheon of divinity, Shiva the Destroyer is a necessary part of the trinity. Uranus, Neptune, and Pluto are all destroyers in a sense, for they shake the foundations of the personal ego structure so that a glimpse of the larger unit of which the individual is a part may be seen. Saturn symbolises the outermost perimeter of the structure of the personal ego; he apparently strives to keep these forces out so that man does not have to accept the humiliating idea that he is psychically one with other human beings; however, there is a fatal flaw in this personality structure, one which always causes the collapse of the structure. When this collapse occurs, the energies of the collective psyche always stream in. When this influx of collective energies occurs, two things can happen. If the man is able to interpret the stream so that he acts as a transmittor or communicator of the unconscious needs of the group, then we say that he is a genius because he has the gift of personifying an archetype so that men can see a reflection of their deepest inner urges in this individual's creations. If the man is unable to keep his concept of himself separate from the collective stream and begins to think that he himself, as a personality, is this stream, then we say that he is mad because he is trying to be the archetype rather than to communicate it and in consequence loses touch with personal reality. The outer planets have strong connexions with both genius and madness, between which two states the borderline, as the saying goes, is very thin.

In spite of this important area of human experience, traditional astrology usually tells us that Saturn in square to Uranus is "unimportant", that Saturn conjunct Neptune has "not much meaning for the individual", and that Saturn trine Pluto only has bearing on the generation into which the person is born. We are also told that Saturn-Uranus contacts precipitate sudden catastrophes, that Saturn-Neptune contacts foster deceit, and that Saturn-Pluto contacts have some association with death and with subversive and criminal organisations. Obviously the human race is not divided up between those who express genius and those who express madness. There are times in the life of every individual, however, when the energies of the collective unconscious impinge upon the ordinary field of personal life; each person has his moments of genius and his moments of madness although they are not sustained. It is at these moments when we come closest to experiencing the true nature of ourselves. These experiences are called peak experiences in depth psychology; they have also been called experiences of "cosmic consciousness" which is unfortunately no more helpful than "peak experience" in trying to describe the indescribable quality of an inner subjective perception of one's whole self. These are deeply personal experiences although they may also be considered as moments when the personality is lost or "dies" in the light of the larger perception of life. It is these experiences which are the field of the outer planets, and it is probable that contacts of these three planets with Saturn create a stronger tendency toward this kind of experience because the flaw in the ego structure is greater. Jupiter-Saturn contacts have some connexion also with this field of peak experience or perception of the self but without the archaic, impersonal, destructive feel that the outer planets bring to the experience. There is nothing of the destroyer in Jupiter; however, it is possible that the destructive aspect of the outer planets is responsible in part for their tremendous power for growth.

The realm of the outer planets is not very accessible to the earthy man who is polarised in his desire nature. But even the earthy man is affected whether he is consciously able to register the effects or not. If the conscious self is not yet sensitive enough to understand these energies, it does not mean that they do not influence or find response in the unconscious. For the individual who has not passed the boundary of Saturn in terms of his level of awareness, the outer planets simply work in the dark; but they continue to have meaning. One may live in an underground cave and be unaware of the sun's rising and setting, but this does not stop the sun from rising and setting. We tend to possess the unfortunate idea that if we do not understand something, it does not exist. The tragedy of the outer planets is that they are so often unrecognised and the motivations which they symbolise are either wholly ignored or considered to be "mystical claptrap". Even when these urges are presented in the light of empiric psychological investigation, they are still "mystical claptrap" to many people. Consequently Uranus, Neptune, and Pluto, when they stream into the field of personal life, often bring tragedy and destruction with them. This is not fate but the persistent blindness of the individual to his own inner rhythms and inner unfoldment.

We are used to assuming that the ancients were ignorant of these planets since the astrology of antiquity only included seven bodies. They were very probably consciously unaware of the outer planets, and there seems to be much truth in the idea that the conscious discovery of each outer planet has corresponded to the emergence into racial or group consciousness of the meaning of the planet. This is an example of synchronicity as Jung describes the term: the simultaneous occurrence of an inner unfoldment and an outer circumstance which have no causal connexion to each other but are connected by meaning. Thus, on a mundane level, the discovery of Uranus coincided with the dawn of the electrical and industrial age as well as with two great political revolutions which resulted in the birth of a new form of government. Inwardly the collective psyche of man had perhaps developed to the point where the ideals of brotherhood, freedom, individuality, and control by the mind of the forces of nature were possible of conscious expression.

There seems, however, to be evidence that our apparently unevolved predecessors were unconsciously aware of these energies because they are presented in mythology in a peculiar and meaningful fashion. All three deities are, in myth, invisible, mysterious, hidden, and not easily approached. Uranus vanishes from the Olympian pantheon after his castration and loss of power at the hands of Saturn; it is never even made clear whether he dies or not if it is possible for a god to die. He remains only in indirect form because the Furies or goddesses of justice and retribution spring from his blood and Venus, the goddess of love, rises from the ocean into which have been thrown his severed genitals. Pluto rules the underworld and rarely emerges from his lair; when he does, he is veiled and invisible and cannot be seen by the eyes of man. Neptune likewise rules a hidden world at the bottom of the sea and also—as Poseidon— shakes the earth from his hidden underground caverns. Mythology has the quality of presenting the contents of the collective unconscious in a pure and unadulterated form because it is distilled from many centuries and many overlayings of individual interpretation. The hidden or unknown quality of Uranus, Neptune, and Pluto is certainly suggestive of the unconscious perception of these energies.

Saturn and Uranus are ancient enemies, and the aspects of Saturn to Uranus are not particularly easy from the point of view of personality comfort. The urge to break free from the confines of matter and material identification, to release the power of creative thought, and to learn to master the forces of nature by the power of the mind is not easily wedded to Saturn's tendency to identify with the form and to isolate himself from anything which is of group concern. Some of the inner struggle of the Aquarian personality, torn between the extremes of his abstract vision, intuitively perceived, and his respect for form and logic, may be understood when he is seen under the rulership of these two planets. The capacity to conceive of an idea and work with it as though it has as much substance and as much reality as a concrete object—which it does through the eyes of the Uranian—is not a widespread talent at present. It touches the world of magic and metaphysics where thought is reality and the power to concentrate on an idea is connected with power over material life.

Recently it has become evident through scientific experimentation that thought has the power to affect matter; this is truly a vindication of the Uranian vision. We are beginning to deduce through the "fringe" schools of healing and medicine, such as radionics and homeopathy, that man is composed of more subtle kinds of energy than the physical body alone and that thought affects these subtle energies and in turn affects the state of physical health. Now, almost two hundred years after his discovery, Uranus is beginning to make himself known to man in a truly meaningful way. It has taken us two centuries to feel the impact of the archetype in the field of consciousness. Through these new eyes Saturn also emerges in a different form, and the opportunity available to the individual with Saturn-Uranus contacts is perhaps along the lines of earthing or making manifest the creative vision of Uranus.

In ordinary personality life these contacts tend to be connected with a kind of bobbing back and forth between the extremes of convention and the extremes of individual self-expression. As we habitually use these terms in relation to Saturn and Uranus, they need to be more closely examined so that the aspect is more comprehensible. Saturnian convention has to do with the formal structures of society and of behaviour which facilitate self-protection and separateness. This is not the subtle adjustment to social and individual need which is a strong feature of the watery type of person, particularly the Cancerian; it is rather a forced emphasis on a form of behaviour simply because it has been done that way before and once held significance. Saturnian convention does not grow with the growth of man's psyche but crystallises in forms of ceremony which become empty shells devoid of life. This, however, is not the function of Saturn. It is the result of the unconscious individual's response to Saturn which is a different thing. Individual self-expression as it is evidenced by the Uranian type is usually adherence to an idea which is perceived by the individual intuitively, rather than absorbed from the environment, and which is conceived to be more true, more real, and more substantial than the conventional structure. It is not necessarily selfish because it may be an idea which incorporates the safety or welfare of the group; and this is usually the case with Uranus. He does not fight for himself but fights on behalf of and as an example to the group. The difference between Saturnian and Uranian codes is that the Saturnian has been demonstrated workable by the past, although this is no guarantee of future relevance, while the Uranian is a reality in the mind and has no demonstration except in the vision of the intuition. Given a contact between these planets, the individual usually tries to ally himself with one or the other, not realising that each without the other is incomplete.

In the ordinary individual who has not worked toward the development of a Uranian consciousness, this capacity to see a whole vision and use the vision as a basis for the ideas by which one lives is largely an unconscious function and is in the process of slowly emerging into consciousness. Uranian energy is then usually expressed in sudden crises which may involve conflicts with public authority, with parents, or with anything which contains the symbolic value of tradition or of opinions rather than ideas directly conceived. What ordinarily happens is that Uranus, disguised as chance, brings about an event which temporarily shatters the apparent safety and solidity of social values and ways of thinking based on tradition. The individual who is not able to express this urge in a conscious manner, who has simply never bothered to think for himself or to stretch his mind up into the heavens instead of rooting it in the earth, is usually at the mercy of eruptions from below which he himself has attracted, unconsciously, in the form of external events. The collapse of the business, the sudden conflict with the law, the disruption of the marriage, the accident are all different masks through which Uranus, symbolising the need to free oneself from identification with the outward trappings of life which are so often thought of as oneself, makes himself known as a collective urge working through the psyche of an individual. The presence of Saturn-Uranus contacts seems to suggest that the time for conscious re-evaluation of the source of ideas is now. The individual is faced with the challenge of demonstrating his own magical powers over circumstance by first declaring his emergence into psychological adulthood by thinking independently. Even if the effect of these contacts is not observable in a pronounced way because it is largely unconscious, in some quarter of life this challenge is offered. If it is not consciously accepted, the individual will usually contrive a way by which he forces himself to accept, and then he calls it chance. If any planet may be said to have a connexion with the law of synchronicity, it is probably Uranus.

This contact sometimes is concurrent with the political or social anarchist, whether he is effective or not. Saturn may react with a good deal of fear to what he feels as a powerful threat from the forces of chaos. Uranian vision usually seems chaotic to Saturn because it has no prior tangible demonstration. It is wholly a gift of the world of ideas. This fear may help to produce a person obsessed by law, or it may contribute to a person obsessed by the need to prove himself free of the law. Either way it is an obsession which stems from a feeling of powerlessness against the enormous power of collective forces. The group of which the individual is a part seems to demand that he make a choice; he feels he must act for or against the larger, more impersonal social structure which surrounds him. He usually tends to identify his personality with one half of the group. If he attempts to isolate himself from the social currents of his time, he is usually compelled by circumstances which he himself unconsciously attracts to abandon his isolation. Whether he likes it or not, whether it is inconvenient or not, the collective psyche calls to him, and some part of his defensive shell is usually sacrificed so that he can grow into a broader understanding of the larger life of which he is a part.

It is probably not strictly true to say that Saturn-Uranus contacts concur with personality traits since these aspects do not have much to do with the personality in itself. They have more bearing on the relationship of the individual to the group and to what happens to his psyche at the point of contact. Some people are more expressive of the spirit of their time than others, and some are consciously aware of their participation while others blindly help to shape the society of the future without understanding the nature of their own suffering and its collective aspects. There definitely seems to be some connexion between one's sensitivity to the ideas symbolised by the outer planets and one's capacity consciously to live these ideas out in practical life. If the vehicle of response lacks sensitivity—that is, if the individual's level of awareness is too narrow to permit him conscious realisation of the importance of the larger world around him—then Saturn-Uranus contacts will still affect him and draw him into the group needs at the expense of his own ego structure, but he will not understand what has happened to him. It will seem to him to be the cruel hand of fate.

Every planet seems to be asked to make a sacrifice when it contacts Saturn, and the nature of this sacrifice is usually in the area of having to resolve a moral conflict between the shadowy and bright sides of the personality by shifting the centre to a broader scope of consciousness. This idea of solving the conflict of opposites by moving the centre of the fight so that it is large enough to contain the opposites within it is basic to both psychological and esoteric thought. We may also find this motif in mythology as in the story of Hercules fighting the Hydra. The Hydra cannot be conquered by the ordinary fighting methods; in order finally to slay it, Hercules is forced to his knees so that he can hold the monster up to the sunlight. It is the complete shift in approach which accomplishes the completion of the labour. Any planetary contact with Saturn suggests a conflict of opposites between the bright face of the planet and the psychic urge which it symbolises, and the dark shadowy face of Saturn who will always oppose it. Out of this struggle comes the possibility of raising the conflict to a new level so that the entire person grows from the experience. To accomplish this he must first see the struggle and understand its nature. Then he can begin to work with his opportunity.

The conflict which ensues from Saturn-Uranus contacts seems to occur between the isolated self and the idea of the group as a unit or living organism, held united by the shared thoughts of its members. The old argument of whether it is possible to remain an individual while being part of a collective unit is brought up here, and for the person who has a Saturn-Uranus contact, it seems to be part of his psychic equipment to demonstrate the reality of this combination of opposites. The psyche appears to urge itself toward being individually fruitful and productive, yet at the same time being group-conscious and able to contribute one's work to the development of the whole. It has been very difficult for us in the past to demonstrate any kind of fusion of these two opposing poles, and the conflict has resulted in political ideologies which sacrifice either one or the other without achieving any kind of integration. In the individual the conflict tends to produce those people who are furious individualists, with a hatred of everything Saturnian, and those people who are furiously loyal to the old system which protects the rights of the individual but has no pity on the individualist. The individual with Saturn-Uranus must generally solve his own problem of integration between these two kinds of law, and two apparently contradictory kinds of authority, so that he can join hands with those to whom he is connected by his humanity and work toward the same kind of integration within the group. This kind of integration seems to be a special gift of the Aquarian personality, and it is possible that with the advent of the next astrological age the same gift can be extended to everyone.

Saturn in aspect
to Neptune

Neptune may be considered to symbolise another facet of the collective unconscious in that he symbolises an impersonal or group urge rather than a personal one, and may require the sacrifice of some aspect of the personality in order to fulfil this urge. While Uranus is connected with collective or archetypal ideas, Neptune is connected with collective feelings, and while Uranian unity with the group occurs through the power of the creative mind, Neptunian unity is a product of emotional identification or empathy. He is symbolic of that urge within the psyche toward submergence of individual desire in the greater desires of the whole; he is really a female rather than a male principle and seems symbolic of mass emotional response. In this role Neptune is also a destroyer because in fulfiling the demand of the mass, he often becomes the enemy of a man's basic personal emotional needs. Neptune is sometimes associated with the entire sphere of the unconscious, particularly with the idea of the collective unconscious, but this is limiting the scope of the psyche to a purely feeling base when in actuality the sea of unconsciousness gives birth to all the functions of consciousness—feeling, thinking, sensation, and intuition. Neptune is particularly connected with the erosion of the differentiated intellect because he is an entirely irrational planet and urges the individual toward identification with the feeling unity of the whole.

The ocean is a suitable symbol for Neptune because of its depths, its constant movement, its mystery, and its value as a symbol for the beginning and end of life, the place of emergence and disappearance. Attempting to come to terms with an archetype like this may seem difficult, or perhaps abstruse; but the outer planets do not lend themselves to easy interpretation by the intellect. The energy of which Neptune is a symbol is hardly able to be described by a keyword; it needs to be amplified by the mythological and psychological connexions before the planet begins to assume real meaning on the individual birth chart. The symbol of the ocean, the source of life, and its association with death by drowning are evocation of a response by the intuition where the intellect may fail to comprehend the symbol. This is an impersonal force, and Neptunian effects are in a sense like death by drowning. The individual is submerged in the sea of collective feeling and loses his individual emotional responses. As a separate feeling entity, he ceases to exist. This experience can be observed any time in the response of a crowd whose emotions have been aroused; the individuals have ceased to exist, but the crowd is now a unit with a single feeling response that is wholly irrational.

As Saturn symbolises the urge to isolate and build a differentiated personality structure through concrete experience, he is quite naturally opposed to the vague self-immolating urges of Neptune. These two planets have nothing in common, and this dissimilarity is aggravated by Saturn's tendency to play shadow to any planet that contacts him. As Neptune is a planet connected with feelings and with mass sensitivity of an undifferentiated kind, Saturn usually assumes the role of the concrete mind, working for the protection of the individual. The nature of the struggle which ensues seems to lie between the person's need to protect his own interests and maintain his separateness, and his urge to transcend himself and lose himself in the sea of common human emotion as an act of self-redemption. The significance of the ritual act of martyrdom or self-sacrifice on behalf of the group needs to be considered before we can come to terms with Neptune's tendency to lead the individual headlong into a denial of his deepest desires. Otherwise we tend to use the term "masochism" loosely as though this urge were wholly pathological. There is an aspect of this kind of sacrifice which is easily observable in myth and folklore and which seems to be connected with the idea that the individual is redeemed and becomes godlike or returns to the gods through self-sacrifice. This is an archaic idea which is far from pathological for it appears to have spiritual as well as psychological validity.

This Neptunian tendency toward self-immolation causes him to be interpreted as a malefic influence. He is certainly malefic to the form side of life and to the personal desires, if these go against the urges of the total psyche. He does not disrupt and sever as Uranus does but rather uses the principle of passive resistance or impotence. A personality which is affected by Saturn-Neptune contains the seeds of its own dissolution in some area of life for there is usually a blind spot, a basic flaw in the shell of the ego, through which the collective call for sacrifice may enter. Usually pity, aspiration, and that exalted kind of romantic love which is so characteristically Neptunian are the triggers which work through the personal feelings to sacrifice the individual to the group. In the ordinary person, Neptune works through ordinary human emotion, but there is usually a touch of exaltation, the giddiness or ecstasy before the self-immolation. There is a breath of Dionysian madness in Neptune although he is generally masked by a mild and self-sacrificing quality. The moment of ecstasy is the moment of self-transcendence, and the individual experiences one of those rare flashes of oneness with life which is called the mystical vision. This is a deeply personal experience which is perfectly real to those who have experienced it and perfectly meaningless to those who have not. There is no way to articulate the psychic effect of Neptune seeping through the Saturnian defenses except to suggest, once again, the image of death by drowning with the touch of ecstasy. This kind of exalted consciousness, coloured by feeling and wholly irrational, can occur through some small act such as the kind of sacrifice one habitually makes for a child. It is the meaning of the sacrifice, as an act of love which is of collective significance, which is the key to Neptune. One feels at one with all humanity at that moment. The way in which the sacrifice comes is only incidental.

It is no wonder that the "hard" aspects of Saturn and Neptune are often associated with drugs and alcohol. Having tasted the ecstasy once, it is often difficult to accept the fact that it might not return. Dionysus is an addictive god because for most individuals the only way in which they can touch the group life is through the feeling nature. Neptune is, in a sense, more accessible than Uranus, for most people feel but not many people know how to think.

Saturn-Neptune contacts are usually associated with the creative imagination and with the individual's power to create in tangible form the outpourings of that imagination. The main quality of Neptunian imagination, whether it is expressed through colour, sound, movement, or words, is that it is archetypal; it touches the deeper levels of feeling which are shared by everybody. The Neptunian songwriter's lyrics evoke a response from the mass because each person responds by feeling that the words have been written for him alone. The Neptunian painter's imagery has the quality of seeming familiar and magnetic to everyone because each person has seen this same imagery before in his own dreams and fantasies. The gift of Neptune is the contact with archetypal feeling experience, and the individual with a Saturn-Neptune contact is given the opportunity to communicate this experience through his own creative expression. He becomes the transmittor of the archetype in much the same way as the Saturn-Uranus individual may transmit the ideas of the group. In some area of life this opportunity is given, and even if the individual is not himself an artist in the usual sense of the word, he can at some point experience and relate to others the ecstasy of having plunged into the collective feeling stream. He may only create fantasies, but there are moments in his fantasies when he is all men, and his feelings are no longer his own.

The individual must, however, pay a price for this plunge. Part of his own isolated ego is eroded by the contact. He can no longer claim to be wholly individual in his emotional experiences; he is not able to say that his desires are unique. Saturn's illusion of isolation and his tendency to consider group feelings banal and full of sentiment usually must give way before the very real experience of the power of the feeling life of the group. Neptune has no sentiment; he is impersonal. Sentiment belongs to the sphere of Venus and the Moon. This is the death by drowning, the baptism into collective emotional life. One's personal desires, as a result, seem petty and insignificant, particularly when they demand the submission of others' desires for their fulfilment. It is no wonder that the ancients thought this experience to be a sacred one, capable of purification and containing the quality of deity.

Unfortunately, as it has taken us almost two hundred years to begin to appreciate the idea of a group mind as it is suggested by Uranus, it will undoubtedly take us another hundred years to begin to appreciate Neptune in a clearer form. So far he has expressed himself in a rather distorted way and seems to work badly with the kind of inner psychic structure evidenced by our society. This may be because we have attempted to repress the feeling function, forcing it underground into the unconscious where it becomes contaminated with all kinds of distortions and peculiarities. Just as Saturn-Uranus people may sometimes become self-appointed revolutionaries or officers of the law, Saturn-Neptune people have the tendency to become self-appointed messiahs. The numinous quality of the collective idea of self-sacrifice becomes distorted by the sense of personal inadequacy connected with Saturn, and the individual may begin to identify himself as a personality with the mass and may believe that it is in some mysterious way his mission to save others by his own sacrifice. He may in reality have this mission; he may also instead be attempting to salvage the dissolving remains of his personal ego. One may never be completely sure with Saturn-Neptune contacts because they very probably incorporate both points of view. Where the Saturn-Uranus individual may be attracted to the realm of law, organisation, and social custom, the Saturn-Neptune person is often attracted to the realm of religion and of the spiritual path.

It is an unfortunate fact that there is no group of people more riddled with delusions of grandeur, megalomania, petty backbiting, struggles for power, emotional blindness, and exaggerated sentiment than those who aspire to the path of discipleship. This appears to be one of the hazards of the path, and it is more subtle and a later stage than the initial Uranian energy which often causes the individual to stop in mid-career and completely reverse his life. In psychological terms it might be said that certain disciplines tend to evoke the response of the collective psyche or put the individual in closer personal touch with these energies. The meeting of the personal psyche, outlined by Saturn, and the collective energies is always a precarious meeting, even if it has occurred a hundred times before. If this contact occurs before the personality has been stabilised and before the psychic qualities which Saturn represents are digested and integrated, then inflation is usually the result. Neptunian inflation occurs because the feeling nature in man is so powerful, and under Neptune one is easily glamoured because the ecstasy of experiencing the group feeling life tends to make an individual forget that there is a destructive aspect to this ecstasy. In order to clarify this idea, it is perhaps useful to consider the last two thousand years which have brought us in touch with Neptunian glamour through the constellation of Pisces and which have given expression to two millenia of religious intolerance, fanaticism, and brutality living happily side by side with the Christian concepts of love, charity, kindness, and self-sacrifice.

We obviously do not yet fully understand Neptune. We only perceive him dimly through the religious symbolism of the mass and through the trends of what we call glamour. These are outer expressions of the psychic undercurrents of the collective unconscious. When a particular fashion, or musical style, sweeps the civilised world and becomes a symbol for a group emotional urge, then we may glimpse Neptune at work. He always expresses through the feeling nature and affects our emotional values. The contacts of Saturn and Neptune seem to suggest that the individual is given the opportunity for integration of these two principles so that the personality can become a vehicle for expression in a creative way of the collective emotions of the group. It is probable that this is only relative integration for it is very likely that we are not yet able to register Neptune except in an imperfect fashion. The vision may only occur during moments in one's life and in apparently small ways. For the person who is able to respond consciously, the opportunity appears to be present for the use of collective feelings as a creative tool.

Saturn-Neptune contacts are important for an artist because they give him the freedom of the group feeling life as a source of inspiration; however, not everyone is an artist. The man who does not express himself in this way must find another vehicle for Saturn-Neptune, and this is often in the area of personal relationships and in his spiritual aspirations. A precarious balance usually needs to be maintained so that the collective feelings do not swamp the personality; otherwise there is indeed madness; however, Saturn-Neptune contacts appear to be a good guarantee of the possibility of this kind of delicate balance. In the average individual Neptune and Saturn are symbols of sentiment and practicality for all he is able to perceive consciously is the tip of the iceberg. He may be unaware of the slow purification of his feeling nature which occurs below the surface through each act of sacrifice and each contact with mass emotion.

The power of any work of art seems to lie in part in its capacity to evoke or constellate the collective psyche, and in acquiring this power the artist must first sacrifice his personality as an isolated unit so that he can become, at least partially, an emissary or transmittor for group feeling. Thus art becomes an alchemical process by which the artist is slowly transformed and redeemed and in so doing, redeems others. These are difficult concepts, but Neptune is a subtle planet. As a group we have not yet developed the sensitivity necessary to interpret Neptune without distortion. Some few individuals succeed to a degree. Ironically, Saturn-Neptune contacts abound among the heroes of the entertainment world, both in music and in films. This is connected with the power to communicate collective feelings and evoke a collective response. These figures speak with the voice of millions when they express an emotion which is unique to them personally yet is also common to all. We do not all express genius in this way, nor can we express madness; however, for those individuals who have Saturn-Neptune contacts, there is always the brief glimpse of genius or madness, the plunge into the water for the brief experience of Neptunian ecstasy.

Saturn in aspect
to Pluto

If we are still a long way from being able to express Neptune without distortion, we are even further away from Pluto who remains an enigmatic figure in both astrology and psychology. In myth Pluto rules the underworld, and he has parallels in the myth and folklore of every nation and every race; regardless of the variations in the upper echelons of deity, there is always a god of the underworld who rules over the souls of the dead and the unborn, and his attributes are almost always the same. He is the only deity in the Olympian pantheon whose word, once it has been given, cannot be altered by either gods or men. Death is irrevocable; when anything ends or has reached its term of completion, it cannot in any sense of the word be recreated exactly the same—whether it is an individual, a state of consciousness, a feeling, a relationship, or a society. The life may always exist and may build another form, but the old form is finished and can never be precisely repeated because the inner quality of life has changed. Death is therefore connected with time in the sense that linear time applies to the birth, growth, fruition, decay and death of a form, while the life within the form is deathless and timeless and is freed by the event of death into greater life. These are esoteric concepts, yet we may observe their workings in the psyche of men. Most characteristic is the individual who is reaching the end of a chapter in his life and is about to begin a new chapter; the individual remains, but the structure of his life is changing and can never be exactly repeated because he himself is different and would give the old structure a different quality. He can never go backwards in the sense that time runs straight forward for him; yet his basic self remains the same. We may also observe this process in the endings and beginnings of social structures, of nations, of religions, of the world of nature. It is worth trying to understand this archetype of death, rebirth, and the eternal cycling around the unchanging centre because like the other two outer planets, Pluto is connected with processes which are far more extensive than a keyword can indicate and which need amplification through symbols to be understood in relation to the individual chart. One of the oldest symbols for this never-ending cycle of death, rebirth, and timelessness is the uroboros, the serpent which eats its own tail. One can say that where Pluto is placed at birth, that is where a man dies and is reborn or where he comes closest to the experience of the archetype; but this is meaningless except in a circumstantial sense unless we understand what value this death and rebirth may have for the over-all growth of the psyche.

Saturn and Pluto have several things in common, and they often overlap in their mythological and religious correspondences. Both have an association with darkness, with destruction, and with the figure of Lucifer, the Dark Prince, or the Beast who symbolises the depths of chaos out of which new life or greater consciousness is born. Pluto is Saturn's only real friend in the planetary hierarchy although, as the saying goes, with a friend such as this, one has no need of enemies. They symbolise two phases of the same psychic process. Both planets lead the individual into darkness, and both carry the suggestion of wisdom through suffering and purification through the ordeal by fire. Both are related to the process of the growth of consciousness which is always accompanied by struggle. In a sense Saturn guards the entry to Pluto's realm for it is the collapse of external values which leads eventually to the burning ground. For this reason there are echoes of Saturn in Charon, the aged boatman who ferries the souls of the dead across the Styx to the underworld. These figures are connected, and both in turn are connected to the figure of the Wise Old Man whose dark face is the Devil. These figures all pertain to the educational value of the experience of pain, and they are immediately evident when we observe that it is only the man who has lost everything who understands that he is not what he has lost but something much greater. In Cerberus, the three-headed monster who guards the doorway to the underworld, there are also echoes of Saturn as the Dweller on the Threshold. The numerous dragons, demons, giants, ogres, and other monsters which the fairytale hero must conquer before he can win the beautiful bride and inherit the kingdom are all related to these planets. These are psychological processes, stages of the growth of consciousness, which are best portrayed by symbols because they cannot be literally and intellectually explained. They are living processes, and the individual who has experienced them knows their reality, both subjectively and objectively.

The usual quality evident in the individual with a Saturn-Pluto contact is obsessiveness. There often seems to be a carefully organised and deliberate movement toward some self-destructive experience, and the person may be fully aware of this obsessive movement yet may not be able to control it. Pluto is connected with the feeling nature, as Neptune is, but it is a different aspect of feeling. While Neptune relates to shared feeling, ecstasy, or self-forgetfulness through unified emotional experience, Pluto seems to relate to the experience of growth through the destructive side of emotion. There is often an element of enforced separation or loss, the irrevocable destruction of something deeply desired or loved. This may be an individual, but it may also be something more abstract—a cherished ideal, a belief, a way of life. The learning of detachment through pain often comes through Plutonian experience for there is a tendency for the individual to become obsessed in that area of life affected by Pluto's position on the birth chart, particularly through desire. Something within the individual must die before he can be free of his obsession, and from the experience he learns mastery over his emotional nature because there is nothing else he can do to survive.

When this process of self-mastery through an inner death is combined with the Saturnian inclination toward identification with form and subsequent disillusionment, isolation, and awakening, it will be apparent that where these two planets are in aspect there is an opportunity for a great depth of self-knowledge and of consequent freedom. This is usually obtainable only through a period of inner destruction through emotional pain. Something within the individual usually drives him directly into experiences which tear away everything he desires and which force him into self-examination until he is able to find a centre which stands outside the world of emotional attachment. This may sound like a rather dramatic pattern, but people with Saturn-Pluto contacts do not lack drama. In some area of life they exaggerate and amplify experience so that it is blown up to mythological proportions. Something of the magical or fated quality of collective experience creeps in. Here the person plays the hero, the handsome prince, the beautiful princess; here he is possessed by the demon, the dark witch, the evil nature spirit. He is not only himself but also the archetype. This is understandable if Pluto is remembered to have some connexion with the collective unconscious.

Saturn-Pluto contacts are considered to accompany a brooding, melancholy temperament, and there is apparently some association with suicide or at least suicidal thoughts. The trines and sextiles do not appear to be any less productive of the intense introversion and loneliness which often accompany the "hard" aspects although they are perhaps less compulsive. Unfortunately the average individual does not always understand what is going on within himself and cannot see the roots of the obsessive pattern. Often it is projected, and it is someone else's obsession which becomes the problem. The urge is an unconscious one for many people who have these contacts, and the psyche seems intent upon driving the conscious personality into the burning ground with or without conscious consent and without help. This contact seems to concur with an intense independence. The individual usually senses that whatever is driving him, the value of his experiences is negated if he seeks too much assistance. Depression, feelings of despair, incessant self-probing are characteristic of Saturn-Pluto. These tendencies often occur only after the individual has first tried to overcompensate and to escape the challenge by living lightly on the surface of life. It is common to find this pattern for a while with Saturn-Pluto contacts, but it does not last very long. The psyche is directing itself toward an intense introversion and a journey into the depths, and if this direction is unconscious, it pulls the individual down through his pain, loneliness, or some kind of tragedy or great emotional shock which he has drawn unconsciously to himself. The individual with Saturn-Pluto will usually not permit himself to get away with anything, and the easy glide through life is not for him. If he attempts to live this way, he violates his inner pattern and usually then goes through his ordeals. If he can understand that this is his chosen direction, then he can cooperate, and the opportunity then is an important one. Through the detachment from his desire nature, the individual is born into a greater freedom to live life because nothing in life can control him any longer.

Rebirth is an archetypal experience, and it may be seen as a motif running through the myths and fairytales of every culture. The king or the god must die in the autumn and returns to life in the spring; the hero dies and is brought to life by the beautiful princess or by the magical helpful animal. Death is always necessary for there to be new life. This archetype has also permeated Christianity in an obvious way. It is not, however, unique to this religion for it is a far older motif. It is probable that for a person with Saturn-Pluto, rebirth becomes a necessity for the psyche at some point during the life, and it is usually a larger rebirth than one isolated attitude or one relationship. It is often the entire shell of the ego which is destroyed so that the person can develop a new centre for his consciousness. Saturn-Pluto contacts seem connected with experiences which shatter the personality structure, providing an opportunity for a more balanced centering to take place. These contacts are also associated with peak experiences where the individual is abruptly catapulted into a new level of awareness which is completely outside the ordinary framework of perception. The meaning of the life within the form becomes apparent, and the inner purpose for the emotional tests becomes obvious. Often these experiences accompany a period in life when the individual has reached the bottom in the emotional sense; he may be on the verge of, or coming out of, a psychological breakdown, may be desperately lonely, or may be experiencing the collapse of his personal life. On the heels of this kind of absolute isolation, the flash of insight occurs, and this helps him to rise up out of his own ashes with a different way of seeing things and a new purpose to his life. These kinds of revelations are common with close Saturn-Pluto contacts, and they inevitably follow on the heels of great pain and despair; the prerequisite seems to be that the individual, reaching the limits of his emotional endurance, gives up desire. The healing power of these experiences cannot be argued with. They may not be spiritual in the sense that any religious symbolism is involved; or they may be of a "conversion" nature. It hardly matters; they are our living examples of the power of the archetype of death and rebirth in the human psyche.

Pluto is usually active by progression or transit at the time that events of emotional importance or crisis occur. Ironically, he is active at the time of marriage which is not supposed to have any association with a subject as terrifying as death; however, the conjugal life is one of Pluto's favourite burning grounds. His primary means of expression is through the desire nature and will. He is connected with passion and the urge to possess and to devour, and the hell of sexual conflict and obsession is a characteristic Plutonian field. It is not physical sex which Pluto is concerned with but the psychic experience which accompanies, and is the meaning behind, the physical act. For this reason the alchemists used the symbology of the act of marriage, the sacred coniunctio, to describe the meeting between consciousness and the forces of the unconscious; and the sacred marriage in alchemy always preceded the stage of blackening, corruption, and death which was necessary for the rebirth of the base metal as gold. Through the experience of merging with another, there is a temporary death and the potential of a rebirth where two become one. This is, of course, the ideal but not often found in reality any more than the alchemists often found gold. In alchemy the base material was called Saturn. The personality, with its confused mixture of warring components, some conscious and some unconscious, must go through the process of purification and death before it can yield the inner integration, the inner self, of which man's various god-figures are symbols.

Although Saturn-Pluto contacts are not personal, they often accompany intense emotional effects such as rage, impotence, jealousy, and frustration. The collective urge toward greater consciousness expresses through the individual in this way. It is helpful for the person with these contacts to understand his inner urges, for in ignorance he may overdo it and may destroy himself with unnecessary brutality. This is a self-destructive combination of planets, but it is the small self, the self symbolised by Saturn's crystallised shell of self-protectiveness, that endures destruction. In psychological terms this is the one-sided differentiated ego working out of a narrow and crystallised viewpoint, cut off from its roots. When this structure is shaken loose, it is a kind of death, for the individual's entire conscious frame of reference becomes meaningless. But transformation is the promised result of the experience. Saturn-Pluto contacts can release great power into the personality, and they should not be underestimated because they occur over extended periods because of the slowness of their motion. It may be that many people are born under the Saturn-Pluto contacts with a collective urge toward this intense kind of self-realisation; the fact that one shares an experience with others does not negate its special individual significance, but rather it strengthens the significance.

Saturn-Pluto contacts, in common with Saturn's contacts to the other two outer planets, seem to have some association with what we call insanity. It is probable that in order for an individual to possess the sensitivity which can contribute to genius, he must therefore open himself to the possibility of madness for the initial sensitivity of the instrument is the same. Saturn is the necessary scaffolding around the building of the self while this building is in construction; or perhaps it would be more truthful to say that it is the revealing of the self, rather than the building, which is accomplished by the unfoldment of consciousness. The scaffolding may range from the unconscious defense mechanisms which stem from fear to the wise and discriminating use of silence and privacy. If this scaffolding is shattered before the inner building is complete, then a new one must be built—a task which may take longer than the individual has to live. Only when the inner integration has occurred can the scaffolding be safely removed. The contacts of Saturn with the outer planets appear to accelerate the process of growth because they lead the individual into experiences which have a collective and therefore powerful and transforming quality. They offer the opportunity for greater and faster growth. They also carry with them the danger of shattering the scaffolding. It is important for people with these contacts to understand the value of the balanced path of development which leads between the pull of the extreme opposites. The shortcut to any stage of consciousness rarely works with these Saturnian contacts because the sensitivity is too great; ironically there is usually a great attraction to the shortcut because of the urgency felt by the individual within himself. It is a very delicate tightrope. The world of the archetypal forces may contain the angelic host, but it contains the demoniacal host as well. Like the alchemist, we may cry, "Purge the horrible darknesses of our mind, light a light for our senses!"

Saturnian contacts with the outer planets always suggest a great capacity for creative expression and self-understanding; they have a transforming quality as well as a destructive one. If the individual is willing to explore not only the world of his own personal psyche but the greater world of the collective unconsious, he can then begin not only to become whole within himself but can also begin to experience the wholeness of the group of which he is a part.

6 in synastry

Having made a closer observation of Saturn on the individual birth chart, it should be fairly apparent that he is not to be pressed aside lightly when the comparison of charts is considered. All things binding and permanent come under his domain, and any relationship without a Saturnian influence has little possibility of either withstanding time and change or of effecting change in the individuals involved. What we tend to forget about relationships is that we do not generally form them for the purpose of being happy; we form them to complete something incomplete, and they are therefore a process of growth rather than an end in themselves. In this is implicit the idea that no relationship which does stimulate growth can exist without some pain and limitation although we tend through ignorance of ourselves to exaggerate the pain and minimise the growth. There is ordinarily so much unconscious projection occurring in most relationships, and so little objective perception of the real nature of the individual opposite us, that any effort to bring the relationship out of the unconscious level and into a conscious act of union inevitably brings pain with it—the pain of confronting oneself. It is this process of mutual growth through the gradual unfolding of self-knowledge that brings the field of human relationships under Saturn's influence although no one would consider him a planet that has anything to do with love.

Saturn's exaltation in Libra is not surprising when all of this is considered, for relationships can be our hardest taskmaster and our most fruitful source of development. The more difficult aspects of any encounter may perhaps be blamed on the "malefic" nature of Saturn; but what is often forgotten is the fact that in our present society the art of relating is not one of the primary values. It belongs to the world of feeling and of intuition rather than to the concrete and logical world of the body and the intellect, and consequently we are quite inept at the subtleties of understanding one another. The real value of Saturn, however, can only be tested against the influence of others, much as the structure of anything can only be measured for strength when pressure is brought to bear against it. Saturn is a measuring stick of the individual's inner power of self-determination; he symbolises that which has become a permanent part of the conscious self through self-motivated effort. He also measures the quality of the individual's defenses against his environment, which are necessary for a time until the inner structure has been built and are necessary afterward to keep the machinery of social interweavings working smoothly.

There is a consistent frequency of Saturnian cross-aspects among the charts of those people who for one reason or another become entangled in each other's lives. And although Saturn can scarcely be considered a planet of romantic attraction, what we call love and romantic attraction is frequently the unconscious reaction to our own projections. It is possible, and in fact very likely, that the average unconscious man will become enamoured of qualities which he thinks belong to his loved one but which in reality belong to the darker and transexual half of his own psyche. This phenomenon has been well explored by analytical psychology but has been sadly ignored by astrology. The underlying impetus in the majority of relationships lies not with the apparent conscious choice of partners, which is neither conscious nor a choice, but with the more ambiguous purposes of the unconscious. If this seems like too complex a mechanism to be attributed to the ordinary human brain, it might be helpful to consider that these terms do not refer to the brain, or even to the personality, but to those other areas of the human psyche which are not quite so familiar and which reveal themselves in fantasies, moods, outbursts, and dreams. In esoteric terminology it might be said that relationships which are set up on the unconscious level are the choices of the soul so that it may learn and progress on its path. We earn the right to love as a voluntary conscious act through the effort of self-discovery, and this effort is usually not made until there has been at least one painful failure. It is the effort and the discovery, not the failure, which are Saturn's gift.

The more esoteric lineage of Saturn in relation to synastry is very rich but deserves a separate study. It is worthwhile noting that we find him in the Garden at the very beginning, playing Satan, and offering the knowledge of the duality of good and evil in exchange for the bliss of unconscious ignorance. The implications of Saturn as "Lord of Karma", particularly from the point of view that karma is simply the "substance" within the personality which attracts circumstances in the outer world according to its inner quality, suggest that the psychological and the esoteric approaches to Saturn are in reality describing the same phenomena in different terminology. It is not sufficient to say that a woman who has natal Saturn placed on her husband's sun within a degree or two of exact conjunction will "limit and restrict" him or that it is a "karmic tie". Neither of these explanations will help the two people concerned cope with the feelings of anger and frustration which may continually boil up between them, nor will they be any closer to doing something about it. It is more important to understand why the effect takes place and what is really being communicated unconsciously. Otherwise the relationship eventually runs the risk of producing an intense level of hostility as its by-product or necessitates one or both people "unplugging" their sensitivity to each other so that they can maintain a pleasant conscious facade. Psychic energy cannot be destroyed by being ignored but will merely seek another channel of expression which may be less comfortable than the blocked one. And hostility which is not recognised and expressed can reappear as a variety of things, ranging from meaningless quarrels to physical symptoms which appear at appropriate times. Or, in more abstruse terminology, this situation can create new karma between the individuals which will draw them back again to work off the unreleased energy or "substance". All of this can occur, of course, in the face of a very deep love existing between the people concerned for psychology has long been aware of the reality of ambivalent emotions.

It is helpful to remember in an analysis of Saturn in synastry that he is a symbol for the individual's point of greatest vulnerability, the area where he has been scarred by the withholding or repression of some quality necessary to his growth and maturity. This may be either on a figurative level, connected with the mind or the feelings, or on a literal level, the most obvious analogy of which would be the child who through a lack of certain vitamins develops a warped bone structure such as rickets. In some ways Saturn may be related to the Jungian idea of the "shadow", the dark side of the conscious ego which contains qualities which we either repress because they are not in accord with our self-image or which we are unaware of because they are in embryonic, or infantile, form. The "shadow" is both positive and negative in character because although it is bound to express some inferior or immature qualities, nevertheless it also contains those qualities in germinal form which are necessary for the rounding out of the conscious personality.

The sense of inadequacy or lack is symbolised by Saturn's sign and house placement, and the lack may affect other aspects of the personality as reflected by Saturn's aspects to the other planets. When studied in depth, a detailed picture is offered by Saturn of that which a man does not wish to see about himself. This is the point where he will fight against the intense inner feelings of inadequacy and frustration with an equally intense need to dominate and control anything which touches this secret and hurting place, like the oyster which buries the irritating grain of sand under layers of pearl. Only when the shadow is made conscious is the intensity relieved, and only at this point can the conflict become a deliberate choice based on a moral or ethical code. Before this confrontation the choice is compulsive and based on fear. It will be apparent from all this what happens when a planet, or the ascendant or midheaven, or the Moon's nodes, or an important midpoint or progressed planet on another person's chart touches this most sensitive point. Unless the individual is reasonably well integrated and has some understanding of the workings of his own unconscious, the initial reaction to a Saturnian contact is usually fear. The person's pride, social conditioning, or self-image can effectively prevent him from admitting this feeling and even from recognising it for what it is. If he were to recognise it, he would be a long way toward understanding and accepting himself. But the quality of self-honesty is not one which is valued in our culture where greater value is placed on external accomplishment and "manners". In fact the individual who seeks another's help in pursuing the path of self-knowledge is considered neurotic or unbalanced when he may simply wish to grow. Herein lies one of the greatest problems with Saturnian contacts: our social trends and values are opposed to the most positive and constructive use of these ties because this involves the path of introspection. Consequently Saturnian aspects generate much unnecessary friction and pain.

Often the reaction on a conscious level to a close Saturn contact is dislike or animosity of a particularly irrational kind. This is good testimony to the maxim that what we hate or fear within others, we find within ourselves. Equally often the characteristic Saturnian phenomenon of overcompensation is displayed, and the person experiences a kind of compulsive fascination toward his "attacker"— and prepares himself, unconsciously, for the eventual conquering and disarming of his foe. This, frighteningly enough, is often called love.

The law of compensation appears to be connected with Saturn and is inherent in Nature as well as in man. It is a biological as well as a psychological function directed toward the preservation of the self or of a species. For example, those animals which have the least competent method of self-defense have the highest reproductive rates to ensure the survival of the group. And often those men and women who have the least developed defenses and the greatest inner imbalance tend to attract the greatest frequency of relationships where there are difficult Saturnian contacts. They unconsciously use this friction to attempt to build up through another what they are afraid of building within themselves—and this is done often at the expense of the other person. So they "limit and restrict" and sometimes come close to a symbolic castration of the function of the partner symbolised by the interfering planet. They may even apparently grow stronger. We have all seen the phenomenon of the couple who start life off with one obviously dominant and the other submissive; and then, a few years later, everything seems to have completely reversed itself, and the once dominant partner now humbly submits. It is not coincidental that Saturn's method of gaining control in mythology was to castrate his father so that he could not create any other life.

The quality which is attacked in the partner, however, has an unpleasant habit of reappearing elsewhere as it is a component of the person's own shadow. And when the relationship has reached the stale impasse which often accompanies this kind of dance, those who have travelled by this road may find they have gained nothing after all for Saturn's strengths do not derive from someone else's broken bones. What we tend to call "neurotic" relationships are often created out of this raw stuff. Unfortunately, when observed with a clear and unsentimental eye, the great majority of relationships in our society are of this type although the stalemate may be successfully hidden because factors like children or the demands of a job can always be used as a distraction. Given the freedom to marry for love, unlike other cultures where marriage has been a family, political, or religious matter, we marry out of need and fear instead, and the fulfilment of these needs does not always take the benefit of the partner into consideration.

Yet if we pursue the line of thought that Saturn is the great gateway to freedom, the presence of Saturnian contacts in a relationship can be an indication that much growth and self-knowledge can be gained if both people make the commitment to be honest with themselves and with each other. A journey can then be undertaken jointly which brings far more richness and depth with it than the starry-eyed fantasies of the psychologically virginal. Nothing will force the hand of the unconscious as surely as someone stepping on one's shadow; the reaction is so immediate, and so predictable if we were only able to step back far enough to observe it objectively, that a great deal of insight may be gained simply by a study of those we either irrationally like or dislike. This is not something to be done with criticism or the desire to judge, however, for the faculty of rational judgment has no place in the realm of the shadow. It is because of this very faculty of judgment, applied out of hand century after century, that we have so much trouble with the dark, Saturnian side of human nature in the first place.

Sun-Saturn contacts

The Sun is usually considered to be the symbol of the conscious or rational ego. He represents the individuality and the conscious expression of goals and decisions. This is particularly true of men, and often not so applicable to women, for many women relate to life through the feelings and instincts and consequently reflect the Moon rather than the Sun. The Sun then becomes the symbol of the unconscious male half of a woman's own psyche, the "animus", and if the qualities which are represented by the Sun's sign and house and aspects are not understood and integrated, then the woman will seek these same qualities in a husband or lover and attempt to live them through him.

The majority of Sun-Saturn contacts in relationships appear to occur when it is the woman's Saturn and the man's Sun which are involved. This is perfectly in line with the idea that the majority of women do not freely express the quality of the Sun, and consequently a tie involving the woman's Sun would be largely unconscious and not so obviously powerful. There seems to be no doubt that Sun-Saturn contacts are very powerful and binding in relationships as well as being more common than the proverbial Sun-Moon or Venus-Mars interchanges.

When one person's Sun falls on another person's Saturn—and although the conjunction is the most intense contact, other aspects seem to be productive of similar effects if they are close enough in orb—those qualities which Saturn works the hardest to hide are displayed in full, glowing colours by his partner. This produces a very potent reaction which is more or less compulsive depending upon the closeness of the aspect. Wider orbs than are generally allowed in synastry appear to be effective when Saturn is considered, and in the case of exact aspects there is almost a feeling of fatality about the interaction which may result in the common opinion that the exact aspects constitute karmic ties. They may in fact denote this; we are not yet in possession of knowledge which can tell us whether this is possible. In psychological terms this feeling of "rightness" or fatality is the usual accompaniment of intense projection of both persons' unconscious qualities on each other—they are in effect falling in love with themselves. Whether it is karma or projection, or perhaps both, is a debatable point. But something certainly happens which is inexplicable in the rational terms of the intellect and is also inexplicable according to the traditional rules of synastry. The longer one is in the company of the other person, the more the contact will be felt, and even a ten-degree orb between the Sun and Saturn will be apparent in time.

There is often an element of reluctant respect or grudging admiration on the part of Saturn towards the Sun because the Sun can express easily and automatically those qualities which Saturn finds it difficult to express and frequently fears or dislikes within himself. If the Saturnian partner has some self-awareness, he will often be openly admiring and may be able to learn a great deal from his partner which will help him in his own self-expression. Only the Sun, the great life-giver, can offer warmth and light to Saturn's chilled bones. But with a person who is relatively unconscious, envy and hostility are often also apparent and the sort of pride which is of the "cut off your nose to spite your face" variety. Being natural opposites in the spiritual as well as the astrological sense, symbolised by their rulership of opposite signs and their exaltation in the signs of each other's fall, Saturn and the Sun are one, at the same time that they form an apparently irreconcilable duality. Each possesses only half the picture. The medieval alchemists knew this when they insisted that lead, which they called Saturn, already contained gold, which they called Sol, within it. The shadow as well as being the dark or destructive side of the personality is also the helpful hidden brother and cannot be ignored or abandoned because these two brothers together make one life. For this reason there is often an element of mutual dependency in Sun-Saturn ties which is so great that the relationship will often endure much buffeting before a break is even considered.

The great danger with Sun-Saturn contacts is that Saturn, if the individual is unconscious and frightened, may lean so heavily on the Sun that he stifles his partner. He may display a curious blindness to the Sun's chosen goals in life because he is busily attempting to live out his own cherished desires through the Sun instead. This can be particularly damaging if the Saturnian person is a parent and the Sun a child; for in such cases the child is rarely permitted to be himself, or to develop along the lines of his own potential blueprint. When this contact occurs with a man's Sun and a woman's Saturn, the woman will often be the unconscious source of power which pushes the man along a path he would not have willingly chosen himself for she is living out her own ego dreams through him at the same time that she preserves the material advantages of appearing to be the submissive partner. When a man's Saturn and a woman's Sun are involved, the man will often unconsciously stifle the creative expression of his partner because he is afraid of what she could become if she were to express it; therefore, he must "keep her barefoot and pregnant in the kitchen" so that there is no possibility of her excelling him. The fact that she may not want to excel him does not occur to him.

These kinds of situations are never very pretty to look at. They occur with frightening regularity, however, and the only possible way out of them which preserves the dignity and self-respect of both people is to bring the whole arrangement out of the darkness. It is then possible for both persons to develop in themselves what each wishes to express so that both may appreciate their partners while maintaining their own inner centres. The relationship of the Sun to Saturn may be compared to a parent-child relationship on the psychological level, and if we are to seriously consider it as a karmic contact, it may well imply that this kind of relationship once existed in literal fact. The Sun, the eternal child who is full of light, new growth, and joy, is a means of conferring immortality to his parent because through him the parent lives anew. Saturn, the voice of experience and authority, can protect and guide his creation; one therefore provides the structure and the other the meaning. Yet if Saturn does not have sufficient purpose in his own life, or if his life has been a story of frustration, he will seek to live vicariously through his child and may forget that the Sun has a right to his own individual expression.

I do not feel that Sun-Saturn contacts, even the square and the opposition, are inherently negative or necessarily destructive in a relationship. The fact that they generally seem so is perhaps more a reflection of the ineptness with which we deal with the feeling side of life than it is a suggestion that the relationship is "doomed". There is often a struggle, and the struggle may be a great strain on the Sun, who rarely appreciates the depth of Saturn's fear and vulnerability because Saturn is so proficient at presenting a cool and uncaring face. But sooner or later, if he is willing to help his Saturnian partner become more fully conscious of where the problem really lies, much good can come of the contact on both sides. Saturn can give direction and support to the Sun and can help him to realise his goals in a practical fashion at the same time that he himself is learning to be more joyful. It is largely up to the Saturnian to come to an understanding of his own fears. These ties are enduring, coloured as they are by Saturn's inclination toward dependency and the Sun's desire to be depended on. Perhaps if our values were different, we might look for Sun-Saturn contacts as the chief indication of an enduring relationship rather than as one of the signals for caution.

Mars-Saturn contacts

Mars contacting Saturn is one of the "bad guys" of chart comparison. Although it is generally acknowledged that Sun-Saturn connexions have their positive side even with a minimum of work, we are issued stern warnings by various writers that a Mars-Saturn tie between two charts bodes nothing but trouble, even the "harmonious" aspects. One is left with the impression that two individuals who find this contact existent between them should run as quickly as possible in opposite directions. One might also assume, on superficial interpretation, that this aspect ought to cause repulsion and dislike, particularly on a sexual level, as Mars symbolises the physical desires and passions. Why then do Mars-Saturn contacts appear with such great frequency when a serious emotional involvement occurs, perhaps more often than the Mars-Venus connexion which is supposed to designate strong attraction? And why, rather than repelling, do they seem—at the beginning, at least—to be concurrent with such intense and almost feverish sexual attraction? This contact has a reputation for producing passion before marriage and increasing coldness and sometimes violence afterwards. Seen from the perspecitve of Saturn's great vulnerability and his tendency to work along the lines of unconscious projection, these seemingly inexplicable effects of Mars-Saturn aspects become much clearer.

Here the qualities of Saturn's sign, or element, or quadruplicity are inflamed by Mars's being placed there; they appear full-blown, concentrated, rendered slightly aggressive, overt and sometimes slightly arrogant, and they are channeled not only into the will and energy drive but, more importantly from the perspective of relationships, into the sexual style and drive as well. Mars symbolises passion, Saturn fear. It is no wonder that the unconscious individual caught by this kind of contact is fascinated like a bird before a snake. He is immediately aware of someone who can display openly and forcefully the qualities he himself is most unable to express—and all with a sexual overtone. Such a contact is compelling rather than repelling in many cases, and the person whose Saturn is involved in this encounter may then become unconsciously resolved on the domination and control of the person who threatens him. The fright may often take the guise of stimulation because there is a challenge offered and a conquest which must be made although these "arrangements" are never conscious in nature. The moment a projection becomes conscious, it ceases to be a projection; and the individual who becomes aware that the threat lies not in the other person but in his own shadow is free of the unusual compelling quality of this contact.

Saturn is a master of disguises as we have already seen. He can personify passion more grandly and theatrically than the most inflamed Mars. This is not a conscious duplicity; it is authentic passion but the causes, which lie on the emotional plane, are somewhat ambiguous. And so they fall in love but rarely live happily ever after because when the conquest is complete—which may take anywhere from a night to fifty years and which generally occurs in the bedroom, the real battlefield of the Mars-Saturn contact—then Saturn generally reverts back from passion to his natural state of coolness and aloofness, thus completing the symbolic disarming which has been his unconscious desire since the first meeting.

This is, of course, an over-simplified description of the underground psychic process which accompanies the Mars-Saturn contact. Generally there are many connexions on the conscious level which bring an element of mutual harmony and appreciation into the relationship for this aspect by itself would probably produce intense and immediate dislike—and generally does—without some "soft" cross-aspects mitigating the situation. It will then combine with what is essentially a natural attraction and complicate matters tremendously. But the frequency of the contact is somewhat suspicious if we wish to believe that the only reason for people getting together is because they like each other. Sometimes it is because they dislike themselves.

It is in this area of unconscious projection, and subsequent frustration, that the tendency toward violence may be found. It is a curious fact that many men who appear to be normally mild or inoffensive by temperament, or who do not at least resort to the use of physical or emotional violence to express their anger, can be aggravated past the point of self-control by a woman whose Saturn falls on Mars. This is also true of women although a woman cannot generally use physical violence in a quarrel without paying dearly for it. During the stage where Saturn begins, sometimes imperceptibly, to draw back into his shell, much emotional pain can be experienced by the partner because suddenly the individual who seemed so full of passion at first has pulled away and become, subtly or overtly, unreachable. This is intensely frustrating to Mars who, if nothing else, favours the path of honest expression. Quarrels or emotionally charged scenes may then be generated by Mars to try to recreate the rapidly vanishing interest of the partner. These quarrels may be slight enough, but they may also assume gigantic and uncontrollable proportions and result in physical harm. Most of them are the result of Mars's trying to get a reaction—and any reaction is better than no reaction at all—from a cool and disinterested partner.

A married couple may live with this contact for a lifetime if the people are bound by other, more loving ties. Then it becomes necessary to attempt some kind of understanding of the real roots of the friction. This also becomes necessary when the contact occurs between a parent and a child for the same kind of cat-and-mouse game may occur on an unconscious level even in the midst of affection and dependency; and it is the child who suffers most for this in his adult years because of the emotional scars. If this contact does exist in a situation where it is impossible or difficult to sever the relationship, great pressure is placed on both people involved and particularly on Saturn, who holds the key to whether the final outcome will be mutually constructive or unnecessarily painful.

One of the difficulties surrounding Mars-Saturn contacts is that we have, in our post-Victorian society, a tendency to cloak conflicts or misunderstandings which are essentially sexual or emotional in nature with the guise of money problems, trouble with in-laws, and arguments about who takes the dustbins out on Friday nights. It is most difficult for the Saturnian to express his feelings anyhow for he often does not even know what his feelings are; he hides them from himself as much as he does from others. A more independent Mars, dimly aware of the net closing about him, may extricate himself abruptly from the situation if he is able, leaving Saturn with a newer wound in the same sore place and an even greater fund, now conscious, of resentment. But Saturn has a way, with any planet, of making the other fellow feel responsible for him so the situation usually runs its course. When two people are involved who have a close Mars-Saturn contact and who know very little about themselves, it would appear that there is not much to commend the union of the god of force with the god of resistance.

If some effort is made, however, the contact need not be this deadly; in fact it can be one of the most productive contacts of all. Some of its promise lies in the fact that it can foster mutual honesty about the entire area of sexual interchange, something which is sadly lacking in many relationships. Saturn himself is not a planet of sex by any stretch of the imagination, but he becomes important in those areas where sex becomes an obstruction. He may even be considered anti-sexual or asexual, leaning as he does toward control and discipline and asceticism. But he will play a sexual role if he is threatened by Mars, just as he will play a romantic role when contacted by Venus or an intellectual one when aspected by Mercury. Like Janus, he guards the gate by watching in all directions, and his main defense lies in camouflage.

While the more difficult aspects of Sun-Saturn contacts may be discussed openly between individuals, the difficult side of Mars-Saturn contacts may not without the possibility of embarrassment and hurt feelings for many people. This is part of the heritage of the Victorian era, certainly, but it also has antecedents in Church doctrines which have been with us for almost two thousand years. As the collective psyche of the group develops, greater honesty may become possible in the sexual area, and one of the results of this honesty is bound to be a more constructive use of this energy in relationships. Psychology may have outgrown its Freudian origins, and the idea of an unconscious dominated by repressed libido is no longer valid in the broader view of the human psyche. But the nature of sexual relations, and in particular the male and female "roles" in a larger sense, are still a major stumbling block in the development of many people. It is possible that a Mars-Saturn contact, when it is found between two people who are involved in a sexual relationship, may be a means of self-discovery through an exploration of the archetypes behind sexual symbolism, and this may be a most effective path for the achievement of wholeness. The feelings of inadequacy, guilt, and confusion which colour the unconscious attitudes of many people toward their own sexuality can be brought to light and dissipated through the positive and honest energy of Mars, and the natural and instinctive selfishness and lack of sensitivity existent in the sexual expression of many people can be balanced by the understanding and depth of Saturn.

When a Mars-Saturn contact occurs in situations where no sexual association is involved, such as a parent-child relationship, the inferences of unconscious undercurrents are nevertheless still sexual in nature. This is a fairly frequent occurence and is inevitable when seen from the point of view that a male child will inevitably see his mother as a symbol of womanhood for the first phase of his life and that a female child will inevitably view her father in the same light. There are bound to be sexual associations attached to parental ties although sex here is meant in its broadest sense and encompasses the emotional aspect as well as, or instead of, the physical. Parent-child situations, or even friendship situations, where Mars-Saturn contacts exist may have some element of projection of sexual values; and this is bound to create difficulty if the mechanism is not properly understood. This does not suggest the proverbial Oedipal complex although that unquestionably can and does occur in real life as well as in psychoanalytical textbooks. It simply suggests that there are many currents at work in all close relationships, and that these currents overlap and create far greater complexity than we imagine exists. It is the refusal to accept the complexity which brings us problems, and our lack of honesty in talking about it; a contact like Mars to Saturn does not intrinsically contain any evil or necessitate difficulty.

Mercury-Saturn contacts

Mercury-Saturn contacts pertain to the plane of the mind and are less concerned with emotional reactions between people. They are common because of this among those who relate primarily on an intellectual basis, such as teachers and their students, and are also frequent among friendships, as well as appearing with regularity among relationships with an emotional bias. With a little careful handling they are a highly productive exchange of energies as Mercury and Saturn are not really inimical to each other and both possess a certain cold rationality.

For the person who is in a relatively unconscious state about himself, however, the mechanism with this contact is similar to other Saturnian aspects. We have seen that the Sun threatens Saturn with his radiant capacity for spontaneous self-expression and that Mars threatens him with self-confidence and undisguised sexuality. Mercury, innocuous and asexual planet that he is, becomes a symbol of intellectual competence and has a remarkable way, if the aspect is close enough, of arousing a feeling of stupidity or mental inadequacy in the person whose Saturn is affected. Those qualities which Saturn finds it difficult to express are displayed by Mercury through a facility at communication and thought, and the speed and nimbleness of Mercury's reactions can be disturbing to the slower, more plodding temperament of Saturn. Saturn may also find Mercury untruthful, at least by his own definitions of truth—but truth is often a relative matter to Mercury. The Saturnian's partner may be no intellectual giant, but Mercury has a way of appearing unusually clever to Saturn.

There is often great admiration displayed with this contact and little hostility; a kind of open and harmless envy of the other person's gifts is frequently shown by Saturn who, in turn, can be an excellent sounding-board and critic, offering stabilisation and practical advice to the often too fluid Mercurial energy. But as with all Saturn contacts, this depends largely on the state of consciousness of the Saturnian person. Admiration for another's dexterity, and a willingness to offer a supporting structure for its development, is one of the best expressions of the contact. But if he feels threatened, Saturn can become overly critical and a constant nag and can be tremendously inhibiting and suffocating to Mercury. Because he feels inadequate, but cannot admit to himself that it is his own slowness that is the difficulty, Saturn may attempt to destroy Mercury's confidence by ceaselessly criticising, or simply ignoring his partner.

Mercury may find Saturn a bore and may move along to more entertaining or sympathetic companions. Because this tie is primarily of the mind, it will rarely bind two people unless there are other contacts which suggest a strong emotional relationship. When emotional ties are existent, then this contact may cause considerable trouble if it is not handled constructively, particularly if the Mercurial partner is actually strongly influenced by Mercury in his natal chart or if Mercury is in Virgo or Gemini.

The importance of Mercury in chart comparison has generally been underrated although some justice has been done recently to his role. But in his connexion with communication, Mercury is obviously important as a symbol of the individual's capacity to express himself to others. The most difficult problem between two people can go a long way toward a solution if they can sit down and talk about it. And the most loving of relationships cannot keep pace with the growth of the individual psyche if the relationship is polarised on the plane of feeling and there is no mutual sharing of ideas and interests. People who have nothing to talk about often find that the most feverish of sexual attractions and the most ardent emotional needs grow to be a bore in time. The husband who wanders into other pastures seeking someone who will understand his thoughts is so common that he had become a cliche, and the wife who feels the walls closing in about her because it is assumed that she can understand nothing except the language of recipes is an equally ordinary situation. It is the mind that differentiates us from the lower kingdoms of nature. Yet it is frighteningly rare that individuals seek an intellectual match; they are much busier seeking emotional and physical companions instead because these needs express themselves with urgency.

A frustrated Mercury will naturally be felt much more strongly by individuals who are predominantly airy in temperament, and Virgo and Gemini in particular can become intensely frustrated, nervous, and restless within the confines of a relationship if they cannot communicate with their partners. Mercury-Saturn contacts can therefore be quite a large problem if Saturn reacts by attempting to fence in or dampen the mental energy of his partner. He then runs the risk of precipitating that most common and most plaintive of lines spoken by the truant husband or wife to the devoted lover: "I love her (him) but she just doesn't listen to anything I say."

Saturn-Mercury contacts may have considerable influence on the thinking patterns of both people involved in spite of the fact that Mercury is considered a neutral and convertible planet with little power of his own. He can offer to Saturn the one quality which is most effective in dispelling shadows: detached analysis. With his help Saturn can achieve a new level of self-understanding, and Mercury will rarely claim anything in return. From Saturn, Mercury can receive that quality which he most sorely needs: concentration. It will be apparent that this contact, even the square or opposition, is potentially a most useful one in any kind of relationship if it is dealt with in a graceful fashion.

Venus-Saturn contacts

The conjunction of Venus and Saturn between charts was once referred to by Evangeline Adams as the signature of eternal friendship. Perhaps this was true of her friends, but the outcome is frequently not so pleasant when romantic relationships are considered, where the connexion is more commonly found. Nor is it easy in parent-child combinations. Although Saturn is exalted in Venus' sign, his more primitive side is not conducive to happy relations. This is the aspect "par excellence" of emotional rejection, and it is a difficult one to deal with unless it is taken as an opportunity to discover whether any reality lies behind the projections of the relationship. Our most cherished illusions surround the realm of love and affection, and these must be given up if eternal friendship is to be gained from a Venus-Saturn contact.

We know that Venus is the chief significator or symbol of affection, love of harmony, and the urge for companionship. As a reflection of the individual's capacity to relate to others, Venus expresses with charm, grace, and ease those qualities which Saturn cannot freely demonstrate. She will also often suggest a sense of taste and refinement in those areas where Saturn finds himself clumsy, inept, inhibited, and cramped. Venus is the eternal lover and the eternal youth, and this can very naturally upset Saturn who may have a tendency to react with jealousy, possessiveness, suspicion, and a feeling of unattractiveness or social ineptness. These feelings are usually concurrent with intense admiration as is generally the case with Saturn contacts; and when this situation occurs between members of the opposite sex—and often enough between members of the same sex—there is some degree of fascination involved. It is not physical in nature, as is the Mars-Saturn fascination, but is often a kind of adoration and affects the level of the feelings.

There is a curious bond between Venus and Saturn which cannot be properly explained except in terms of the closeness of the shadowy or dark side of the psyche with the "anima" or transexual symbol of the soul; in the process of individuation, whereby a person gradually discovers and becomes that which he has always potentially but unconsciously been capable of being, the confrontation or realisation of the nature of the anima can only come after the shadow has been integrated for one follows on the heels of the other. In more esoteric terms the soul, the Beloved, cannot be perceived until the Dweller has been passed. None of this is of any use to the practical astrologer, nor is the idea that Capricorn is connected with Venus as well as with Saturn in esoteric astrology. But it seems to be an empiric fact that Venus-Saturn contacts, whether they appear on a natal chart or in the comparison of charts, have the tendency to bring first, great unhappiness of a peculiarly personal kind and second, great opportunity for the establishment of an honest relationship— something which is rarely seen. This is a most important contact, and when it occurs between charts, there seems to be the possibility of utilising the relationship in the fullest sense as a symbol of an inner union so that the outward situation reflects the inner marriage.

There is some work to be done first by the average individual whose Saturn is affected by Venus. He is likely to be especially sensitive to his own emotional constriction in the presence of Venus and usually experiences a sense of clumsiness and inadequacy. He may feel unloved, unappealing, overly serious, and stiff around his Venusian partner and is likely to compensate for this by convincing himself that it is really Venus who is superficial, shallow, flirtatious, disloyal, and vain. He may react with a particularly unpalatable combination of envy, resentment, and a need to dampen or stifle the lighthearted, carefree, self-indulgent grace of the Venus temperament.

It will be apparent that Venus-Saturn contacts are one of the main indications of jealousy between people, and this is true also of friendships and of parent-child situations. It may be difficult to imagine a parent being jealous of his child, but this is a common situation and one which, if it is left unrecognised, can cause great pain to the child who is the unfortunate inspirer of his parent's envy. Venus-Saturn jealousy is not based on a fear of sexual inadequacy or infidelity which is the province of Mars-Saturn contacts. It tends to be expressed more as a possessiveness which is based on the feeling of being inherently unlovable and thus constantly demanding the formal demonstrations of love and loyalty to ensure against the possibility of emotional rejection. Venus-Saturn contacts have a tendency to stimulate two people into legalising their relationship when it might have been better left loose and free or when a better reason than the need for emotional guarantees might have been sought. This is of course the typical reaction of an unconscious Saturn; but this is the reaction of the majority of people. In order to overcome his tendency to stifle the pleasures of his partner, Saturn must first be able to enjoy himself which is not an easy task when confronted with the easy spontanaeity of Venus.

It may be something within the partner which makes him seek Saturn for a bedfellow in spite of the fact that difficulty usually follows through mistrust and fear. Tracing inner motivations through the realm of the personal unconscious sometimes discloses a bottomless hole where the root of it is never found, and it is possible to analyse too much. Some people are more "Saturn-prone" than others, either to seeking relations where they must deal with a partner's Saturn or to having their own Saturn bombarded. It may be that the path of developing a fully conscious relationship is as valid a spiritual discipline as the path of meditation or yoga—and that, as it is considerably more difficult, its rewards may be proportionately greater in terms of being able to overcome at last the sense of separateness. This is the more esoteric promise of Saturn in Libra. Perhaps those who are "Saturn-prone" in their relationships sense this, and this is the best path for them.

Not all relationships are built around love, and it is only comparatively recently that marriages are based on the choice of the heart rather than of the pocketbook. A relationship may occur out of expediency, out of a need for financial security, or a general loneliness. It may also occur because an additional responsibility such as a child makes it impossible to consider any alternative situation. Some relationships occur under family pressure or for religious or moral reasons. Often Venus-Saturn contacts will be seen in these situations for the other side of this tie is the duty-over-love side, and it will frequently occur in relation to money—our concretised symbol for emotional possession and exchange. Saturn may not always react with the desire for emotional possession; he may decide that material possession is more worthwhile. Venus has two faces as she governs two signs, and it is characteristic of people to express the same attitude toward possessions as they do with their affections.

Saturn will often contrive to make Venus obligated to him by assuming control over her material security. He may be tight-fisted or resent the freedom which money gives and therefore withhold it. There is frequently a tie of financial obligation involved with Venus-Saturn contacts which binds two people long after the affection has ceased to exist. This is common where a woman is dependent on her husband's income or where there are children who must be supported. Sometimes this situation is reversed, where the woman controls the inflow of money, and this is offensive to the majority of men because social conditioning insists that the man be the breadwinner. Along with the usual hurt feelings in these cases, there is also often a bruised ego. In most of these situations it is the inner sense of guilt which constitutes a powerful tie; and this feeling of guilt is characteristic of an unconscious Saturn.

Venus-Saturn contacts intrude on a most delicate area of human psychology, and although they are unquestionably difficult in a relationship of close proximity and intimacy, they can also help to bring into the light all the complex and convoluted unconscious motivations which poison people's relationships with one another. It is generally the truth that hurts the most with these aspects, but if the truth were confronted, it would be possible to raise the entire relationship to a higher and completely different level—one of mutual cooperation rather than of dependency. Like Mars-Saturn contacts, these tend to relate to areas which people prefer not to discuss with one another. For this reason they are often far more difficult than their nature suggests. Perhaps the dream of the eternal friendship is sufficiently powerful to help two people overcome their natural apathy toward self-knowledge so that they can help each other to achieve it.

Moon-Saturn contacts

Moon-Saturn aspects between charts have a reputation similar to Sun-Saturn contacts as they are often given a fatalistic or "karmic" implication if sufficiently close in orb. There is certainly a compulsive quality about these, as well as all, Saturnian contacts if the orb is under three degrees. Moon-Saturn connexions suggest a definite area of difficulty between two people, yet they are common enough in marriages and friendships and if handled with understanding, have a definitely positive and constructive side. They seem to be productive of a bond of emotional fidelity as the protective, sympathetic, and mothering nature of the Moon responds readily to the obvious vulnerability of Saturn.

The Moon symbolises the feeling nature and the natural flow of the instinctual, unconscious side of the personality. To the Moon's eagerness to experience new sensations, Saturn can prove rather stifling. He may react to her obvious emotionality with feelings of fear, vulnerability, awkwardness, and a sense of his own lack of emotional responsiveness. Unlike the Sun who gives forth light and energy of his own, the Moon's gift is her sensitive response to others on the plane of feeling, and it is this open and easy sensitivity that Saturn both envies and fears.

This contact may cause irritation and resentment if it is not understood. Saturn may feel himself to be callous and constricted when confronted by the Moon and may react by attempting to structure and confine the fluidity and responsiveness of his partner. The Moon may feel cramped and inhibited and, on some vague level, disapproved of, like an errant child. Because of the lunar sensitivity, she is easily discouraged and hurt by Saturn's criticism and apparent emotional coldness. Saturn's tendency to offer free and unsolicited advice, and to display resentment if his advice is not taken, is exaggerated by this contact. The Moon may be constantly subjected to structuring and analysing by an overly conservative and somewhat gloomy parental replacement, and this can be particularly interesting when it is a parent whose Moon is involved and a child whose Saturn is at work. The Moon can become increasingly self-conscious in the presence of Saturn for nothing she does is right.

The Moon is a symbol for the unconscious, the primitive and instinctual self, and denotes those qualities which have been integrated from childhood, from hereditary patterns, or—if the idea of rebirth is considered—from the longer past. She is therefore representative of the line of least resistance, the behaviour which is instinctual and which reacts rather than acts. She is a reservoir of experience on the personal level from which the conscious will of the Sun can draw emotional support and instinctual wisdom. It is not difficult to understand why the Moon is a natural threat to Saturn for his experiences and knowledge are also of the past and may be related to childhood, to parental influences, and perhaps to the "long history" of the individual, but his past is one which is unpleasant to recall and which has taught him self-defense. Saturn and the Moon both suggest unconscious levels of behaviour, based on past experience, but one is a defense against the environment while the other is a flow outward toward the environment. Saturn attempts to create space between himself and the things or situations which have hurt him while the Moon attempts to draw everything to herself as part of her own subjective feeling experience. The Moon clings to those areas which are most disturbing to Saturn, and this becomes apparent even in the realm of personal habits. It is common to find Saturn irrationally irritated by a small and often meaningless personal idiosyncrasy of dress or habit expressed by the Moon for it is only a symbol of a deeper disturbance.

Since the Moon also seems to be connected with the private self-image which a person cherishes in his imagination—the guise which he wears in his fantasy-life—the Moon's qualities are most likely to be expressed in close relationships, particularly in a domestic situation, where it is not as necessary to maintain a facade. Any other planet falling on the Moon from another chart tends to bring forth a response of a positive kind from the Moon as this private self is in some subtle way understood or encouraged by the other person. For this reason we tend to feel more spontaneous, free, and capable of expression of the private self around those whose planets kindly aspect the Moon, and this is one of the facets of the Sun-Moon tie which is traditionally indicative of compatibility of temperament.

When Saturn contacts the Moon, this private self is certainly understood, at least after a fashion—although overlaid heavily with projection—but it is discouraged or disapproved of. At least this is the impression which Saturn may give although the actual situation is probably closer to greater longing and needfulness, carefully masked. Consequently there is often a certain embarrassment which the Moon feels in the presence of Saturn, the kind of feeling which sometimes occurs in dreams when the dreamer discovers that he is naked in the company of a group of people. Saturn, in his attempt to protect himself from his own vulnerability, may unconsciously become critical, nagging, and demanding, and may attempt also to undermine the Moon's confidence in order to gain her attention and emotional fidelity. There is usually great emotional needfulness present with a Moon-Saturn contact, and this in itself is not negative as it can provide the opportunity for a deep and meaningful relationship as well as a means for the development of inner strength and self-understanding. The difficulty usually lies in Saturn's reluctance to demonstrate his needfulness and to face his own sense of inadequacy. He may express a cool, critical exterior instead, and this can be painful to the sensitive Moon.

Moon-Saturn contacts occur frequently in enduring relationships which points strongly to the more positive potential they hold. It is possible to explain their frequency by the more cynical or pessimistic view that many people are conditioned by emotional rejection in childhood to identify love with pain, and they cannot function with a love which is accompanied by acceptance and happiness. The nuances of relationships when viewed from the perspective of Freud and Adler are certainly depressing; however, although much of this is undoubtedly applicable and although contacts like Moon-Saturn aspects between charts suggest a less than healthy reason for an attraction initially, it is possible that a deeper meaning to the relationship exists between the less attractive convolutions of the personal unconscious and that with patience and effort this deeper meaning may be perceived by two people who are willing to seek it. It is only when this area has been glimpsed that a reasonably accurate evaluation of the potential of the relationship in the long term is possible. Although there is much self-consciousness, inhibition, and hurt that often accompanies Moon-Saturn contacts, these reactions may be worked through and understood so that an enduring bond can be found to be existent underneath.

The Moon must often bear the brunt of Saturn's gloom and moodiness. Moon-Saturn connexions are common where the complaint is voiced that one is "picked at" mercilessly by another person, especially in the area of trivial habits and mannerisms. This may be particularly uncomfortable if a parent's Saturn affects a child's Moon for nothing the child does will be right in the eyes of his parent, and the child is not usually in a position to understand that this criticism is only the darker face of need. This is also a touchy contact in business relationships, especially if Saturn holds the authority, for he will make life generally uncomfortable for the Moon in the line of "duty" when purely personal antagonism is the real motivation. Unleashed in the domestic life without mutual understanding, it is a contact which breeds nagging and discontent, generally over personal habits. Behind all this lies the Moon's essential irrationality; she behaves as she does because that is simply how she is, and she is this way because it is the way she has always been. This makes no sense to Saturn who has spent much time constructing carefully designed defenses. A man will express his Sun sign largely because he consciously chooses to act in this way, and he will express his ascending sign largely because his experiences have taught him to develop these qualities as a necessary tool for the effective functioning in his environment. But he will express his Moon because he cannot help it; this is his past and his heritage and his line of least resistance. It is the lack of structure and control which is so infuriating to Saturn who desperately wishes that he could, just once, forget to reason or forget that he is separate.

Moon-Saturn contacts require the complete cooperation of both people. Both planets are connected with the unconscious and both tend to react rather than act; but because of their depth, both the Moon and Saturn if studied as components of the psyche can yield a great deal of understanding. Two people with these contacts tend to possess a clear and uncomplicated channel into each other's most private inner life in terms of the personality, and if this channel is not muddied with hostility and fear, it can help to create a powerful and meaningful bond.

Jupiter-Saturn contacts

In the combination of Jupiter and Saturn between two charts we have yet another polarity or blending of opposite principles on yet another level. It will be apparent by this time that Saturn forms a duality with every other heavenly body for his energy does not synthesise naturally with the energies of the other planets. What is always denoted in Saturn contacts within one chart or across two charts is the opportunity to resolve or integrate one of the fundamental dualities of human experience through conscious effort.

The Sun and Saturn, as we have seen, are opposites in a symbolic sense, and they are perhaps the most important pair of opposites to be considered from the point of view of the personality. They are, in psychological terminology, the conscious ego and the shadow. The great magnetic power of Sun-Saturn contacts between two people is well-known if not fully understood. The Moon and

Saturn are also opposite, but this duality occurs more on the plane of the form and the instinctual nature. These two planets rule opposite signs, and these signs have natural rulership over the vertical axis of the chart, symbolising our heredity, our origins, and how we are bound by this past in our expression outward to the world. The Moon and Saturn therefore represent two phases of the past and two aspects of the unconscious; and in combination across two charts they tend powerfully to affect the emotional, instinctual, and domestic aspects of a relationship. Mars and Saturn form a duality which is well known by astrologers and, among other things, signify impulse and control or desire and fear. Venus and Saturn create the duality of companionship and isolation, and even Mercury and Saturn form the duality of mind and its prison of form.

The combination of the "greater malefic" with the "greater benefic"—it yet remains to be seen which is which—symbolises the encountering of the two paths of concrete knowledge and experience with intuitive perception and faith. These are the two largest planets in the solar system and mark the dividing line between the personal planets—all of which deal with the urges of the personality and its threefold equipment of mind, feelings, and body—and the outer or "higher octave" planets—all of which have some connexion with the urges of the collective unconscious or the soul and the group life of which the man is a part. Jupiter and Saturn represent the bridge between the higher and lower levels of consciousness. Any combination of the two, natally or in synastry, offers an opportunity, for through the intuitive faculty—Jupiter—may be perceived at last the shadow, the Dweller.

Cross-contacts of Saturn with the personal planets affect two individuals primarily on the personality level although the person whose Saturn is involved also has the opportunity to reach a new level of self-understanding through the contact. These cross-aspects hinder or stabilise the urges of each person and as such are extremely common in close relationships because for the majority of people relationships are fields for the development of the personality. Saturnian contacts with the outer planets, and with Jupiter as well, affect two individuals on a more subtle level, hindering or stabilising the urges of the inner man or the soul. Together Jupiter and Saturn can provide to both people the necessary qualities for passage into a more expanded field of awareness: knowledge and wisdom.

In mythology Jupiter was the child of Saturn who swallowed most of his offspring whole because of his fear that they would do to him what he had done to his own father, Uranus. Only Jupiter was saved and hidden in a cave while a stone, wrapped in a blanket, was offered and accepted as a substitute. At the appointed time, when Saturn disgorged the lot because he could not digest the stone, Jupiter seized control and locked his father in Tartarus, the darkest region of the underworld, under the guardianship of Pluto to keep him out of mischief. From the depths of Tartarus, the myth tells us, Saturn still howls and bangs on his bars demanding release. For, like the other gods, he is immortal and cannot die.

We know now that mythology has great psychological relevance as well as being entertaining, and this myth is characteristically rich in symbolism on several levels. A little study may reveal that the relationship between Jupiter and Saturn is nicely stated in allegorical form here in terms of the growth of the human soul. It is important that this deeper aspect of the contact be considered for if we interpret cross-aspects like these in a wholly superficial manner, we are missing the significance of the major opportunity which is offered for personal growth. Every situation contains something which can be utilised for growth and none more powerfully than a relationship between two people.

Jupiter believes, instinctively and without intellectualisation, in the positive outcome and beneficent aid of those qualities and situations represented by his sign and house placement. Not only has he always had an abundance of these things, he continues to expand and attract a greater abundance for his faith vindicates itself. It is also not blind faith but rather an inner knowing based on the intuitive perception of the whole which guarantees to him—although he may not understand the details—a positive outcome and meaning for his own life. More than any other fiery planet Jupiter is synchronous with Jung's concept of the intuition, that faculty of consciousness which permits the perception of the over-all meaning of things, the cause behind the effect. Jupiter has also been linked with the image-making faculty, the powers of visualisation and fantasy. These faculties are primarily means of perceiving symbols which are the language of the unconscious self. It is said that people who come strongly under Jupiter and Sagittarius are lucky, and they certainly appear to be—but rather than luck, it is an inner acceptance of the positive outcome of any situation, an unconscious understanding of the meaning of that situation, and a capacity to visualise what they wish to experience in such a way that they shape it themselves.

Jupiter is a natural threat to an unconscious Saturn who fears the qualities of Jupiter's sign and house because he has been hurt by the lack of them. He is reluctant to take any risk without having a tangible guarantee of the eventual success of his efforts. The usual mundane effect of the interaction is that Saturn attempts to dampen Jupiter's enthusiasm, punch holes in his confidence, replace his optimism with caution, and check the flow of his intuitive acceptance of meaning. Jupiter can be a prodigal planet and governs excess; we have only to examine the myths of his escapades to get some idea of the complete irresponsibility of his nature. It is to be expected that Saturn's reaction to what he deems wastefulness and recklessness is disapproval of a rather old-maidish kind. Jupiter finds Saturn unduly pessimistic and overcautious and frequently an impossible bore because there is a lack of spontanaeity in Saturn's nature. To even a more sensuous Jupiter, the good things in life are a man's right because life itself is essentially meaningful and positive and full of opportunity. To Saturn the painful things in life are a man's natural lot, and any happy or bright periods are ephemeral and without meaning unless they have been earned through great effort.

The Jupiterian can learn much from Saturn if he will take the time to stop and listen, for imagination and ideals have no purpose if they cannot be demonstrated and utilised in the mundane world for the growth of the group. Saturn in turn can learn much from Jupiter in the way of tolerance and in the understanding that practical experience is not necessarily a more valid means of perception than the intuition. These two planets fall neatly along the perceptive axis of sensation and intuition and symbolise two opposing and apparently irreconcilable means of apprehending life's experiences. They are reconcilable if it becomes possible to raise one's consciousness out of the arena of the battle and shift the perspective above it, when the opponents then become observable as two valid but incomplete halves of expression.

Jupiter-Saturn contacts are rarely destructive even in the most unconscious cases for Jupiter is far too magnanimous a planet and will rarely react with anger or spite. Some of his good nature is bound to rub off on his Saturnian partner. The deeper side of Jupiter's nature will unfold under Saturn's care, and the search for answers to the larger questions of life can yield the dignity and wisdom which we generally associate with the better qualities of the planet, the human half of the centaur who is inextricably connected to his animal half and recognises its necessity for motion but who holds it firmly in harness.

Like the figure of mythology, Jupiter wins any battle which may ensue because of his natural authority, that of the inner man. This is not a particularly common contact in relationships because neither of these planets deals directly with the personality; their tie is connected with the broader, more abstract area of the ideals and the development of wisdom. Nevertheless it is an important contact because it is the tie of the teacher and the student in the ways and lessons of life, belief measured against experience first and inner or subjective experience measured against outer tangible experience later. The student eventually, if he masters his lessons, will outgrow and instruct his teacher to the benefit of both; but the roles shift, and each one learns from the other.

This is an interesting contact to be found between two people. It is sometimes synonymous with spiritual or religious differences between people although it will sometimes also affect the more earthy level of finances. But Jupiter, like Mercury, is a planet of the mind, ruling what is termed the upper mental plane or plane of creative thought while Mercury is given rulership over the lower mental plane of concrete thought. It is interesting to note that one of the esoteric teachings on the subject of rebirth is that when the personality dies and the temporary vehicles of the body, the emotional nature, and the concrete or rational intellect are dissolved at the end of an incarnation, the higher mental body or capacity for vision remains for it is a permanent attribute of the soul. From this rather abstruse concept it may be seen that Jupiter has very little to do with the personality and its life in the physical world; he is the first touch of the soul, seen through symbol and vision, which leads eventually to the battleground of Saturn.

Saturn-Saturn contacts

In order for two people to have a Saturn-Saturn conjunction across their natal charts, they must either be born close together or at intervals of approximately twenty-nine and a half years. The interval of one Saturn return is common with parents and children as many people in our society are pressured into marriage in their early twenties and have had at least one child by the time they reach their thirtieth birthday. When this contact occurs between parent and child, a relationship of a particular significance is indicated, and there are certain difficulties which do not occur when the contact of Saturns is absent. There are also certain opportunities offered which, unfortunately, are rarely taken because of the confusion, emotional and mental, which surrounds the average person's motives for having a child in the first place.

The Saturn return in an individual's birth chart marks a point in his maturing process where all that he has built in the way of defenses, inner and outer, now stretches over every area of his mundane life—as Saturn has now transited each house on the natal chart—and he is able to view this defense network as a whole and perceive what is real and what is illusory in the structures that he has built. If he has built well and has aimed toward qualities of character rather than external forms, then this period can mark a peak of accomplishment and the reaffirmation of an inner sense of purpose. If he has built poorly by depending on and identifying with his external attributes and circumstances, then everything may be knocked out from under him, and he may be forced, by the momentum of his own unconscious currents, to start again with a different premise and a different perspective on his life. That which is transient or borrowed is dissolved, and only that which has become a permanent attribute of the man's character remains. For this reason many people undergo a crisis at the time of the Saturn return and often do a sudden about-face in marriage, business, ideals, or life-style because the old ego structures suddenly are seen in a new and not very flattering light.

When a child is born during the period of a man's Saturn return, the child becomes part of the internal crisis of his parent; and with natal Saturn placed on the parent's Saturn, he is a constant reminder for the rest of the man's life of the pain, conflict, and new awareness which accompanied that period. One of the implications of this pattern is that, as Saturn symbolises a point of fear and defense, a child born during his parent's Saturn return is a reflection of the need for security and permanence in the parent. If this occurs, then both the parent and the child share the same kind of fear and the same manner of expressing it; and they may use this against each other.

Very simply stated, Saturn strongly aspecting Saturn tends to suggest a combination of individuals who bring out each other's insecurities. This is particularly true of the close conjunction, which is common enough in marriages or relationships between persons of the same age, as well as being true of the squares and oppositions which occur at seven- and fourteen-year intervals. The latter seem to go along with more friction and open hostility than do the conjunctions, but none of the various combinations are particularly easy because each person seems inadvertantly to activate the other's shadowy or "inferior" side. No one likes to see his clumsier qualities reflected in another's clumsiness, particularly if these qualities are ones which we have gone to a great deal of trouble to hide. It may even become necessary to "pick on" the person who attracts our projections because of his own similarity, thereby allowing us to vent our anger toward ourselves safely upon another. Saturn-Saturn contacts are often the mark of the unconscious scapegoat.

This combination may result in both people's feeling rejected, shut out, and hurt although as a rule neither one will admit that he has been wounded. Because it is the unconscious side or shadow which is affected by the contact, there is little rational behaviour involved; primarily the relationship will consist of persistent antagonism, resentment, and mutual feelings of constriction and lack of appreciation, but much of this resentment may be forced underground if there is a positive conscious tie which makes it impossible for the two people to voice their grievances. When other planets contact Saturn, it is generally in the hands of the person whose Saturn is involved to redeem the unpleasantness through self-understanding and the patience and cooperation of his partner. When two Saturns are involved, each is afraid to make the first move because they bring out so much defensiveness in each other, and stalemate results. Both people may attempt to manipulate the situation unconsciously so as to vindicate their own private views and resentments, and both may express the opposite to what they truly feel. Consequently both may continue to feel abused and misunderstood.

The only way out of this sort of impasse is for both individuals to face the situation simultaneously and make a mutual effort. This is obviously impossible in the case of a parent-child relationship if the child is young, but it is not only possible but virtually necessary with two adults. An unconscious Saturn can cause so much trouble singlehanded that he can completely topple a relationship which might otherwise have developed in a constructive fashion. It is rare that two people grow at the same rate of speed or in the same direction or reach the same point of awareness at the same time; yet couples constantly take the gamble of discovering that they are headed in contrary directions when they marry before Saturn has made his return on the natal chart. It may occur that the severance of the relationship is necessary when this discovery is made, but avoiding the discovery will not improve the relationship. Particularly when a Saturn-Saturn contact occurs, it is necessary first for each person to face his own shadow and make some attempt at integration of his own pesonality and clarification of his goals and ideals. Then a sharing of this often upsetting but nevertheless precious material can ensue. The first bridge has then been crossed in the gradual mutual disarmament which must occur with any attempt to make positive use of a Saturn-Saturn combination.

Saturn fears the other side of his own face with these contacts, the side which of course he cannot see because he is too busy projecting it in the other direction. What he sees as coldness, criticism, and rejection in the other person is merely the outward display of the same kind of terror of being hurt or proven inadequate that he himself is feeling. In misunderstanding himself he cannot possibly understand his partner and misreads the signals, fighting back by offering coldness, criticism, and rejection in his turn. This creates the proverbial "vicious circle" which becomes progressively more difficult until either an emotional crisis occurs or the relationship ends. But there is always pressure, on both sides, and this pressure forces growth more effectively than anything else.

One is reminded of the story of the schoolboy who, passing an acquaintance on the way to class, would not say hello because he was sure that if the acquaintance favoured him he would say hello first. The other boy, because he felt the same, would not acknowledge the first boy; and in consequence they ignored each other and decided independently to dislike each other because each felt the other was a cold and indifferent snob. Unfortunately most people are still schoolboys emotionally, and it is hardly necessary to continue the metaphor. This is a great waste of the potential of a Saturn-Saturn contact which always provides the opportunity of the short, fast route up the sheer cliff face to a realisation of the contents of the personal unconscious of both people, or in other words all the qualities each one works carefully to hide from himself and others. It may be argued that a little mystery is a good thing and that one ought to let sleeping dogs lie. This is certainly easier, and if the individual chooses this less painful and also less conscious route, let him beware of involvements with those who have any planet, particularly Saturn, in close aspect to his own natal Saturn.

When Saturn-Saturn contacts occur between parent and child, we may have an exaggerated example of what has been euphemistically termed the "generation gap". The gap, however, runs far deeper than the natural antipathy between the young and the old. The parent, who has the larger responsibility because he is theoretically an adult and controls the child inwardly and outwardly for the first few years of its life, will often aggravate his child's feelings of inadequacy or fear because something subtle and intangible in the child's psyche reminds the parent of his own buried fears. This is a pretty subtle arrangement, but anyone who has taken the time to study the motions and laws of the unconscious will understand the almost diabolic (or angelic) subtlety which occurs. When this kind of situation occurs, increasing coldness over the years may be the price paid and mutual pain as well because each desperately needs the other's love, understanding, and approval yet cannot voice his need. Often complete alienation takes place for a period of time. A great deal can be accomplished to use this contact as a means for mutual growth if the parent is able to swallow his pride and present himself as a fallible human being rather than as the voice of authority who cannot err.

When this combination occurs between persons of the same sex in friendship, it can be a very binding tie because the tensions which are inevitable in the male-female interchange are not as evident, and no one understands one's deepest fears better than someone else with the same fears. When the relationship is more intimate, particularly with a sexual relationship—not because Saturn has any direct relationship to sex but because he encourages isolation across which the act of sex is, hopefully, a bridge—difficulties begin to occur because it is important for each person to play the role of the animus or anima to the other one which necessitates some falsification of behaviour. During periods of stress, when transiting planets are affecting both Saturns, crises can occur which either force revelations or destroy the relationship.

It seems to be a facet of human nature to need some degree of privacy, and no one likes to feel that he is totally exposed with all his weaknesses laid out for public consumption—no matter how much understanding or sympathy he may receive. Saturn contacting Saturn may be a little too close for comfort in this respect. For Saturn to escape from his baser side and develop his deeper virtues, he must have the balance of an energy which is as free and spontaneous as he is tight-fisted for it is by the tension of opposites that he grows and evolves. For this reason Sun-Saturn and Jupiter-Saturn contacts are particularly helpful because these planets are giving by nature. When two people are both unable to express in the same area, an act of will on both parts is required to break apart the crystallisation. It is fitting that the contact of Saturn to Saturn across two charts is rarely discussed in astrological literature although it is a very important one from the point of view of the psychological growth of both people involved. For this contact produces the clearest and truest of Saturnian manifestations and consequently discussion is usually avoided.

Uranus-Saturn contacts

The three known outer planets are connected with states of consciousness which have little to do with the physical world, and consequently they deal with levels of which Saturn himself has no experience as he is bound to the concrete realm of existence. Uranus, Neptune, and Pluto are often suggested as symbols for different aspects of the collective or transpersonal unconscious of humanity and of individual man as he participates in his group heritage. As we have no hope of comprehending this shadowy world through the powers of the intellect, we are told in esoteric teaching that Saturn "cannot follow a man past the gates of initiation". His function, esoterically considered, is to train, discipline, and condition the evolving soul through the offering of opportunities to acquire wisdom through experience, life after life, so that the soul may eventually pass freely through those gates. Like the scaffolding around a building, his usefulness is finished when the building is complete. In psychological terms, if we consider Saturn as having some connexion with the "shadow" or darker, repressed side of a man's personality, his "personal unconscious", then it follows that integrating the Saturnian principle, which involves the rounding out and expansion of the conscious personality, brings one finally to the borderland of the collective unconscious—a step which is a necessary part of the individuation process of analytical psychology. The confrontation with the collective forces may be a difficult one, but at least the man has acquired freedom in his personal life—something which few people ever achieve although all long for it.

Seen from this point of view, Saturn is our greatest and truest friend if we are willing to follow his path according to his own rules. He will infallibly lead man toward self-knowledge and integration, although his own function is in a sense left behind or absorbed when this stage is reached. In this guise Saturn is Lucifer, whose name means "bearer of light", and he is kin to Prometheus who stole the fire of the gods and offered it to man and was condemned because of this voluntary sacrifice to eternal torture. There is some slight suggestion here as to the real nature of that "brightest of the archangels" who, as Christian doctrine tells us, fell from Paradise through pride and the sin of separateness. One may begin to wonder whether this symbolic fall is, in a deeper sense, the greatest of voluntary sacrifices. Someone, as they say, has to do the dirty job. The character of Saturn as the greater malefic, when considered in this light, is subject to some reevaluation.

When Saturn in his role of shadow on one person's chart is contacted by the outer planets on another's horoscope, he swings about to confront what he feels to be an abyss opening behind him by using as his defense all that he knows of the realm of personal, concrete experience. There is usually some numinous quality about the other person which is mysterious, frightening, and a threat because there is the feeling of the dissolution of the structure which Saturn has worked so hard to build. Uranus, Neptune, and Pluto evoke a different response from Saturn than the inner planets do because they are past the personal boundary and partake of the power of archetypal or mass energies. They play by different rules. Obviously the average individual may display very little "archetypal energy" in his everyday life; but he will inevitably manage to evoke this kind of response from the person whose Saturn is affected for he will seem to be a personification of something the Saturnian person cannot cope with. Most of this kind of exchange is on an unconscious level. But we know enough about the workings of the mind to realise that it is precisely on this hidden level that the most powerful currents occur in relationships.

Therefore contacts of Saturn with the outer planets have a rather mysterious and fatalistic reputation, if they are considered at all. Most of the time they are passed aside in traditional synastry because the planets involved "move too slowly", or have no bearing on the individual, or they are classed together as "karmic" and then dropped from discussion. Certainly many millions of people are likely to be born with Pluto in the same degree of the same sign as he does so much retrogradation over the same few points; but if these aspects are exact, they are powerful and have meaning to the individual and provide a channel through which collective energies can come through and affect the lives of particular people. Probably many millions of people also have the Moon in the same degree as one individual's Saturn, but he does not meet all of them nor become involved in close relationships with them. We are used to assigning a cause-and-effect interpretation to contacts in synastry, and we assume that two people are attracted together wholly because certain links exist. Probably it is subtler than that, and once they have arranged to meet (and the chance factor here is fairly unlikely), it will be found that they share certain configurations which make it possible for a mutual exchange to take place.

It is a mistake to disregard Saturn's ties with the outer planets in synastry on the basis that these links are general rather than specific in meaning. The two areas of group consciousness and individual consciousness are not mutually exclusive, and we are both individuals and part of a collective life at the same time. But mass life and individual expression are contradictory because mass life requires a submission to the instincts which are collective in nature. The outer planets have little to do with instincts, however; this is the sphere of the Moon which is traditionally given rulership over the public. Uranus, Neptune, and Pluto have to do with purposeful group participation rather than blind mass response. The very frequency of exact contacts between Saturn and the outer planets in close relationships should be cause for suspicion and investigation. It seems that when these contacts occur, major steps in the growth of consciousness are stimulated.

As the outer planets appear to have some link with the world of the collective archetypes, it is of some value to explore their mythological antecedents. Mythology is purified of personal components because it is distilled over a long period of time through many generations of men, and only those symbols which have value to the group remain while all colouration by the individual is lost through the process of time. Consequently, we are justified in thinking that much truth may be found from an astrological point of view about each planet from an examination of its mythology.

Uranus was the primordial god of Heaven and ruled with his mother and his wife Gaea, the Earth, over the worlds of spirit and matter. They are the first of the great male-female polarities which stem from Chaos, or, as the Chaldeans said, the "One about Whom naught may be said". We know that the incest theme of the mother-lover is a very ancient one for the light or sun of consciousness springs from the darkness of the unconscious as its child and then must marry or integrate with this same dark irrational principle to recreate wholeness. Beyond this image, we are given little information about Uranus in myth which is fitting for a planet which could only have been sensed unconsciously and therefore remained hidden until its physical discovery in 1781.

Only the downfall and castration of Uranus at the hands of his child, Saturn, is mentioned by our ancestors in their symbolic portrayal of the evolution of consciousness. This is an amazing symbol which suggests a very ancient enmity between the two motivations within a human being which these planets represent. It would be an insult to the richness and beauty of the symbol to make so pragmatic a statement as the fact that we may see the castration of the intuitive mind by the insistent identification with matter in the course of our history as well as in the relationship between two people trying to work with a combination of these planets. But the trouble with a symbol is that it cannot be explained in any way which does it justice.

From the blood of Uranus sprang the Furies, who were personifications of the forces of justice or of the cause-and-effect principle we call karma. From his severed genitals, when they were thrown into the sea, emerged Venus, the goddess of love and beauty. Here is another series of symbols worthy of inspection.

After this we hear no more of Uranus in mythology. We do not even know whether he perished from his wound or where he went after he lost his throne. Many astrologers seem to display the same confusion as to the workings of Uranus on the individual chart. No character is assigned to him in mythology, and the only attribute suggested is his fertility which was destroyed by Saturn and reborn as Venus. Astrologically we assign to him the rulership of invention, genius, originality, individuality, and the urge for freedom. His chief characteristics are his suddenness and the abrupt flashes of intuitive knowledge which he evokes through an airy sign, and esoterically he is given rulership over the etheric body of man, that web of energy upon which the mould of the physical body is built and which serves as a conductor between the mind and the feelings and the physical brain and body of man. The etheric body or vital body is no longer an esoteric concept; it has at last made its appearance in the laboratory and been duly photographed, and it is now under extensive research as the possible source of life.

For many people the energies of Uranus are too fine to be utilised, and so he has the reputation of being either a dumb note or a malefic. The intuitive mind, which is capable of synthesising inner and outer perception, does not function particularly well in the man who is centred in his feelings or in his body—or even in his concrete intellect. He is, however, a powerful motivation toward freedom from identification with matter and works in this fashion unconsciously if not consciously in every person. Uranus seems to be linked with the archetypal figure of the magician in the Tarot deck, who is a fusion of mind, feelings, body, and soul and therefore has mastery over all four worlds.

When this principle contacts Saturn in another person's chart, the result can be quite explosive. A very close conjunction has something of the quality of a prison inmate watching a free man walk past just outside the barred window. The reaction of an unconscious Saturn is rarely pleasant; more often than not it is bitter envy. If Uranus is not being consciously utilised, then the individual may allow his Saturnian partner a spell of apparent thralldom; he may even be expressing his independence and still allow the constriction out of cool pity for Saturn's obvious emotional difficulties. His symbolic castration yields only love and an inexorable kind of justice for if vexed enough—and this planet is easily vexed—the person may break violently free. He may not do this with the personal passion and hate of Mars, however, but with the same cold, impersonal detachment that a man might feel in breaking a chain around his foot.

The usual level of expression for this contact is in the direction of "what other people think" as opposed to "what I want". The Uranian quality is too rebellious and disrespectful of authority for Saturn's taste, and Saturn may be particularly envious of the apparent confidence that the Uranian type has in his right to be his own lawmaker. Even the most eminently conventional man will appear to be a bit of a rebel in the eyes of one whose Saturn is placed on his Uranus.

Saturn is no match for Uranus as the faculty of intuition

insures that the Uranian receives his knowledge from a source which is apparently, to the Saturnian, godlike and out of reach. He has a better reason for his social behaviour than Saturn who works largely out of fear; for Uranus does exactly as he pleases because he knows that all social structures for behaviour are relative to individuals and are not divine absolutes. He knows this because he is his own divine absolute. If the person whose Saturn is involved in this contact attempts to control his partner, he is very likely to be left with chaos, disruption, and the shattering of his carefully nurtured social opinions and defenses. As a result of this, his entire way of life may be changed in part or all of his life, and the new way will usually be richer, broader, more tolerant, and less bound to the voices of the past and of his own fears.

Uranus confers an important lesson and symbolises a universal law: one cannot hold another's will in captivity. This is generally demonstrated even in the most personal of exchanges when the contacts between these two planets are close in a relationship. Uranian energy is a clean, positive force because it has little of the personality about it; it symbolises the collective ideal of freedom of thought. Uranus sweeps away illusions and breaks apart calcified patterns of thought with a loud snap. The person whose Saturn is involved may, however, not think it particularly positive when he is in the middle of it and feels himself threatened by something intangibly outrageous about his partner. The Uranian is a law unto himself, receiving his commands from his own higher nature even if he only displays this in one area of life. In the case of those people who are not responding in a conscious manner to Uranus, this intrinsic self-ness shows through, although in a subtle fashion, to the person whose Saturn is contacted. And the surest way to bring Uranus into conscious activity is to attempt to stifle him.

Thus these planets can do each other a great service. Saturn can awaken in Uranus his latent individuality by attempting, out of fear, to control it, and Uranus teaches Saturn, in defying his control, that the limitations of a personality structure built on defense cannot hold back the development of the creative mind.

These contacts are fairly common in close relationships. It may be inferred that when they do occur, an opportunity exists which is more extensive than personal comfort or happiness for this combination seems to have more connexion with big leaps of consciousness. Although there is no personal emotion involved on the part of Uranus, as there is with contacts of the inner planets to Saturn, the two individuals are likely to be highly significant to each other's growth. This is particularly true if the person whose Saturn is involved makes the effort to understand himself for the bright, clear light of Uranus can save him much time and effort in jolting buried things to the surface of consciousness.

It is a major step in a man's development to shift from being one of a mass to being an individual, just as it is also a major step to shift from being an individual to a consciously cooperative member of a group. All three steps are connected with the process of Saturn's unfoldment within the individual from a blind, hurting spot to one of deep self-understanding and control. Uranus can help Saturn to recognise that the great "They" are not always right and that eventually it is a good idea to build a code of behaviour on inner convictions rather than external opinions. Saturn can in turn help Uranus to recognise that it is sometimes necessary to display caution and diplomacy in the expression of the will.

When applying these ideas to the practical effects between two charts, it is often helpful to consider that the affairs connected with the house in which Saturn is placed and the house which he rules are those affairs which will probably be subjected to the shattering and transforming process initiated by the Uranian partner. This applies both to the more superficial and the deeper meanings of these houses. Saturn expresses his energy of either constriction or a sense of discipline and responsibility to the house where Uranus is placed and the house which he rules. In this way the interchange may seem to express itself on the mundane plane. The inner effects, however, are more important, and these deal with a restructuring process in Saturn's defenses and unconscious narrowness so that the man whose Saturn is contacted can build his inner structure on a firmer base and for a higher set of reasons. If consciousness is brought to the relationship, it can be an excellent partnership; even if left unconscious, it will be highly productive even though painful. These two planets, although they have been enemies on the collective psychic level for a very long time, have the possibility of unity through the medium of group consciousness symbolised by the sign which they co-rule. The collective unconscious of man may evolve very slowly, but nevertheless it evolves.

Neptune-Saturn contacts
In mythology Neptune was given dominion over the waters

and the subterranean passageways of the earth when the rulership of heaven and earth was taken from Saturn and divided up among his three sons. Pluto was of course given the underworld, and Jupiter the heavens; and the surface of the earth itself was given to man who was, as it were, caught between the hammer and the anvil in much the same way as he is now caught between the pressures of the unconscious which tear him in different directions. The ocean is a fitting symbol for that aspect of the collective unconscious which does not differentiate but which relates to all things as a whole. It is this aspect that causes the unconscious to appear inimical to the intellect of man which by its very nature differentiates and assigns separate meanings to things.

The mythological Neptune could be quite inimical and was capable of arbitrarily overwhelming ships and their passengers as well as precipitating earthquakes, floods, and tidal waves. We may occasionally glimpse some of the impotent horror of the ancient mind as it attempted to understand such a capricious deity in considering the same impotent horror which one feels at being overwhelmed by the forces of the collective unconscious. Our term for this is insanity; the ancients considered it possession by the god who shared much in common with Dionysus and the other fertility deities in that he had some connexion with irrational states. We are used to viewing Neptune as a kindly influence astrologically, the "higher octave" of Venus, symbol of universal compassion and love elevated above the level of personal relationships. He is certainly related to the urge for union with that which is greater, not through the symbol of the sacred marriage rite but rather through death by drowning—the dissolution of the separate identity. If we were able to express the Neptunian energy in an uncontaminated form, he would undoubtedly reveal himself as the vehicle of final transfiguration, the experience of the unity of life. Unfortunately there are very few men who can consciously express this urge, and because it is a collective one, it can only be glimpsed if the shadows have been absorbed and made part of his conscious expression. The archetype of Neptunian ecstasy is paralleled in the declarations of mystics throughout the ages, but the man who has not dealt with his shadow (Saturn) is in the position of becoming hopelessly inflated with his own sense of mission and messianic purpose.

Although he is not harmless, Neptune is not a malefic influence by nature. It is only in the misunderstanding of his energies that he becomes dangerous, and unfortunately the majority of people are simply not in a position to understand him any better because the path of devotion has been riddled since the dawn of Christianity with moral fanaticism and the spirit of bloody martyrdom. None of these qualities are Neptunian in nature; they are Martial. But we have saddled them together, and some good clean Mercurial analysis—always avoided by the Neptunian person—is the only thing that will help us.

Neptune's second method of pursuing his ends, after that of complete submergence, is that of impotence. By his apparent passivity, he leads to that point where neither reason nor passion are of any use because the individual has attracted circumstances to himself which provide him with the vehicle to acquiesce to greater and wiser forces. These greater and wiser forces often wear the guise of a not very great or wise parent, lover, friend, or business partner; but it is the experience or acquiescence which is important and not the means by which it occurs.

Neptune, like Uranus, can overwhelm Saturn because his energies belong to a level which Saturn cannot understand. Consequently any contact between these planets within a relationship usually has the greatest effect on the person whose Saturn is involved. With infinite patience and gentleness Neptune can accept Saturn's attempts to bind him for Saturn, made uncomfortable by the apparent inclusiveness and capacity for indiscriminate empathy which is characteristic of Neptune, will often try to make this into a very exclusive and discriminating empathy for him alone. We can see the same kind of mechanism at work here that is suggested by a Uranus-Saturn contact. Even if the individual is not expressing Neptune in a particularly conscious way—and few do except through the creative media of music or theatre—this fluid and magical quality will be apparent to the person whose Saturn is affected. It is an entrancing quality at the same time that it is a terrible threat for although Neptune seems to say, I completely understand and love and accept you, he will say the same to everyone indiscriminately. It is this apparent faithlessness or deceptiveness which disturbs the Saturnian; but it is not deception at all. It is simply an error in interpretation on the part of Saturn who because the dissolving of barriers is unfamiliar to him, feels as though he has been betrayed.

It is a characteristic of Neptunian contacts in general in synastry for there to be an element of elusiveness and a sense of deception or betrayal in the relationship, and it is usually the

Neptunian who helps stimulate these feelings of betrayal in the partner because he will respond as an actor to the manner born. He cannot say no because he is forever seeking a cross on which to crucify himself, and at that moment it seems that all his emotional energies are for the sole private consumption of his partner; but he is just as genuine in his feeling toward others at the time that they, too, imagine they are being exclusively granted the Neptunian magic. Only those who respond to Neptune can understand how painful and apparently unjustified it is for them to be accused of betrayal when this was the last thing they had meant to do. They can never understand why so much trouble has been caused for they are always gentle and kind. It is a very common and very ancient story. Saturn is the most liable to be hurt of all for he is the most vulnerable and the least able to share what is precious to him.

The result of all this subtlety is the unpleasant feeling of disillusionment which is justifiably associated with Neptune. It is particularly bitter for Saturn because he is a rigid and inflexible planet in terms of his effects for the majority of people. This is due to the rigidity and inflexibility of the conscious attitude which has forced certain attitudes and feelings to be repressed and to form the "shadow" in the first place. Saturn's direction in the unconscious man is toward self-protection, and he sees in the unreliability of Neptune a reflection of the ultimate futility and illusion of his efforts. This is an uncomfortable feeling, and consequently he attempts to possess the Neptunian personality—something like grabbing a fistful of water.

Neptune can inflict very deep hurt on a person who has not come to terms with his Saturn for the man will then be extremely vulnerable on his dark side. Although the Neptunian type is frequently considered amoral or immoral because his behaviour is so fluid, his wisdom is that of the unconscious which does not set up moral values and which tends to show up all consciously reasoned values as relative rather than absolute. To this kind of person, all things have their place. To Saturn, this is the destruction of all order for he is trying to struggle with the building of an ego and does not dare to let go of his black and white evaluations for fear the new and rather shaky structure will collapse. He is right in this for the structure can collapse under the weight of Neptune, who sees all colours and knows that choice in the end is meaningless; however, in the end Saturn must go back and rebuild his structure, allowing for the inclusion of a new element—compassion. Neptune in turn may learn that his intent of harmlessness often creates the most harm for impotence can be the cruellest of weapons, and it is sometimes better to say no at the beginning and inflict a clean wound.

Neptune-Saturn contacts tend to produce this kind of pattern even if there is very little fluidity in the life of the person whose Neptune is involved; for because of the contact, the Saturnian will see what is expressed only unconsciously and will react accordingly although often unknowingly. It is an important although subtle combination. If Uranus-Saturn aspects convey the fact that one cannot control another's will, then Neptune-Saturn aspects communicate the fact that one cannot own another's feelings. These are hard lessons to learn, but it may be assumed that if two people remain together and attempt to work these contacts out on a constructive level, the act of willingness provides or guarantees the possibility of a solution.

Pluto-Saturn contacts

As Pluto spends up to thirty years in one sign, he is considered to have little meaning to the individual; however, if one takes into account his association with certain collective psychic energies, he has potentially a very powerful effect on individual man since each person must make his own pact with these collective energies. Like the other higher octave planets, he is available for the consciousness only of those whose instruments are suited to receiving him. Otherwise he remains a dumb note on the individual chart and works only in an unconscious fashion. He affects relationships with great power, but these effects may also remain unconscious.

In mythology Pluto chose as his domain the underworld and the guardianship of the dead. Because of this ancient association, we tend to attach a rather satanic quality to his astrological character. But Hades bore not the slightest resemblance to our Christian idea of hell. Certainly Tartarus, the grimmer aspect of Hades, is associated with punishment, but the retributions of Tartarus were directed toward men who had sinned against the gods, not men who had sinned against men; and only the gods themselves could pronounce judgment. If we try to translate this into psychological terms, we may find that our greatest sins, from this point of view, lie not in the violation of a moral or ethical code but in the violation of the dictates of the unconscious which is older and wiser than our conscious personalities. This violation we commit daily in our rejection of the faculties of intuition, imagination, and instinct. If we carry this translation further, into astrological terms, we may find that the "ordeal by fire" which is often associated with Plutonian transits and progressions only ensues when the conscious man sets himself up as the final authority on how his life should be lived and opposes the urges of his inner psyche which may be attempting to tell him that everything must end so that it can grow in a new direction.

Saturn himself was imprisoned in Tartarus after Jupiter overthrew his rule. But also to be found in Hades, side by side with Tartarus, were the Blessed Isles of the great heroes, where peace and eternal beauty reigned. Two rivers were associated with Hades: the Styx, which represented the borderland between the dead and the living, and Lethe, where human souls were baptised in the waters of forgetfulness before they returned to take a new earthly body. Pluto himself, when he made a rare visitation above ground, wore an invisible helmet so that no man's eyes could see him. Few men's eyes see him now. And once a soul was committed to his care, no other god nor any force in heaven or earth could free that soul without his consent. Vast riches were to be found in the domain of Pluto, but these could not be removed either without his consent.

There seems to be strong evidence that Pluto is connected with the archetype of immortality which rather than being a static state is one of constant deaths and rebirths and perpetual growth on the pattern of a spiral. If this is so, then each man carries within him this archetype for it is part of the collective heritage of our race. There is that within him which seeks to accomplish its own autonomous growth through a series of endings and beginnings, and the end result of this growth would seem to be wholeness; but wholeness itself is relative since it suggests integration, and there remain higher and higher states of consciousness which may be integrated into the growing whole. This kind of abstraction may appear to have no practical value when it comes to interpreting two charts, but in reality it is extremely practical because if we can conceive of a drive of this kind existing within the human psyche—conscious or unconscious— then certain kinds of behaviour are then to some extent explained by it. It is the task of modern depth psychology to gain some understanding of this "urge for wholeness" which seems to be so total that it is often willing to sacrifice the life of the individual to accomplish its purposes.

If Pluto carries with him the experience of death—and death

is meant as a relative concept since it is the death of a particular form so that the inhibiting life can be set free to build another and better form—then he also carries with him the experience of the creation of form as well, and this links him with the experience of the sexual act. The associations of sex with death have already been touched upon in dealing with Saturn in Scorpio, in the eighth house, and in aspect to Pluto on the natal chart. This same association also holds true in synastry where the power of the archetype, stripped of any personal feeling, is perceived by another person through the medium of a very vulnerable Saturn.

Saturn contacts with Pluto are not so inimical as they might at first seem because the natures of these planets, both guardians of the gate in their own spheres, have certain features in common. In character there is a similarity, and the features of sternness, self-control, and love of power are shared. Saturn must control the external world because he feels threatened by forces from outside himself; Pluto on the other hand must control his internal world so that he can accomplish his purposes of destruction and rebuilding cleanly.

It is the quality of eternity about Pluto which is so frightening to Saturn; somehow it seems that he is able to experience anything including the complete destruction of his world and yet something constant remains and grows stronger. Pluto has a capacity to feed on emotional crises for it is on the level of desire that most of the deaths and rebirths of an individual's life occur. Because the majority of men are polarised on the plane of feeling—or, in other words, because their desires are more important to them than anything else—it is on this level that the purification process of Pluto is most apparent. Frustrated desire creates an overload of unexpressed psychic energy which must be released through some other channel, or it backs up and destroys some part of the personality that created it. There is often a quality of accumulated energy which is about to erupt at any moment surrounding Pluto on the horoscope and also in a more subtle way surrounding people who have Pluto prominently placed or respond to Scorpio strongly. This quality is often sensed as cruelty although it is only the impersonal destruction of a natural phenomenon rather than planned malice which is involved. These suggestions of immortality, of pent-up energy about to burst loose, and of an apparent cruelty or ruthlessness are sensed by the individual whose Saturn is affected by another person's Pluto, and this will generally precipitate an immediate power struggle if the Saturnian person is not aware consciously of what is taking place.

The effects of this combination in a relationship are often very dramatic although this may occur on an inner and semiconscious level. There is usually the sense of a battle of wills for Saturn will first attempt to dominate the situation by asserting his control. Pluto will usually respond to this challenge in the manner traditionally associated with his mythological counterpart: he can afford to sit still and wait because his word is irrevocable, and in the end he always wins. This may sound like an exaggeration of feelings, and it is rare that two people who are closely involved will acknowledge this kind of struggle. But it should be remembered that Pluto brings with him the energies of the collective unconscious, and because he is connected with an archetype, he will frequently evoke this kind of feeling in the person who is being attacked. Even in someone who is not recognised for his strong will, another person's Saturn will usually activate this quality. The matter about which the struggle takes place may be small, so small that it is silly; but it sets a precedent of an important kind, and generally both people can sense that it is desperately important who wins this battle because it will decide who in the end controls the relationship. For this reason the quality of drama is almost always present.

Something is usually destroyed in the Saturnian as a result of this confrontation. He may find that it is necessary to completely reevaluate himself and understand his own defensiveness because his defenses are useless against Pluto's energy as they are useless also against Uranus and Neptune. The person whose Pluto is involved will usually initiate the end of a phase of life and the beginning of a new one for the Saturnian person, and this may be judged more closely by an examination of the houses involved. The effect on the Plutonian partner is usually the feeling of one more experience because Pluto thrives on this kind of confrontation.

The main impact of Saturn to the three outer planets lies in the fact that Saturn is the last outpost or shell of the personality and is, for the majority of people, occupied in fortifying his city walls so that no one else can get in. Before a man has come to terms with and integrated his darker half, it is rare that he can experience any feeling of a common bond with the rest of humanity because the shadow stands between him and others; he uses it to reaffirm his differences and assures himself that he is better, wiser, more rational, and more right than they because the more inferior or immature qualities are conveniently tucked away into the shadow. Consequently everyone else looks darker, and the man looks lighter to himself. To this kind of man the energies of the outer planets are like the intoxicating air of the mountain peaks; but he is afraid of heights. They threaten his illusions because they carry the reality of common or collective experience where there are no differences, no barriers, and no bases for judgment. When this contact occurs within a relationship, the person whose Uranus, Neptune, or Pluto is involved with the contact becomes the symbol for these collective forces which are wholly unconscious for the Saturnian; and this symbol is threatening as well as fascinating.

It would appear that the mechanism of projection is extremely common with any Saturnian cross-contact, and this projection is the source of the trouble which usually ensues with such contacts. If the individual could see himself and could withdraw his projection, he could then also see his partner clearly and would find that he was not threatened after all. These projections become especially difficult when the outer planets are involved because so much of the mechanism is totally unconscious on the part of both persons. It is as rare to find someone who can consciously channel the energies of Uranus, Neptune, and Pluto as it is to find someone who has integrated Saturn for the latter is the necessary prelude to the former. Also it is dangerous to reach this point in development since identification with collective energies suggests the appropriation of something by an individual which in reality belongs to all, and this we call madness or megalomania. People instinctively and wisely back away from tampering with Uranus, Neptune, and Pluto for they are stern deities when aroused. It is no wonder that the ancients referred to them as hidden—beyond the sky, beneath the surface of the waters, and buried deep in the earth.

7 conclusion

The science of psychology is a relatively new one, and it has only barely begun to demonstrate its real potential as a means of shedding light on the ambiguities of human nature and the mystery of human suffering. In unfolding as a truly useful tool for the man who seeks greater meaning in his life, as well as a healing method for the person suffering with a pathological problem, psychology has had, unwillingly perhaps, to begin to develop along the lines suggested by the meaning of the word itself: a study of the soul. The gap between the world of psychology as an empiric study of effects and the world of esotericism as an intuitive study of causes is slowly diminishing. The two worlds are now beginning to overlap although each aggressively clings to its own terminology. Perhaps more than any other single individual, Carl Jung has been responsible for building a bridge over the chasm between these two worlds, although adherents to each group have so often refused to walk across that bridge.

This new direction of psychology includes but does not limit itself to the analytical approaches of Freud and Adler. It is heading, however, straight toward an apprehension of phenomena such as the peak experience, the mystical vision, the altered state of consciousness—in short, the realm of esoteric teaching and the spiritual path. It has, perhaps wisely, maintained a stubborn insistence on its own terminology so that the reek of the seance parlour does not contaminate this new exploration. Therefore we do not speak of the soul but talk instead of the self or the total psyche; and this is full of wisdom because words carry emotional values and we cannot afford to bring our old emotional values into a new field of study. It is possible that in this new direction of psychology, the key to a more inclusive approach to astrology may also be found. Astrology, like any other science, must be able to keep pace with the acceleration in knowledge which is now occurring in every area of life. It has shown its capacity to do this in a technical sense with the development of harmonics, midpoints, and other contributions of modern astrological research. It has not, however, shown a capacity to keep up with the human side, and we are still trapped under the dead weight of malefic planets, afflictions, good and bad characters, and superficial behavioural diagnoses which show no understanding of motive. It is here that psychology, the newest science, can offer much help to the oldest science.

I do not feel that it is possible to comprehend a birth chart in a deeper sense without having some grounding in the fundamental principles of psychology. The very basic and apparently simple division of man's psyche into conscious and unconscious puts the interpretation of the birth chart into a completely new perspective, offering nuances, subtleties, and lines of definite orientation which are otherwise completely missed. Much may be explained in the light of the study of motives which cannot be found no matter how much technical dissection is done in relation to the birth positions. That mysterious, elusive entity which psychology calls the self—that thing or life which looks out through a person's eyes, to which he refers when he says, "I"—has not yet been found among the glyphs and symbols of the horoscope; it may be seen working through a behaviour and a personality suggested by that horoscope, but it remains standing outside the framework, aloof, objective, numinous, and able to be invoked at any point during the life so that the personality—and the chart—acquire a new and more meaningful expression.

I also do not feel that it is possible to come anywhere near a comprehension of Saturn without this additional perspective for I believe that Saturn is the key to this invocation of the self with its transforming potential. In esoteric teaching, Saturn is the planet of discipleship, and a disciple is simply someone who is learning. He is not malefic; he is not a negative influence and is only inimical to those who cannot understand the educational value of pain. His path is not that of the martyr or the disciplinarian but instead contains the seeds of joy. His lineage is ancient and impeccable, and his associations in the world of myth, religion, folklore, and fairytale are innumerable and varied, yet always coloured by the idea that instead of running away from the devil, if one goes up and kisses him on the lips, he becomes the sun.

What I may personally feel, or intuit, or experience, or think about Saturn has not really been articulated for even if I were to amplify this analysis with a hundred times greater detail or attempted to structure it in a hundred different ways, the presentation would necessarily be inadequate because Saturn is a symbol and a symbol cannot be comprehended by words but must be approached through the intuitive faculty; however, an attempt has been made to suggest that he is far, far more than he seems and is, as a psychic factor, our greatest friend, source of strength, and bringer of light if we approach his birth sign, house, and aspects with a more extensive knowledge.

There is finally the very practical question of what one can do about self-development, once the challenge is recognised and is seriously accepted. In the early days of psychology, only the sick person was expected to be concerned with the convolutions of the unconscious because the unconscious was supposed to be a dustbin into which was poured each man's private accumulation of filth. Only a man who was suffering was considered to have the right to treatment for the pursuit of psychological help meant that one was half-mad by his own admission. Now we know better; the unconscious has shown itself to be not only a dustbin but also a life-giving, creative force with all the attributes of deity. We are also beginning to recognise that sickness is a relative term, as is normality. One may express the symptoms of a psychic sickenss by being sane, normal, and well-adjusted to a sick society. There are many kinds of sickness, and not all of them show in a pathological way. There is a sickness of the soul which results in a sense of meaninglessness, and this sickness is more prevalent than the common cold and far more difficult to cure. Only the man who has seen the vision, who lives only to create a work of art, who has glimpsed the seven circles of heaven and the seven circles of hell, is free of meaninglessness. And most of these men can do nothing for the rest of us because they are mad. We have worked so hard for sanity and social adjustment that we have destroyed our life-giving roots, and the creative flow of life has dried up and left a dusty shell.

Fortunately another movement is now occurring, and we are beginning to look at the idea of self-development as a commitment to that which is highest and best in us instead of as an admission of defeat. The appearance of numerous groups, schools, workshops, and courses of study in self-development through all kinds of techniques, ranging from meditation and yoga to creative fantasy, seems to suggest that a deep collective need for this kind of work is being expressed. Here an individual can develop himself yet be part of a group without sacrificing his privacy, and this is perhaps an Aquarian idea which is emerging with the beginning of this new astrological age. This does not mean that it is going to be easy; but it seems that we are beginning to discover the meaning of individuality within group consciousness. The collective psyche of man is changing and is spewing out new symbols, new values, new structures, and new ways óf approaching a new concept of God, and this kind of change is characteristic of the changing of an astrological age. It will take some time before these outpourings assume any kind of stability, but the broad outline is emerging. In the hands of psychology and astrology lie two powerful and significant tools for self-understanding and self-development. And all this is accompanied by new research on the part of science into the subtle constitution of man and new developments in healing through alternative medicine. It is becoming possible to explore and develop oneself and to be concerned with one's inner life without being judged as a lunatic, a neurotic, or a hippie. If a man decides that he wishes to begin the Quest, he had best begin with that aspect of his psyche which is symbolised by Saturn: his shadow. And for this Quest, the emergence of groups and schools and workshops in every country of the world makes it impossible for him to say, "But there is nowhere to go."

I wish to end with a quote from Jung's *The Undiscovered Self*:

"I am neither spurred on by excessive optimism nor in love with high ideals, but am merely concerned with the fate of the individual human being—that infinitesimal unit on whom a world depends, and in whom, if we read the meaning of the Christian message aright, even God seeks his goal."